"Each new Amelia Grey tale is a diamond . . . a master storyteller." —*Affaire de Coeur*

"Enchanting romance." —*RT Book Reviews*

"Devilishly charming . . . A touching tale of love." —*Library Journal*

"Sensual . . . witty and clever . . . Another great story of forbidden love." —*Fresh Fiction*

"Grey neatly matched up a sharp-witted heroine with an irresistible sexy hero and let the romantic sparks fly." —*Booklist*

"Delightful . . . charming and unforgettable." —*The Long and Short of It Reviews*

"A beautifully written tale . . . delicious historical romance." —*Romance Junkies*

"Such a tantalizing and funny read, you won't be able to put it down." —*Rendezvous*

"Fun, fast-paced, and very sensual." —*A Romance Review*

"Well written and entertaining." —*Night Owl Romance* (Reviewer Top Pick)

Also by Amelia Grey

The Duke in My Bed

THE
Earl Claims
A Bride

Amelia Grey

St. Martin's Paperbacks

This is a work of fiction. All of the characters, organizations, and events portrayed in this novel are either products of the author's imagination or are used fictitiously.

THE EARL CLAIMS A BRIDE

Copyright © 2015 by Amelia Grey.
Excerpt from *Wedding Night with the Earl* copyright © 2015 by Amelia Grey.

For information address St. Martin's Press, 175 Fifth Avenue, New York, NY 10010.

ISBN: 978-1-250-04221-7

Printed in the United States of America

St. Martin's Paperbacks edition / August 2015

St. Martin's Paperbacks are published by St. Martin's Press, 175 Fifth Avenue, New York, NY 10010.

10 9 8 7 6 5 4 3 2 1

Chapter 1

He which hath no stomach to this fight, let him depart.
Henry V *4.3.35–36*

Winter 1817

The last thing Harrison Thornwick wanted to do was shoot the man, but he didn't have a choice.

Harrison's head was pounding and his eyes were blurry, but his spine was straight as an arrow as he stood back-to-back with—with . . .

He grunted a tired laugh.

Well, hell, Harrison couldn't remember the tosspot's name. They'd been playing cards all night at one of the gambling hells on the east side of Bond Street and both he and Mr. No Name were deep in their cups. It was a wonder Harrison was still upright and thinking at all.

No Name had accused Harrison of cheating after he'd won all the man's money and prized stallion, too. And then the bloke had the nerve to call him out. Harrison tried to quiet him, but pointing out his shortcomings as a card player had enraged the dandy all the more. The only thing that had mollified him was Harrison picking up the glove the man had thrown to the floor of the club.

If he wanted to get shot, Harrison would have to oblige him.

"Dueling is against the law," Harrison's second reminded him in a subdued voice as he extended the pistol to him.

"I know."

"Either that gentleman has a death wish or he doesn't know you are one of the best shots in London, even when you are none too steady on your feet as you are now. Do you really want to do this?"

"No. I don't like dueling, and I hope this is my last. I never like shooting a man."

"Then perhaps you should just conveniently miss this time and not wound him."

Harrison took the pistol without bothering to look at it. "He called me a card cheat."

"He's drunk and so are you."

"I'm not the one itching to feel a lead ball in my shoulder this morning. He is. You know I gave him ample opportunity to repair the injury. I cannot accept the affront without redress. This point will be settled here and will be settled now. My honor demands it."

"Very well," the second said and stepped away.

Harrison had shed his hat, cloak, and gloves in preparation for the duel. As was the custom, he'd allowed his second to inspect the pistols, make all the arrangements, and resolve the details with No Name's second.

A dozen or so bloodthirsty witnesses formed a silent bulwark at the edge of the field of honor. They held their impatience well. Harrison knew the small crowd was ready to get on with the matter and be off to their slumber.

So was Harrison.

"On the count of ten, gentlemen," someone called, "turn, lower your weapons, and fire."

Harrison placed his forefinger on the cold metal of the trigger and lifted the barrel of the pistol level with his chin.

"One . . ."

The ground crunched as Harrison took a wide step and a calming, shallow breath. He didn't know whose property they were on, but it had been a short carriage drive outside London. The area was all it needed to be: wooded and isolated.

"Two . . . three . . ."

The last vestige of night had faded. Scattered whorls of fog had evaporated, and the early-morning sky was shaping up to be a bright shade of blue even though the winter air was damned crisp. Sunlight glistening on the crest of the horizon was visible through the spindly limbs of the barren trees.

"Four . . . five . . ."

Harrison couldn't help but think it was going to be a good day—after he got this nasty business out of the way.

"Six . . ."

"Wait! Stop!"

Harrison halted and looked around. A tall, robust gentleman clutched his hat to his head and ran out of a thicket of trees with his coattails flapping behind him. He skidded on traces of silvery dew covering the hard ground before stopping between Harrison and his opponent, gasping to catch his breath.

"I've been looking for you, Mr. Thornwick," the man finally got out.

"And you found me at a most inopportune moment," Harrison said dryly.

"But thankfully before it was too late."

Harrison eyed the interloper suspiciously, but it was Mr. No Name who said, "Who the deuce are you?"

The meddler cast his large, slightly bulging eyes toward the man and lifted his chin disdainfully. "Sir, I am Mr. Alfred Hopscotch."

"I don't know you," No Name snarled. "So who do you think you are to stop this duel?"

"I am the Prince's emissary," Mr. Hopscotch said testily. "I'm here on his official business."

"Yes, and I am the King's brother." No Name cut his eyes around to Harrison and grunted a slurring laugh. "Did you hire this man to come here and save your bloody life, Thornwick?"

Harrison squinted against a sudden bright ray of sunlight that broke through the tree limbs. His answer was to turn his back on the man and resume the dueling stance.

"Keep counting," Harrison called.

"Step aside, sir," No Name said. "Or stand your ground and get the bullet that's meant for him!"

"Seven . . . eight . . ."

"No, I beg of you, Mr. Thornwick, wait."

"Nine . . ."

Harrison hoped like hell the Prince's man had the good sense to move out of the way.

"Ten."

Harrison pivoted on his back foot, lowered his body as he swung, aimed, and fired his pistol at No Name's shoulder. The man folded with a yelp, his shot wild and plugging a nearby tree.

Smoke from Harrison's gun barrel swirled and then quickly evaporated in the frosty air. Several of the onlookers rushed to the fallen man's side while other gentlemen were already pulling money out of their pockets to settle their wagers.

Harrison walked over for a look, too. Blood had stained the man's white shirt and quilted waistcoat, and was seeping through his fingers held tightly against the shoulder wound.

No Name looked up at him with a furious glare in his wild eyes. "Did you come to gloat?"

Harrison stared at him and said, "Don't ever call me a card cheat again." He walked over to the carriage that had brought him to the dueling site. Several of the young blades and onlookers followed him, some offering mumblings of congratulations and deserved claps on the back while others quietly counted their winnings.

"Well done," Harrison's second said, handing Harrison his coat. "The shot missed his bone. He'll have a hell of a pain in his shoulder for a few weeks, but nothing that won't heal properly with time."

"It took great restraint," Harrison admitted, returning the pistol to the second.

"I'm sure. No one likes being called a cheater and a coward in the same breath."

The stranger who had interrupted the duel elbowed his way through the muttering crowd gathered around Harrison and in a loud, impatient tone said, "I must speak to you now, my lord. I have important information for you."

Harrison frowned at the man as he shoved his arms into the sleeves of his coat. "I am not a lord, sir."

"That's what I've been trying to tell you. You are. The Prince charged me with finding you and giving you the unfortunate news that your brother, the Earl of Thornwick, and his heir have died. You, my lord, are the new Earl of Thornwick."

Gasps from the tight circle of men rent the air, and shock rippled through Harrison. His mind immediately recoiled from the words he'd heard. It took several seconds before he managed to say, "What?"

"I'm sorry, my lord."

The pounding in Harrison's head increased. A loud roar swooshed through his ears as denial rose up within him. Cold, dry air caught in his lungs, pressing like an anvil on his chest.

The ramifications of the man's words sank deeply into his soul, wounding him, and he whispered, "My brother and his three-year-old son? Dead? Are you sure?"

Mr. Hopscotch ran a nervous hand down the front of his waistcoat. "Yes, my lord. There's no doubt. A fever quickly ravaged a nearby village and spread throughout Thornwick."

"*That one an earl? Can't be!*" Harrison heard a man whisper.

"*He'll never take care of the place,*" another gentleman said. "*He doesn't know how. It'll be in ruins in less than a year.*"

"*For sure,*" came the reply. "*He doesn't know anything but drinking, gambling, and dueling.*"

"*He certainly does all three of those bloody well,*" someone else whispered.

"Damnation" blew softly past Harrison's lips on a throb of hellish emotion he couldn't hold inside.

"I know," Hopscotch said. "It's tragic. Since you are the new earl, the Prince wants to make certain that you don't go to Thornwick and expose yourself to the fever, too."

"My brother's wife and daughters?" Harrison asked as alarm nipped him. "How are they?"

The man blinked rapidly. "Gone, too, I'm sorry to report. Most of the servants as well."

A low groan of anguish rose from Harrison's throat but he managed to swallow before it sounded. Beautiful, sweet Maddie with her raven hair and soft brown eyes dead. And her twin infant girls gone, too?

Harrison turned away from the man and threw his fist into the side of the carriage before clamping a hold on the door handle to shore himself up should his knees fail him and buckle. The pain that shot through his hand whipcord-fast couldn't dull the shattering grief that echoed through him. Over the years he'd lost his parents and two older brothers, but their deaths had been years apart and somehow easier to bear than hearing of the loss of the rest of his family.

"The Prince says it is imperative you to come to London immediately so he can speak to you about a most important matter. My carriage is right over there. I'll take you."

Mr. Hopscotch had continued talking as if he had no clue about the torment thundering through Harrison. "Being an earl is of little consequence to me right now," he ground out.

Hopscotch nervously clutched his hands together in front of him. "But it must matter, my lord. The Prince can't risk losing you, too."

Harrison jerked open the door of his carriage before looking back to the man and saying, "I'm going to bury my brother and his family."

Chapter 2

Wake not a sleeping wolf.
Henry IV *1.2.153–54*

Spring 1818

Harrison put his two fingers to his lips and whistled. When the driver of the wagon looked up at him, he called, "Over there," and pointed to a lean-to built to store the lumber that would be used in rebuilding Thornwick.

Late-morning sun warmed the back of Harrison's neck as he stood on the back lawn, his gaze scanning the gently rolling hills in the distance. As far as he could see, and then some, it was Thornwick land. His land. Still, at times he didn't want to believe everyone was gone. That he was now the earl. There were a few times when he was a youngster that he'd wished Thornwick would be his one day, but those were foolish, childish wishes that weren't supposed to come true. He never wanted to lose his family.

The trees, shrubs, and scrub grass were showing their

first signs of green. Harrison looked behind him at the burnt-out shell of what was once the massive three-story manor house where he'd grown up. It was situated on a spacious, grassy knoll. The more than twenty rooms that were in the main section of the house had been gutted; a dozen others in the guest wing had fared little better. The expanse of flawlessly manicured gardens and lawn outlined by a tall yew hedge and perfectly trimmed topiary trees hadn't been touched by the destructive fire, and neither had the carriage house and two paddocks that accommodated his more than two dozen horses.

Not only had the fever taken his family, but the Thornwick he'd loved, the house that had been in his family for over one hundred years, had been destroyed while he was off carousing. But there was so much more lost than just the house. The urns, the china, the furniture could all be replaced. Even the hundreds of books in the library could be replaced. It was the portraits of all the previous Thornwicks that had hung in the gallery, and the priceless volumes of recorded family history, that were gone forever. All of it had been lost and on his watch.

His brother had written and asked him to come home, but he ignored the request as he had so often in the past. While he had been drinking, gambling, and dueling his family had perished and the manor had burned. Over the past weeks, Harrison had often remembered the hastily spoken words he'd overheard that morning he'd learned that he was the new earl. They all doubted his ability to properly manage Thornwick and keep it prosperous. And with good reason. He'd never given anyone reason to believe he could do anything other than continue his debauchery. But that was before the title became his.

Thornwick was where he'd learned how to ride, shoot,

and wield a sword. During long, cold winter nights he
became proficient at cards, billiards, and chess. On this
land he'd chased his older brothers, climbed its trees,
fished its streams, and hunted its game. But it was never
supposed to be his.

The fourth son of an earl wasn't meant to outlive his
brothers and their sons to inherit the title. Certainly not
by the age of thirty. A different kind of ache suddenly
pierced his chest. And to lose Maddie, too. His first love.
His only love. His thoughts drifted back to the Season
she'd made her debut. He'd tried his best to capture the
heart of the dark-haired beauty and win her favor. But
it soon became clear she had eyes only for his older
brother, and in time Harrison had accepted that. Though
it hadn't been easy.

Damnation, none of it had.

Not the grief of losing them all and losing Maddie
twice. Not the struggles of these past weeks of discov-
ering what was expected of an earl, learning to see that
an estate was managed, and functioning well enough
that once the house had been rebuilt there would be a
Thornwick for the foreseeable future. Fourth sons were
educated but never groomed to take on all the responsibilities that came with bearing the title of earl. It was
assumed they would never need it.

Harrison had never had any responsibility to anyone
or anything. There was never a reason. The oldest son
was always revered, but the youngest was either treated
like an infant and indulged or completely ignored. Harrison made certain he was neither by challenging, testing, and besting his older brothers from a very early
age. He'd missed them when one by one they'd been
sent away to school, but he soon found replacements for
them in his friends Bray Drakestone and Adam Greyhawke when it was his turn to be shipped off to Eton.

When Harrison had left Oxford, his father had bestowed a more-than-generous allowance on him, and from his cards, bets, and all manner of wagers he added a considerable amount to that each year. All his father had expected was that he live the comfortable and respectable life of a gentleman and not sully the Thornwick name.

Harrison hadn't been able to manage that small request. His father should have known better than to ask that of him with scoundrels like the Duke of Drakestone and Adam Greyhawke as his friends. The three of them had scandalized London's social elite more times than Harrison could count. Harrison was a rebel at heart, and neither his father nor anyone else had ever been able to make him follow the rules or do what he was told.

He'd always done whatever pleased him because he had no reason not to. But now he did. He had Thornwick, or what was left of it. And he would rebuild it. Bigger and better than it was before. He owed it to his father and to his brothers to make it the grand place it once was.

He didn't know a damned thing about buying books, furniture, and all the other items that filled a house, but he'd learn. And despite the assertions of the gentlemen at the duel that day, Harrison would take care of Thornwick.

The first load of supplies to reconstruct the house had arrived earlier in the day, bringing with them a small measure of peace to Harrison. There had been a steady stream of wagons carrying lumber, ladders, hammers, nails, and all manner of materials to start the rebuilding of the manor first thing tomorrow morning.

When he'd arrived at Thornwick the ashes were cold. All the servants had either fled or died of the fever. There was no answer to his question whether the fire had been an accident or deliberately set in order to stop the rampages of the fever. For days no one wanted to go near the house. Neither did Harrison, but not from fear of the fever. Guilt. More than once his brother had asked him to come for a visit. He should have missed the parties, the hunts, and the gaming hells. He should have gone. If he'd been a good brother, he would have been there to help, not drinking, gambling, and dueling. Maybe he could have saved them. Or maybe he would have died with them? Not that he wanted to die. His scandalous ways saved him from the fever but also kept him from saving his family.

Guilt was a hard thing to deal with.

The day he arrived, he cleaned out one of the shell rooms, scavenged what few pieces of furniture he could, and made his home among the ruins. Within a week, he didn't have a stitch of clothing that wasn't smeared with soot. He'd found an older couple in a nearby village willing to help him with the cleanup; others had come later. He'd sent for Thornwick's managers and solicitors and immediately started familiarizing himself with the inner workings of the vast estate, but there was still a lot to learn.

"My lord, there is a Mr. Alfred Hopscotch here to see you."

Harrison's stomach clenched. He turned to see Summers, one of his workers, standing behind him. He had a vague recollection of the first time he'd met Mr. Hopscotch. It wasn't a fond memory.

"He's not alone," Summers continued. "He brought some of the Prince's guards with him."

That seems odd.

"Did he say what he wanted?"

"Just that he's an emissary of the Prince and he must

speak to you at once. Given that, I didn't feel I should question him further."

Harrison nodded once. "I'll see what he wants. Where is he?"

"By his carriage in the front of the house. I apologized for not having a room where we could invite him inside."

Harrison glanced at the stacks of lumber and smiled. "Not yet, Summers," he promised. "But we will."

As soon as Harrison rounded the corner Mr. Hopscotch walked to meet him. "I'm sorry to disturb you, my lord, but I must. The Prince and I have sent you several letters requesting you come to London, and you've ignored them all."

"I'll have to beg the Prince's pardon," Harrison said, looking down at his soot-stained shirt and trousers. "It's been a little difficult to keep up with correspondence from my home recently."

Mr. Hopscotch cleared his throat rather loudly and mumbled, "Yes, I'm sure. We were sorry to hear about the fire. The Prince realizes his mistake in asking that you come to London immediately upon hearing of your family's deaths and sends his apologies for the grave error in judgment. But it's been over three months now. The Prince is most anxious for you to return to London by the time the Season starts next week."

"That would be difficult," Harrison said, hoping to hurry the man on his way. "As you can see, the rebuilding of Thornwick is just beginning. I'm needed here. Please give my apologies to the Prince."

"I'm afraid he won't take no for an answer this time, my lord. I must have your word that you will be at the first ball of the Season, or . . ."

Harrison's eyes narrowed as the man's words trailed

off. That comment seemed rather high-handed even for a Prince who was more used to getting his way than Harrison was. "Or what?"

Mr. Hopscotch held up his hand and snapped his fingers twice. Four sentinels appeared, two from each side of the carriage. Each guard rested a blunderbuss on his shoulders, and their swords hung at their sides.

Summers wasn't kidding when he said the man had brought armed guards.

"Or these men have strict orders to escort you directly to Newgate."

Harrison smiled and then chuckled. Evidently there were some things about being an earl he still had to learn. When the Prince called he meant for you to come.

"Prison?" Harrison said good-naturedly. "For ignoring the Prince? That's a bit harsh for a civilized society, isn't it?"

"It's more than that, my lord," Hopscotch said, remaining serious. "He feels he has given you ample time to mourn your family and now he must insist that you do your duty as an Englishman and an earl. He wants you to marry quickly and produce an heir."

"Marry?" Harrison scoffed another laugh. "The Prince can't be serious. I can assure you bringing a bride to Thornwick at present is the last thing on my mind."

"But it's very much on the Prince's mind. You must realize that should you meet your demise before you have an heir, the title would fall to your cousin Guilfoyle. The Prince will do everything in his power to keep that from happening."

Harrison knew Guilfoyle. He was a stiff coxcomb, but he wasn't a bad sort. In fact, his reputation was a hell of a lot better than Harrison's. He'd never heard of the man racing his curricle down Rotten Row when half the ton was out for an afternoon stroll, or shooting a man in a duel.

"Start explaining," Harrison said, still not wanting to believe it really mattered to the Prince who actually held the title Earl of Thornwick. "I want to know exactly what the Prince wants with me and why."

"There are many reasons he is so interested in you in particular. You are good friends with the Duke of Drakestone and the Prince is pleased about that, but chief among the others is because of your cousin Guilfoyle. He has ties to the top military officials in France. As you know, his wife is French and her uncle is a high-ranking officer in their military. Quite frankly, the Prince doesn't trust your cousin as far as his loyalties are concerned. He is the last person the Prince wants taking a seat in Parliament to help govern and fashion the laws of England. Why, the man's even educating his son in France."

"None of that is of any concern to me, Mr. Hopscotch. Rebuilding my home is."

"But it is a major concern to the Prince. You have never given him any cause to worry about where your loyalties lie even though you've spent time abroad."

"And I don't intend to," Harrison said, restlessly shifting his stance.

"Splendid. Your marriage to a proper young lady with an heir on the way would make the Prince very happy."

Harrison considered this entire conversation nonsense. Marrying was the last thing on his mind and the Prince was just going to have to accept that fact.

"That is not likely to happen when I haven't met a lady I want to wed."

"The Prince suspected that," Mr. Hopscotch said casually, seeming unconcerned with Harrison's growing irritation. "He's pleased to let you know that he has chosen someone for you."

Harrison laughed out loud, but Mr. Hopscotch never twitched a hint of a smile. "You want me to believe the Prince has actually chosen a bride for me?"

"It's true, my lord."

"And if I marry His Highness' pick of the litter, has the Prince indicated yet whether we shall provide the world with a male or female child within nine months?"

Refusing to acknowledge Harrison's attempt at humor, Mr. Hopscotch shrugged. "I must admit that there are some things the Prince has no control over."

"Please, tell the Prince I appreciate his interest in my marital status, but right now the only thing that I have on my mind is rebuilding my family's legacy. After that is done, I will look for a bride to be mistress of Thornwick."

"I'm sure you are quite capable and can accomplish both at the same time, my lord. The young lady is bright, lovely, and more than suitable for you. Her grandfather was a baron and her father a distant relative of the King himself."

Harrison looked from the guards to Hopscotch. "Even if I were inclined to marry, which I'm not, I wouldn't have the Prince choosing a bride for me. Now, if you don't mind, I've work to do."

Mr. Hopscotch nervously fiddled with the ends of his neckcloth. "I'm afraid I can't leave without your word that you'll come to London next week."

Harrison felt his frown deepen. "Does the Prince think I will allow him to control my life and pick a bride for me without question?"

"Certainly not. Question all you want, but the Prince knows you will acquiesce in the end."

The man seemed very certain. A feeling of unease crept up Harrison's back. "And why does he know that?"

"Because you broke the law by dueling."

"What the devil?" Harrison took an agitated step toward the man.

"That's right," Mr. Hopscotch said with all confidence. "So no, you don't have to marry the lovely lady he's chosen for you, but if you don't the Prince will see to it that you spend at least the next five years in prison for attempted murder while dueling."

Harrison scowled. "He wouldn't."

"He would. And it would all be perfectly legal. You dueled a few months back. I can attest to it myself and find at least half a dozen more gentlemen who will swear to it in court, including the man you shot."

A flare of temper swept through Harrison. "You bloody blackguard. I didn't want the duel. I tried to walk away from the man. He's the one who insisted."

Harrison took another menacing step toward the robust man. He heard the shuffle of muskets being lowered and tromping footsteps. He looked over Hopscotch's shoulder and saw that the guards had walked closer and had their blunderbusses pointed directly at his chest. Harrison wasn't a foolish man. He stopped and slowly lifted his hands in the air. It would be his luck that one of the guards was eager to pull the trigger.

He had finally gotten the message: The Prince meant business. He would be damned before he was shot over a young lady who couldn't snare a husband any way but by force.

Mr. Hopscotch turned and motioned for the men to lower their weapons. He cleared his throat nervously. "Perhaps I am what you call me, but your feelings for me will not change what the Prince wants or what he will do to get it. He will see to it that the courts have whatever evidence they need to fulfill his wishes. If I snap my fingers again the guards will arrest you and take you straight to Newgate, where you will be accommodated before, during, and after your trial." He paused. "You need to make the right decision, my lord. I'm told the courts are very slow when Parliament is in session."

Harrison had never liked being told what to do. But he didn't want to risk losing Thornwick, either. He was the one who stayed away when his brother asked him to come home. He was the one gambling and drinking when his family died and the house burned. Now he was the only one left. It was his responsibility to build it back. And he wasn't going to let prison or anything else stop him from doing that.

"If I decide I will marry this spring, I will choose my own bride," Harrison said in a deadly quiet voice.

"That would be very awkward for the Prince. As I mentioned, the young lady's father is a relative of the King."

"So the Prince wants to favor the man with a title for his daughter?"

"It wouldn't be prudent of me to comment on that. I trust you understand."

Harrison hesitated. Hell yes, he understood, and he didn't like it. "Tell the Prince I'll come to London next week and meet her, but I'm not promising I'll marry her."

"One step at a time. I understand." Mr. Hopscotch smiled for the first time and fiddled with his neckcloth again. "Good enough for now. She's making her debut at the Great Hall, which is hosting the first ball of the Season. I'll see to it that someone presents Miss Angelina Rule to you."

Miss Rule? God help me.

Even her name made Harrison want to grind his teeth. Rules weren't anything he wanted to become familiar with.

Mr. Hopscotch tipped his hat to Harrison. "Good day, my lord."

Harrison watched the man walk to his carriage, his soldiers following him. If Miss Rule's father had to call in a favor from the Prince to leg-shackle a husband for her, there must be something wrong with her. Harrison didn't even want to consider what that might be. *He* would choose the next mistress of Thornwick.

But if the Prince kept his word and Harrison was charged with dueling, could he fight the charges and win? It certainly wouldn't help him that there had been several convictions for dueling in recent years. But Harrison wasn't without friends. Bray was a duke. Perhaps he could give Harrison some advice on how to avoid the Prince's ultimatum.

In the meantime, he didn't want to be managing the rebuilding of Thornwick from that hellhole called Newgate. He had a feeling the Prince would have him thrown in there if for no other reason than to prove to Harrison he could.

Harrison wasn't completely heartless. He wanted a wife and heir one day. He supposed all men did. But he didn't want to be forced into marrying a young lady just so the Prince would feel safe from the possible clutches of a French sympathizer.

"Damnation," he muttered under his breath.

He was still learning what being an earl was about. He had no inclination to learn about being a husband and father, too.

Chapter 3

So quick bright things come to confusion.
A Midsummer Night's Dream *5.1.111*

Angelina Rule leaned over and gazed dreamily at the man. He looked just the way she wanted him to: tall, lean, and broadly built with wide shoulders and chest. His frame was lithe with a slim waist and sturdy, powerful-looking legs. The color of his eyes was an amazing and intriguing mixture of deep forest green and golden brown. His features were strong, aristocratic, his lips full and well-defined with just a hint of amusement lifting the corners.

She smiled at the attractive gentleman, and she liked the way he smiled back at her.

Something disturbed her concentration.

Angelina looked up from the miniature she was painting, squinted in the light of the glaring sun, and listened for a moment. All she heard were the peaceful sounds of the early-spring morning in her back garden. She turned and glanced at Sam, who lay on one of the warm stepping-stones that led to the back door of the house. He had raised his head; his short floppy ears had perked up, too. As usual, Rascal was too lazy to be bothered by sounds that weren't offering food. Perhaps all that had distracted them was a distant driver shouting at his ill-tempered horses.

Angelina blinked several times to adjust her eyes and went back to tediously painting a bow on the neckcloth of the gentleman with a fine, delicate brush. Having already decided that the handsome rogue would have on a sage-green waistcoat to match his eyes, she pondered whether to give the clothing shiny gold or leather-brown buttons down the front.

Another sound. This time she was sure she'd heard whimpering, and so had Sam. The mix of bull terrier and only God knew what else rose quickly from the step and took off barking and barreling toward the rear gate. That got the old hound's attention and she hightailed it after Sam, adding her deep warning bark.

Angelina ripped off the spectacles she used when painting miniatures and laid them on the table. She reached down and picked up the large tin dome she used to cover her work when she left it outside and settled it over her brushes, palette, and the lid to the snuffbox. Long ago she had learned the heart-wrenching way not to leave her paintings outside unprotected from butterflies, beetles, and all manner of insects that wanted to land and crawl around on the fresh paint.

"Sam, Rascal, quiet!" she called as she rose from her chair, picked up the hem of her dress, and headed after the dogs. Before she threw the lock, Sam was already nudging to get past her and out the gate.

"No. Sit. Stay." The brindle-colored dog obeyed immediately, but Rascal, being mostly hound, continued to bark and scratch at the gate. "Sit," she said again. And then more forcibly she added, "Sit, Rascal!"

Rascal grumbled and barked again but reluctantly obeyed. Angelina opened the gate just enough to wedge her way through and closed it quickly behind her. She looked twice up and down the tree-lined lane that separated the rows of houses before spotting a small brown dog curled near a hitching post.

"Oh, you poor dear," she said, hurrying over to him. She gasped when she knelt down and saw he was lying in a wet, boggy spot of dead grass. He was only a puppy, terribly malnourished and shivering.

Dark, frightened eyes stared at her. He had the coloring and shape of a beagle, but she doubted the bloodline was pure. Strays seldom were. There were cuts and scratches on the animal's head and upper body. The outline of his ribs was clearly visible beneath his short hair. Her heart went out to him so with no thought but to help and comfort, she reached for him. He snarled and snapped at her.

Angelina jerked her hands away and sat back on her heels. Sam and Rascal must have heard the stray's warning because they started barking and clawing at the gate again. She called to quiet them.

She then spoke calmly to the shaking, frightened puppy before her. "Well, Mr. Pete," she said, giving the dog the first name that popped into her mind. "That is no way to introduce yourself to someone who is only trying to help you. You look like you need a friend. Now, I'm going to sit here with you for a while and let you get used to me. When I ease my hand toward you again, I want you to sniff, not snap. Understand?"

A few minutes later Angelina had the trembling dog wrapped in the skirt of her paint-stained apron and, holding him carefully, she opened the gate and stepped inside. Sam, being at least some part bull terrier, stiffened his legs and formed an attack stance. He growled up at the stray. Rascal followed suit by curling her lips, but Angelina was having none of that from either of them.

She looked down at her pets and said firmly, "That's enough from you two. Cease right now. I found you both on the street and I can return you to the street. Mind your manners and be quiet or out you go with the rubbish."

Sam listened to her command and remained quiet but furiously wagged his short tail. Rascal barked at her as if to argue. Sam had been easy to train into submission, but the hound had to test Angelina over and over again before giving in and heeding her commands.

"Just for that," Angelina told Rascal, "you will stay out here with Sam and not come into the house with us."

The two dogs followed her to the door, obviously hoping she would change her mind and they would get inside, but she kept her word and shut them out. After quietly slipping into the house, she peeked inside the kitchen. It was empty. She smiled.

"Looks like today is your lucky day, Mr. Pete," she said softly. "Mrs. Bickmore must be taking her rest before she starts preparing dinner."

Angelina looked around the room and quickly spotted a loaf of bread on the woodstove. She hesitated. Mrs. Bickmore wouldn't be happy, but she wouldn't say anything, either.

After she placed the puppy on the floor, she grabbed a plate and knife from the cupboard and cut off a quarter of the loaf. She then uncovered the pitcher of milk and poured a small amount over the bread before adding a dipper of water and then putting it in front of the starving animal. In three greedy bites the plate was clean. He looked up at her with his big brown eyes, licked his chops, wagged his tail anxiously, and whined pitifully for more.

Angelina looked from Mr. Pete to the bread and milk.

"All right. A little more bread, but no milk this time. Only water. I can't overfeed you or you'll be sick. And don't eat this one so fast," she added as if the puppy could understand and would obey her. "After you finish and are feeling a little stronger, I'll wash your cuts and put some ointment on them."

It wasn't the first time she had pilfered food from the kitchen to feed a stray and she doubted it would be her last. She took another large slice off the loaf and made a plate for him. And contrary to her instructions, he ate the second just as ravenously as the first. She reached down to pick up the empty plate and saw her father's boots.

Caught.

She winced.

Angelina slowly rose and tried to step in front of the puppy even though she knew there was no way the eagle-eyed Archard Rule hadn't seen and heard Mr. Pete. Her father was a tall, thin, and handsome man who was almost regal in the proud way he carried himself. His light-brown hair had recently receded slightly from his forehead but nothing else gave away the fact that he was well past forty.

"Papa, I didn't know you were home."

"Obviously," her father said as he crossed his arms over his chest and began to gently tap one booted foot on the floor. "Feeding the family dinner to yet another stray?"

She looked from his frown to what was left of the raided loaf. Her father had been gone more than he had been home for the past three weeks, and when he was home, he was either distracted and aloof or short-tempered and irritated. She didn't want to add to whatever had been bothering him, but she couldn't have left Mr. Pete on the side of the road.

Angelina squared her shoulders. "He's injured and starving."

"All of them are," he said testily. "We can't feed every dog left to beg on the streets of London."

But that didn't keep her from wanting to take care of them all.

"I know you've told me more than once not to pick up any more strays, Papa, but he's just a puppy. He can't be more than a few weeks old. He doesn't know how to scavenge for food yet. He's so little."

"We already have three dogs," he said, the tap of his foot getting louder.

"Well, really only two in that Molly belongs to Grandmother."

"Angelina, your grandmother lives here and so does her dog."

She folded her hands together in front of her, sighed, and lowered her lashes over her eyes for a moment. It had always been difficult for Angelina to know when to just be quiet and give her father time to think and adjust to whatever point she was trying to make. But she had to press on if she was to have any hope of keeping Mr. Pete. It would be heartbreaking if she had to put the shivering puppy, sitting so quietly at her feet, back on the street to fend for himself.

She glanced up at her father and was surprised by the tightness that showed around his mouth and eyes. Clearly something serious was bothering him. If they had been talking about anything other than the future of this puppy, she would have backed away from the conversation and queried as to what was wrong.

"Mr. Pete looks to be at least part beagle. I know he'll be a pleasant, mild-mannered pet."

Her father's blue eyes widened and he threw his hands up into the air in disbelief. "You named him?"

She blinked rapidly. "Well, I—yes, I had to call him something," she defended. "I don't think he'll get very large and he won't eat much."

"He almost ate a whole loaf of bread," her father said on an exasperated sigh.

"I doubt he'd eaten in days."

"Heaven have mercy, Angelina, you would turn this house into a kennel if I let you."

Angelina thought she sensed the sound of weakening in her father's tone so she said, "I'm sorry, Papa. But see how quiet and well-behaved he is. He hasn't made a sound since you walked in. I promise he will be no bother to you."

"Oh, all right, you can keep him, for now," he said, shaking his head. "I've too many other things on my mind at present to deal with this."

Angelina threw her arms around her father's chest and hugged him tightly. "Thank you, Papa."

"I just hope you will still be thanking me later," he mumbled near her ear as he hugged her to him for a second before setting her away. "Put him in the room where the others are kept at night and come into the drawing room when you finish. But change your apron first. You look like a ragamuffin. I've already asked your grandmother to join us. I have something important to discuss with you."

Thrilled that she had won, at least for the time being, Angelina started untying her soiled apron. "I'll take care of him, wash up, and be right in."

A few minutes later Angelina was almost floating with happiness as she walked into the drawing room.

Her grandmother Lady Railbridge was sitting in her usual spot on the floral-printed settee.

"Good afternoon, Granna," Angelina said to her youthful-looking grandmother. Unlike Angelina who took after her tall and blue-eyed father, Lady Railbridge was petite and brown-eyed with chestnut hair that had only recently begun to show a smattering of silver woven in its thick depths. The only thing that gave away her age was the thick blue veins showing beneath the thin white skin of her hands.

Her grandmother had come to live with them and help care for Angelina after her mother died four years ago. Lady Railbridge looked so much like her daughter that it had given Angelina tremendous comfort to have her nearby.

The older woman smiled and reached out her hands to Angelina. "Let's have a look."

Angelina chuckled lightly and placed her palms down in her grandmother's soft hands. "Very clean, Granna," she said. "No sign of paint under my nails." She turned her hands over. "Or in my life lines."

"That's my perfect young lady," her grandmother said, sporting a pleased smile that always reminded Angelina of her mother.

For the past year her grandmother had been readying Angelina for the fast-approaching Season. From an early age Angelina had a tutor to teach her writing, reading, and sums as well as the finer things a young lady was supposed to know such as French, embroidery, and playing the pianoforte. But from her very first art lesson, Angelina had fallen in love with painting. She loved to create and re-create scenes from life or her imagination, or sometimes copy from original oils on canvas, ivory, fans, shells, or most anything the paint would adhere to. With the first ball of the Season only a week away, her grandmother was insisting she be more careful when washing the paints off her hands.

She had teased Angelina a few days ago by saying, "My biggest fear is that you will take your gloves off at a duke's dinner table and there will be paint stains running up your arms."

Angelina kissed her grandmother's soft cheek and then glanced over at her father. Her stomach tightened. She felt again that something was wrong. He stood in front of the fireplace, his back to them. His head was lowered and the regal tilt of his shoulders slumped. There were times he let grief over losing his wife overwhelm him; today must be one of those times.

Feeling a spark of guilt for testing his patience about the puppy, she laid an affectionate hand on his shoulder and said, "Papa, don't worry. I will find another home for Mr. Pete."

He sighed heavily and slowly turned toward her. His eyes had narrowed, his forehead was wrinkled into a tight frown, and his lips had formed into a thin grimace. At that moment she thought that he actually looked older than her grandmother.

He stared at her for so long she became anxious and said, "Papa what's wrong?"

"I know it's a poor choice of words to use, Angelina, but I have good news and bad news."

"Oh, dear," her grandmother whispered behind Angelina.

The fine hairs on the back of her neck tingled, and she swallowed slowly. "I'll take the bad news first," she said calmly, knowing that no news could ever be as bad as when she'd heard four years ago that her mother had died in her sleep.

For as long as Angelina could remember her mother was sickly, needing more and more medication as the years passed. Angelina had done her best to help care for her. Still, it was a shock when she went to sleep one night and didn't wake the next morning.

A tired, rueful sound passed her father's lips before he said, "You have always been far braver than me, Angelina."

"Nonsense," she said with more confidence than she was feeling. She wasn't brave at all. She was terrified she'd hear he had some dreaded disease and little time to live, but instead of telling him her fears she said, "This way, the good news will help soothe the bad."

"Archard, stop stalling and tell us what's wrong," her grandmother injected in a worried tone. "Angelina, come sit by me."

"I'll stand," she answered her grandmother, though her legs were already feeling weak.

"I'll get right to it then," her father said, though he hesitated again. "No use in delaying longer. I'm afraid I'm in dire jeopardy of going to debtors' prison."

A jolt of shock jerked her. "What?" Angelina whispered.

Debtors' prison? My father?

"Archard, no!" Granna exclaimed and rose to stand beside Angelina.

"It's true," he answered, not meeting his daughter's or his mother-in-law's eyes. "I foolishly invested everything we own in a fool's game of chance and lost."

"Even my accounts?" Granna asked.

His gaze darted to his mother-in-law. "You must understand that in the end I had to. I had borrowed money to ease the burden of our increasing creditors and then had to borrow more to pay the first lender, and then the second. It's a nasty group of jackanapes who have me twisting in their grip. I've not been able to break free from them. Now there is no one left to borrow from and I have no means of paying back any of them. We've lost everything."

Amid the crushing blow of helplessness, Angelina immediately wondered what she could do to aid her father. He had changed after her mother died, drinking more than usual and staying away for days at a time. She knew her father spent time at his clubs, and gambled from time to time. But how was it possible that he'd allowed his debts to mount so extensively?

"What do you mean by 'everything,' Archard?" Lady Railbridge asked what Angelina was thinking but couldn't voice.

Her father's regal shoulders flew back and he turned an irate gaze toward her grandmother. "What do you think I mean by it, my lady? Every investment I had, every piece of furniture in this house, every piece of jewelry that would have gone to Angelina, every pence, pound, and shilling. Everything including eighty percent of my yearly allowance going to a tightfisted money lender! The only reason this house isn't included is because it belongs to my second cousin."

Angelina could not hold in her gasp. She squeezed her hands into tight fists and winced. He truly was in danger of prison?

Her grandmother's eyes flashed wild with worry. "I don't understand. What did you do to get in this position? Cards? Dice? Something else?"

"Must I give all the sordid details, Lady Railbridge?" he asked indignantly. "Will you not leave me some thread of self-respect? Will only the airing of the intimate, sullied details of my downfall satisfy you?"

"No, Papa, no," Angelina said, blindly stepping into the conversation. "She doesn't want that."

"Good, because I won't subject myself to that evil,"

he said emphatically. "Neither of you knows what it's like to be the poorest man in a family of titles, prestige, and legacies, always depending on the generosity of a wealthy relative to take pity on you and give you an allowance, which I might add is so meager that it can scarcely pay the rent, let alone the grocer, tailor, and the few servants. Yet I have been expected to care for my daughter in the grandest of ways and live the life of a gentleman on such a pittance all these years. We wouldn't have done as well as we have if not for your grandmother moving in, bringing her maid to aid you, and helping with expenses. So yes, yes, I wanted better for you than I've been able to give, and I'm not ashamed of doing my best to get it for you." His voice suddenly faltered. "I regret that I made such a muddle of it, not that I tried."

Angelina's heart went out to her father for the pain he was feeling. She knew it hadn't been his intention to end up in this horrid situation. She must find a way to help him.

"Papa, if things were this desperate for you, why did you allow us to spend so much money on gowns, gloves, headpieces, and other clothing for me for the Season? Just last week you brought me more gold and silver dust for my paintings. I don't understand. Why didn't you say something?"

His eyes softened and she saw genuine love for her in his eyes. "Can't I indulge my daughter if I want to without asking anyone's permission? You wanted it, I wanted to get it for you."

She was astounded, silent for a moment. "Surely you know I would rather have you at home and your debts paid than to have the dust and all the finery you've purchased for me these many years."

"No, no, don't you see, Angelina," he said gently

taking hold of her shoulders and gripping them affectionately. "All I did was for you. So you would have the best of everything. You deserved a proper Season just like all your cousins have had so you could catch the eye of a titled gentleman."

"A title?" she asked, confused, heartbroken, and a little angry. "Papa, you know I've been waiting for Captain Maxwell to return from India so we could make a match."

"An army officer, Angelina," her father said, suddenly sounding irritated again. His grip tightened on her. "I've never agreed to such a meeting with the captain. Besides, you don't know when or if he is ever returning. He could even be married to someone else by now. It's my responsibility to take care of you and see that you have the very best. The day you were born I promised your mother I would see you properly wed, and I'm going to do it."

"But what will this news of your possible imprisonment do to Angelina's chances of making a good match when the Season starts next week?" her grandmother asked.

"Granna," Angelina injected. "I'm not worried about the Season right now. I don't want Papa to go to prison."

"I may not have to," her father said, letting go of her to rub his eyes with his thumb and forefinger before looking at her again. "That is the good news I promised. I have been working on a plan for your future. Though it took me quite a while to accomplish it, the Prince finally agreed to see me a couple of weeks ago."

"The Prince?" her grandmother said breathlessly.

"Yes, even though we're distant cousins by marriage, as you know, I haven't seen him since he became the Regent."

"I know that's always bothered you," Granna said.

"I admit it," her father agreed, pulling on the tail of his coat. "Apparently he is much too busy for his poorer cousins now. Not surprising. However, having no other choice, I kept soliciting him and finally met with him a few days ago."

"You never said a word to us," her grandmother commented.

"There was no reason to. You couldn't have done any more than I was doing. I was forthright with him about my circumstances. At the time, he had nothing favorable to offer, but then yesterday I had a note from him, asking that I visit him today. His news was better than I could have hoped." Her father stopped, squared his shoulders, lifted his chin, and took in a deep breath. "The Prince knows of an earl who is in need of a suitable wife. With your grandmother being a baroness and me his cousin, the Prince believes you will be a perfect match for the earl, Angelina, and I agree. If you marry him by the end of the Season, the Prince will settle all my debts and I'll avoid disgracing myself, you, and the family name."

Her grandmother whispered, "An earl."

Anguish blazed through Angelina, choking her. Not marry the man she had dreamed about for three years? Her father in debt and facing prison. It was too much to take in. She didn't want her father to go to debtors' prison but she didn't want to marry the earl, either. She wanted to marry Captain Maxwell. What her father said was true, no promises had been made between her and the captain, but she knew he was waiting for her.

Hoping she'd heard her father wrong, she asked, "An arranged marriage? For me?"

"Yes, and all my debts will be settled," he added with

a twitch of a smile. "When you meet the Earl of Thornwick next week, if he finds you acceptable, he will marry you."

The fine hairs on the back of Angelina's neck spiked in protest. "If he finds me acceptable?"

"The Earl of Thornwick, Archard!" her grandmother exclaimed, jumping into the conversation again. "You can't be serious! That man is an outrage, a scoundrel if there ever was one. You know his reputation. He is not acceptable for her."

"That's not for you to decide, my lady."

"Well, it doesn't appear you are capable of determining that."

Angelina's breaths came short, fast, and heavy. She'd heard about the notorious Earl of Thornwick from some of the ladies in her reading society and her sewing circle. She stepped back and slowly sat down on the settee while her father and grandmother continued to talk.

From the gossip, she knew the Earl of Thornwick was devilishly handsome, a rake, and that he had only recently become an earl. He was known far and wide by his association with two other rogues. The three of them had scandalized London for years with raucous behavior that kept polite Society in an uproar, racing their curricles through crowded parks and disrespecting rules of convention at every turn. His lordship even had the nerve to walk down several streets in Mayfair with a mistress on each arm.

To hear the young ladies talk, neither he nor his two friends had a shred of decency among them when they were younger. She had no reason to believe that had changed. But even after all those horrible things were said about Lord Thornwick, every lady attending agreed she was dying for the earl to ask her to dance and hoped that she would be the one he would find favor with and marry.

Not Angelina. She found it difficult to believe the ladies actually wanted to marry such a man. A man who followed no rules and had no order in his life. She would have eyes only for the honorable and distinguished Captain Maxwell. A military man. He would know all about following orders, obeying rules, and being a true gentleman.

"You are talking about his past," she heard her father say though she had no idea what her grandmother had said to prompt that answer from him.

"He's settled down now," her father continued. "All that was before he became the earl. Why, he hasn't even been in London for weeks now."

"I'm sure that's because he was in a duel not three months ago and shot a man."

Yes, Angelina had heard about the duel, too. There was much gossip in her reading society about it. Everyone thought the reason the earl hadn't been in Town was because he had been shot, too, and was recovering from his wounds. They had all speculated as to what the duel had been fought over. An insult, a woman, or a wager? The ladies in her group had giggled and decided it must have been because he was having a torrid love affair with the other man's wife.

If that was true, did her father really want her to marry such a man?

"All gossip!" her father insisted strongly. "I have it on good authority that the earl has changed. Besides, what he has done or not done is of no consequence to us. Only that he be a good match for Angelina."

Angelina rose and said, "Papa, I don't want you to go to prison but I don't want to marry the earl, either. You know I've had my heart set on Captain Maxwell. We must think of something else."

"Nonsense. Besides, what else is there? Haven't you heard a word I've said? We are destitute. I'm completely without further resources with no way to obtain any." He looked down at her with eyes a lighter shade of blue than her own. "I've already made the arrangements with the Prince for you to meet Lord Thornwick next week. I've just returned from seeing my creditors and, because of the possibility of the Prince paying them in full, all have agreed to give me a two-month reprieve. Don't you understand, if your marriage to the earl takes place by the end of the Season, the Prince will take care of everything. I'll be free. If not, there will be no further delays. I will be quickly sentenced to one of the debtors' prisons."

Angelina's throat swelled. She wanted to help her father. She had always tried to help her father. He was in this predicament because he'd been trying to help her. How could she give up on her dream of becoming Captain Maxwell's bride?

But what else could she do?

Swallowing the lump in her throat, she asked softly, "Papa, is there no other way?"

"I'm afraid not." He lowered his eyes and shook his head. "I wouldn't force you to marry anyone you find despicable, my angel," he continued, in an affectionate tone. "I legitimately owe the debts, and I'm willing to go to prison if I must."

"Archard, that's cruel." '

He looked up. "It's the facts, my lady."

A stiff, aching pain seemed to crowd into every part of Angelina's body and soul. "I'll do it," she said. "I'll meet the earl and if he will have me, I will marry him."

But I will never like it.

"The earl will give you a much better life than an army officer could hope to," her father answered with a satisfied glow in his eyes. "It's settled then. At the opening ball next week you will be introduced to the earl. I have no doubts whatsoever that he will find favor with you. How could he not?"

Angelina remained silent.

Her father then muttered, "I'm sorry about all this. It's not how I wanted your Season to be. I've done the best I can for you under the circumstances. I'm not asking for gratitude. Acceptance will do." He reached down and kissed her on the forehead. "Now go see about that new stray you brought home and don't think about any of this for now." He turned and strode out of the drawing room.

Shivering from the raw emotions that gripped her, Angelina took in long, deep, silent breaths. She had no idea how much money was involved in her father's gambling losses, but from all he said, they must be considerable. She wondered if Captain Maxwell had enough money to pay her father's gambling debts if she married him. Would he want to if he could? How could she broach the subject with him? They had no understanding between them. Just sweet smiles and the promise of a dance when he returned. Would the honorable Captain Maxwell even want to talk to her if he knew her father was in danger of going to debtors' prison?

She felt her grandmother's warm, comforting arms go around her. Still she didn't move.

"Mark my words," Granna said. "All this will work out for the best, Angelina. I'll go see about having some tea brought in. It will make you feel better."

Angelina's father's words faded to the back of her mind as her thoughts drifted to Captain Maxwell.

Suddenly her breathing slowed, her shoulders relaxed, and she calmed. Thinking about him always soothed her.

Angelina remembered the first time she saw Captain Maxwell. Her grandmother's friend had come for tea and brought someone with her, but Angelina didn't know who. She waited at the top of the stairs for them to leave so she could see. That's when she saw Captain Nicholas Maxwell for the first time. The officer must have sensed she was watching him because he turned, looked up at her, and smiled. Her heart had melted like snow on hot bricks.

Angelina had never seen a more handsome and appealing man. The red coat of his uniform with its shiny brass buttons and gold fringe epaulets was impeccable, prestigious, and dashing. He looked so gallant and very much the protector of innocents with his sword hanging by his side. Ever since that first glimpse of him, whenever she painted a gentleman, she always gave him Captain Maxwell's enchanting smile.

That was when she was sixteen. In the last three years, she'd seen him a few more times and spoken to him twice. Last year, when he'd stopped at the door and looked up at her, he'd asked when she would make her debut in Society. Another year, she'd replied. He'd smiled at her and said he would look forward to seeing her when he returned from India.

"Save me a dance," he said with a smile.

According to her grandmother, Captain Maxwell's aunt said he was expected home from India in time for the first ball of the Season.

Next week!

Her stomach muscles contracted at the thought of seeing him again. She wondered if he'd been longing to see her. If he wanted to marry her. But even if Captain Maxwell didn't want to marry her, how would she manage to live with a man like the earl? A man who had no order or discipline in his life. A man who had seldom followed Society's rules—in fact, deliberately flaunted them.

No, she wanted an honorable man. A man who wore a uniform and looked like Captain Maxwell. She would meet the Earl of Thornwick. She may even be forced to marry him, but she would never welcome him into her bed.

Chapter 4

Who loses and who wins; who's in, who's out.
King Lear *5.3.15*

Harrison could dance as well as the next man, but he'd never found it entertaining. To him there was something unnatural about a man skipping, hopping, and moving around to music. But here he was in the middle of a hot, crowded dance floor surrounded by people who, like him, looked utterly ridiculous light-stepping to the rhythm.

He and the young lady he was with followed the leaders and helped form a canopy of arms for others to dance under two at a time. There was no doubt his partner was lovely, quite shapely he guessed beneath the high-waisted gown, and completely infatuated with her accomplishments. She could play the pianoforte and sing at the same time, she always wrote the most stirring verse in her poetry society, and she received nothing but praise from everyone for her elaborate embroidery samples. If it took appreciation for things like that to make him a respectable earl in Society or a dutiful husband, he was at the point of thinking maybe Newgate wasn't looking so bad.

At last, he and the talkative miss had their turn skipping under the covering of arms. Gratefully the dance ended soon after that. He could only count it a blessing that her name wasn't Miss Rule.

He quickly left the sparkling-eyed doe with her mother and fled to the champagne table that had been set up in a far corner of the ballroom. Harrison couldn't say he'd actually been interested in a young lady since Maddie. He'd had his share of beautiful ladies, delightful women, and exotic females in his bed, and he'd enjoyed them all. But he hadn't come close to having warm, soft feelings for any of them.

Harrison had arrived in London three days ago. Since Mr. Hopscotch's last visit, he'd thought long and hard about not coming at all. There was another option available to him. He could have left the country, but that idea had no appeal. After his brother had married Maddie and she had their son, Harrison had spent two years traveling from the Americas to India and almost every country in between. He had no desire to see any more of the world.

Thornwick was his home now. He wanted to rebuild it, protect it, and preserve it.

For as long as he could remember, he'd lived the life of an unrestrained scoundrel. He had no obligations to anyone, no responsibilities for anything. That had changed when Thornwick and all it entailed had become his. His penchant for drinking, gambling, and staying out all night had ceased. Learning about Thornwick was his only passion.

Marrying and having a family hadn't been something he'd spent much time thinking about, either, until Mr. Hopscotch had arrived and given him the ultimatum to marry Miss Rule or go to prison for dueling. Harrison had concluded there was probably only one way to prevent either of those things happening and that was to select his own bride, marry, and produce the heir the Prince so desperately wanted. It was something he would have done eventually. The Prince's declaration had just accelerated the inevitable.

He was warming to the idea of having sons to watch grow up and play on the grounds of Thornwick as he and his brothers had. At the moment, he just wasn't keen on having a wife to produce those sons. When his friend Bray was born his mother had moved into her own house and she and Bray's father never lived together again. Harrison didn't see any reason why that type of situation wouldn't work for him if need be.

It was unfortunate for him, and a damned nuisance, too, that now that he had decided he needed to seriously consider having a son, he must first choose a bride.

And that was why he'd decided to make the journey to London and attend the Season. That was why he was at the ball early and why he had already danced with three young ladies very much like the one he'd just left.

Fate had given him Thornwick. It was now up to him to produce an heir, and not leave the task for his cousin Guilfoyle to fulfill. Harrison had decided he wanted to do that for himself. If it would please the Prince and keep him out of prison, all the better. Not that Harrison thought for a moment a French sympathizer could do much damage in England's Parliament, but if the Prince did, Harrison would try to oblige him.

Looking around the room, Harrison hoped to spot Bray. Perhaps Bray would have some ideas on how Harrison could stay out of Newgate and out of the parson's mousetrap, too, long enough to choose his own bride.

Harrison took a sip of champagne, and from over the rim of his glass caught sight of a striking golden-brown-haired young lady standing near the entrance of the ballroom. His stomach contracted as he brought down the glass. His gaze traveled swiftly over her at first and then went back for a slower look.

She wore an alabaster-colored gown trimmed in wide gold braid at the high waist and cuffs of her sleeves. The scooped neckline draped low enough to give a hint of the gentle swell of full, tempting breasts. She was tall, slender, and looked as beautiful as the paintings and statues he'd seen of Venus. She had the strong, capable appearance of the goddess Athena. But this young lady was not cold, hard stone. In fact, all she needed was a pair of wings on her shoulders to look like an angel. He knew she would be warm, soft, and delectable in his arms.

As he watched her, it seemed to him that she was intently searching the ballroom. Her gaze quickly flitted from one gentleman to another like a butterfly checking all the flowers on a bush before selecting just the right one to land on. Harrison's breathing increased as he watched her attention draw closer and closer to where he was standing. Would her eyes hesitate or brighten when they swooped across his face? Would they linger and take the time to thoroughly look him over as he had her the instant he'd seen her?

Harrison's lower body gently swelled at that possibility and he thought, *I want to be the gentleman she's looking for.*

He was attracted to her in a way he hadn't been attracted to a young lady since Maddie. Quickly her gaze caught his and stayed for a few seconds. Just about the time he thought she was interested, her sight skipped past him and continued her exploration of all the gentlemen in the room. He smiled to himself. She might not have had the same reaction to him as he'd had to her, but she had paused and for now that was enough.

Was she searching for a beau, a lover, or a husband?

No, his mind quickly shut down that line of thinking. He didn't want to consider the likelihood that she already belonged to another. Right now, he only wanted to meet her. Then he would continue from there.

It had been much too long since a young lady had intrigued him at first sight. He hoped that when he met her, she wouldn't want to tell him how good she was at stitchery, painting, or some other talent most ladies thought captivated a man. That she could arouse him on sight—that impressed him and that interested him.

As he continued to stare at her a petite, older lady and tall gentleman suddenly flanked her and the three of them stepped down into the ballroom. He watched her alabaster-colored skirt swirl around her long legs until she was swallowed by the crowd.

He chuckled to himself. Harrison didn't believe in love at first sight. He wasn't even sure he believed in love. But he did believe in want at first sight. Just as had happened with Maddie years ago, his mind, his body, and his soul told him he wanted that young lady to be his.

When Harrison turned to set his champagne glass on the table behind him so he could follow her, someone clapped him on the shoulder. He turned to see his good friend Bray, the Duke of Drakestone.

"Why the devil didn't you send word you were back in Town?"

Harrison couldn't very well tell him the truth—that

he had ruined every shirt he owned with soot and had to visit the tailor before he could be seen in public.

"Why bother to send over a note when I knew I'd see you tonight? I expected to see your lovely duchess by your side, though."

Bray and Harrison had been friends since their first year at Eton. The two of them, along with fellow student Adam Greyhawke, had managed to get into one madcap escapade after another all the way through Oxford, their teens, and on into their twenties. In fact, their raucous behavior hadn't stopped until four years ago when Adam married and Harrison left to tour the world.

"And she will be. My mother whisked her away to meet someone the moment we walked into the ballroom. I was on my way to pay respects to the dowagers and widows when I saw you standing over here without your usual swarm of young ladies vying for your attention."

"Oh, so your ritual of having the first dance of the evening with one of them is not going to change now that you are happily married and no longer the most eligible bachelor in London."

"No reason it should."

Harrison gave him a doubtful look. "I have a feeling it was Louisa who insisted you continue the tradition."

"It was." Bray grinned and then said, "When it comes to whatever Louisa wants, I don't usually mind. I wasn't sure you were coming to Town for the Season. How are things at Thornwick?"

"Better," he said, knowing Bray wouldn't press him for details he didn't want to share. "The rebuilding started last week."

"Good to hear. You plan to stay in London for the Season?"

"I'm not sure I have a choice right now."

Bray seemed to study on that comment before saying, "That sounds ominous, my friend. What's happened to cause this?"

"How well do you know the Prince?"

Bray shifted his stance. "Not very. Why?"

"It's too involved to get into tonight." Harrison took a drink from his champagne. His gaze automatically scanned the ballroom, looking for the golden-brown-haired angel he'd seen. Someone had already led her onto the dance floor.

Not surprising that she had already caught attention. She was easily a diamond of the first water and the belle of the ball tonight.

"Are you going to talk to me or stare at the dance floor?"

"You always see too much."

"There've been many times in the past when you were glad I did."

Harrison grinned. "You need not remind me of my foolish youth."

"Are you looking for anyone in particular, or have you already found her?"

Harrison smiled and ignored Bray's probing question. He knew his friend was fishing for what had caught his attention, and Harrison wasn't ready to divulge anything.

"Let's meet at the Heirs' Club this week," Bray said. "Now that you're in London you need to officially apply for membership."

"After all these years." Harrison's thoughts drifted back to the many times he'd walked through the door of that club and acted as if he owned it. "When we were younger I would have signed over my yearly allowance to a footpad to be a member. I didn't want to be a member this way."

"Understandable considering the circumstances. No one wants to gain entrance the way you did. Still, no need for you to continue to participate as my guest when you can have all the privileges of a member."

Harrison thought back over the many times he and Adam had played cards, billiards, and dice when they could get away with it in the Heirs' Club. It was the most exclusive of all the private gentlemen's clubs in London because in order to be a member you had to either have a title or be an heir to a title. No others need apply.

Bray was the only son of the Duke of Drakestone, so when he came of age he was reluctantly accepted for membership. Some of the older, stuffier members had tried to keep him out, fearing Bray and his unruly friends would disturb their quiet and orderly establishment. And Bray, Harrison, and Adam had from time to time. Or at least more times than Harrison could count anyway.

"What do you think the board members will say about now having two of the three *scoundrels* in the Heirs' Club?" Harrison asked.

"I have a feeling they will be saying, *Damnation! What the hell are we going to do with the two of them?*"

"And they'll complain about it for years."

"But we won't care."

"Not a damned whit."

Harrison and Bray laughed, remembering that it was at the Heirs' Club they'd planned an ill-advised journey to Dover where they'd jumped from one of the highest cliffs into the dangerous rocky waters below. Fate had smiled on them and somehow saved them all from certain death.

"Speaking of Adam," Harrison said, "have you heard from him recently?"

The laughter faded from Bray's features and he shook his head. "How about you?"

"Not a word since we visited him last year," Harrison answered.

"I wrote him about your brother and family. The fire. I had hoped he'd be in touch with you."

"I can understand why he hasn't," Harrison said, remembering how he felt when he heard about the deaths of his brother, Maddie, and their children. He didn't even want to imagine what it must have been like for Adam to have lost his wife and babe during childbirth.

"Maybe we should go see him again," Bray said. "What do you think?"

"That it's a good idea. He seemed to be all right with our visit last spring, didn't he?"

Bray nodded. "Let's make plans to do that at the club, too. I'll ask for a time from the review panel and send you a note."

"Good."

"Time for my duty on the dance floor with one of the dowagers or widows. Then I'm going to find my bride and dance with her. I'll see you later in the evening."

Harrison finished off his champagne and watched Bray disappear into the crowd. The music started again and in the distance Harrison saw the swirl of colorful skirts, the clap of joyful hands. He breathed a sigh of relief he wasn't on the dance floor in the midst of the revelry.

He swung around and placed his empty champagne glass on the table and was reaching for another from the server when he heard from behind him, "Good evening, my lord."

Harrison stiffened slightly. He recognized Mr. Hopscotch's voice. Undoubtedly, the man was there to present Miss Rule to him. Harrison hesitated a moment and then slowly turned to look at the Prince's man. Then his gaze immediately flew to the lovely golden-brown-haired young lady at his side. Harrison's heart started beating faster, a surge of heat settled low in his loins, and for the second time that night his stomach did a slow roll.

"Lord Thornwick, if I may have a few moments of your time, I would like to present Lady Railbridge, her granddaughter Miss Angelina Rule, and her father Mr. Archard Rule."

Miss Rule was the angel he'd been admiring a few minutes earlier. Fate was either smiling on him or playing a cruel joke on him.

Only time would tell which, but for now, he would consider this a sweet surprise.

Chapter 5

O you gods! Why do you make us love your goodly gifts,
and snatch them straight away?
Pericles *3.1.22—24*

Harrison only half listened to the formal introductions. His concentration was on Miss Rule. His gaze swept slowly up and down her face. Now that he was close to her he could see her delicate bone structure. Her skin was the color of pale ivory and her complexion flawless. Her lips were full, beautifully shaped, and made for kissing. Soft, sweet kisses that satisfied a man all the way to his soul. Her shiny golden-brown tresses had been loosely gathered to the top of her head, and wispy curls framed her face. There was no hump on her back, and no wart on her lovely nose, but with the darkest blue eyes he'd ever seen, she was giving him the evil eye.

That intrigued Harrison.

Miss Rule didn't appear any happier than Harrison was about the situation confronting them. By the glare in those lovely blue orbs, he'd say that contrary to what he'd been thinking, she hadn't been waiting around just to snare an unsuspecting earl in a parson's mousetrap—

not him specifically anyway. That made him feel a whole lot better about his current circumstances.

She was making it clear to him right from the beginning that she didn't like being told who to marry any more than he did. He liked the fact that she was showing her fighting spirit.

Long ago, Harrison had learned to size people up quickly. One glimpse of the grandmother told him Lady Railbridge wasn't happy about the possibility of her granddaughter marrying him, either. That was no surprise and fine with him. He never minded the odds being stacked against him. That just made life all the more interesting. Besides, right now he wasn't trying to win favor with either of them. But it was good to know the grandmother's feelings all the same.

And Miss Rule's father—well, he looked as if he thought he was the bird sitting on the best limb of the tree. And perhaps right now he was. That made it easy to know who was behind the Prince's machinations to have Harrison marry Miss Rule.

Though Harrison couldn't help but let his thoughts wander back to who Miss Rule had been searching for in the crowd. Definitely not him. It was her debut night, so who had already caught the young lady's attention?

After pleasantries were exchanged, Mr. Hopscotch excused himself and left Harrison to continue a conversation with Mr. Rule about the mechanics of the latest steam engine while Miss Rule and her grandmother chatted quietly. More than once Harrison felt Miss Rule's gaze on him, and a couple of times he was sure she knew he glanced at her, too.

A dance was announced so Harrison turned to Miss Rule and said, "Would you like to dance? With your father's permission, of course."

"Yes, yes, she'd be delighted," her father answered

quickly. "Please go ahead, as one is about to begin. Enjoy yourselves."

Harrison nodded and said, "Excuse us." He lightly placed the palm of his hand at the small of her back and gently ushered her forward.

At his contact, her back stiffened slightly. Touching her before they reached the dance floor and the music began was forbidden. But breaking the rules had always been so much easier for Harrison than following them.

"I really don't want to dance, my lord," Miss Rule said as they threaded their way through the crowd.

"Then you are a lady after my own heart. Neither do I, but you surprise me. I thought all ladies enjoyed dancing."

She cut her eyes around to him. "It's never been my favorite pastime, but my grandmother insisted I couldn't catch a husband if I didn't know how to twirl in ladylike fashion about the dance floor. However, what I meant just now was that I don't want to dance with you. Neither you nor my father gave me opportunity to decline."

They stopped at the edge of the dance floor and she tilted her chin up and faced him. Her nose was even with his chin, the perfect height for him.

"So you are suggesting I wait for an answer from you next time and ignore your father's urging."

Her brow furrowed slightly as if suddenly she wasn't sure. Then she exhaled softly and answered, "Yes, that's what I'm saying."

"Simple enough. I can do that," he agreed easily. "Should I walk you back to your father and grandmother so we can start over?"

Her eyes searched his with a look that told him she wasn't expecting him to be so accommodating, and he really hadn't intended to be. But he was glad he'd surprised her.

He noticed a slight shake of her head, and she said, "No, of course not, but I'm curious about something."

"Concerning me?"

"Yes. I know why I am being forced to marry you, my lord, but I have no idea why you would want to do this."

He tried to stop the smile from spreading across his face but had no luck as he said, "So you don't think your beauty and obvious intelligence are reasons enough for someone to want to marry you?"

"No, of course, I——I wasn't searching for a compliment, my lord," she said with a flush tinting her cheeks.

He inclined his head. "I never thought you were. I was merely stating the facts as I see them."

Her focus stayed locked on him. "I was told you needed a suitable wife but I don't know why."

That was the Prince's thought, not his.

He held her gaze. "Are you under the impression I wanted marriage to you?"

"I was led to believe that, yes, but why not just choose your own bride?" she questioned.

Why indeed.

"Maybe I didn't have a choice?"

It was her turn to mock his comment with a rueful smile. "I would find that difficult to believe, Lord Thornwick," she countered. "Who could force you to marry? You are an earl. A young, handsome earl."

He casually folded his arms across his chest and shifted his stance. "Now you are the one handing out the compliments."

"As you said, I was merely stating the facts. I don't believe even the King could make you marry someone if you didn't want to."

Not the King, but the Prince.

Obviously Miss Rule didn't know about the Prince's pressure on Harrison concerning the threat of Newgate. Perhaps he should keep it that way. The fewer people who knew it was Miss Rule or prison for him, the better.

This young lady wasn't throwing sweet, seductive glances his way and her full lips weren't pouting false promises, but she had his attention. Harrison knew how to handle young ladies who were trying their best to capture his favor and snare him, but he didn't have much practice with ones who showed little interest in him.

His gaze fell to her lips and lingered there for a moment. Oh, yes, he was attracted to her.

Suddenly a weariness stole across her face. She lowered her lashes and looked down at the fan she held in her hand as if she might somehow draw solace from it. "I can't believe I must marry you," she whispered. "It's not what I wanted."

Harrison could understand why a young lady would be distressed at the thought of an arranged marriage to a stranger. He contemplated telling her he didn't like this idea any better than she did.

Wanting to soothe her, he said, "Don't despair, there hasn't been an agreement of marriage between us yet, Miss Rule."

Her lashes flew up and she met his gaze without flinching. "Oh, you're right," she said quickly as a frown tightened the corners of her mouth. "How could I have forgotten that I was told you would meet me tonight, and look me over to see if I measure up as acceptable to you?"

So someone had told her what he'd said to Hopscotch. He could understand her not liking that prospect. He wouldn't, either. But he couldn't just accept the Prince's demand that he marry her without question. Especially when he hadn't met her at the time. Now that he had, of course, he was certainly entertaining the possibility. There was a reason she caught his eye the minute he saw her.

"I can assure you," she continued, "I don't like being treated as if I am a thoroughbred stallion you want to purchase."

"Mare," he corrected good-naturedly, thinking the best thing to do would be to change the subject to a lighter tone. "You would be a mare, not a stallion."

A swoosh of exasperation rushed past her lips. "I know the difference in horses, my lord. I was merely using the stallion reference as an example."

Someone bumped his shoulder in passing and he realized the music had started. The dance area was filling, but Harrison made no move to usher her onto the floor. Their tête-à-tête was far more enjoyable than dancing.

He stepped closer to her and softly said, "I have no doubt, but still you should have said mare or maybe filly."

She lifted her chin a notch as if to counter his statement, seeming oblivious to the dance they were supposed to have, too. She had fire in her eyes and a determined set to her mouth. He took another step toward her, far closer to her than he should be standing in a roomful of watchful and condemning eyes. He caught the sweet scent of her freshly washed hair and lightly perfumed skin, and all he could think was that she was very inviting.

"Oh, all right," she said, clearly exasperated with herself. "I'll admit it was a poor choice of words on my part. I shouldn't have referred to myself as any kind of horse."

Harrison gave her a hint of a smile. It pleased him

that she thought about not doing it before she gave in. He listened to her labored breathing. His attention fell to the slow rise and fall of her breasts. Though he hadn't expected it, yes, she was acceptable. More than acceptable.

"Horses are beautiful, powerful, and magnificent, Miss Rule, and so are you." His gaze swept up and down her face. Unintentionally, his voice turned husky when he said, "I like what I see when I look at you. I find you very acceptable."

She drew in a long breath. Her eyes rounded and her lips formed a delicate O that made him want to pull her close to him and kiss her lovely lips.

Her shoulders lifted and she said, "I don't want to marry you because my heart belongs to another."

That brought Harrison up short and his breath stilled in his lungs. He hadn't expected her to say that. What the devil was Hopscotch doing trying to get him to marry a woman who loved another man?

He took a deep breath and backed away from her. "If your heart belongs to another, why not just marry him?"

He watched her swallow hard. He could see her pulse working furiously at the hollow of her throat. For the first time since they'd met, her gaze combed the ballroom behind him.

Obviously not finding the person she wanted to see, she returned her focus to his and said, "My father has his reasons."

So it was as Harrison thought. Her father was forcing her into marriage. But why? For the title? Money? Perhaps it was something more sinister than either of those, or maybe something as simple as not wanting his daughter to marry the man she wanted.

But it really didn't matter what the reason was. If her heart belonged to another, it changed everything for Harrison. He had feelings for Miss Rule similar to those he'd had for Maddie when he first met her. She had favored the older, titled brother to the younger rogue. Harrison had to guard himself against that kind of pain. He never wanted to be that vulnerable again.

Harrison also had no desire to become involved in a family squabble among a young lady, her father, and her beau. And he certainly had no wish to take a woman who had another man on her mind to bed.

Suddenly he couldn't stop himself from saying, "My guess would be that your father's reason is the gentleman who holds your heart doesn't have a title."

"You'd be wrong," she said defensively. "It just so happens he has a very prestigious title, *Captain*. He was awarded the commission by Wellington after the Battle of Waterloo."

"Ah, military. In the King's service, is he?"

Her breathing relaxed and her eyes softened. "Yes."

Harrison knew it was difficult for young ladies to resist men in uniforms.

"Officers certainly know how to be gentlemen," he said. "I suppose he was the one you were looking for when you first stepped into the Great Hall and searched the ballroom?"

"Yes, but—" She stopped. Her forehead wrinkled. "How did you know—" Her eyes widened. "You had someone point me out to you, didn't you? You wanted to see me before you would even agree to an introduction."

It wasn't true but if her heart truly belonged to another, it didn't matter. He remained quiet and left her to draw her own conclusions.

She flipped her fan open and fanned herself. "I've never had anyone infuriate me as you have, my lord. You are a wretched soul."

He was a wretched soul. He'd stayed in London gaming after he'd received the letter that his brother was ill

and needed him. It didn't get much more wretched than
that. But he'd never had a reason to be any other way
until he'd inherited Thornwick.

"Pardon me, Lord Thornwick, but may I interrupt?"

Harrison heard the familiar voice behind him and
turned to see the Dowager Duchess of Drakestone stopping beside him. Bray's mother. He'd first met her when
he was ten years old. Through the twenty years he'd
known her she'd never changed. She was still beautiful,
forthright, and haughty to the point of madness. As the
youngest of four boys, Harrison had learned early in life
not to let anyone intimidate him. No one ever had—but
this woman had come damned close on a few occasions
when he was first a guest in her home.

"Of course, Duchess," he said, bowing and then taking her hand and kissing the backs of her gloved fingers.
"May I present Miss Angelina Rule to you?"

"Indeed you may," she said and gave him a brief
smile. "She is the reason I stopped to speak to you."

"Duchess," Miss Rule said, and gave her a low curtsy.

"I couldn't help but notice your fan, Miss Rule. The
painting on it caught my eye as I was passing by." The
duchess held out her hand. "May I?"

"Of course, Your Grace," Miss Rule said, handing it
to her.

She spread the fan, and Harrison could see that the
scene appeared to be a brook or stream with flowers,
greenery, and colorful butterflies. Whoever had painted
it had done an excellent job of making the sunlight glis-
ten on the water.

Her Grace looked up at Miss Rule and asked, "It's
superb. Who did you purchase this from, my dear?"

"Oh, I, well I—"–

"I can understand you wanting to be protective of the
artist and keep him all to yourself," the duchess said,

handing the fan back to her. "He has an exquisite touch and delicate flair. I wonder how he managed to get such a realistic shimmer to the brook."

"A fine layer of silver and gold dust is sprinkled on the paint while it's still wet."

The duchess smiled. "Clever. Have him send over some of his work for me to choose from. You don't mind, do you?"

"I can't do that because I——"

"All right, never mind," the duchess said, once again not allowing Miss Rule to finish her sentence. "He can use a courier to deliver them if he wants and remain anonymous. I don't mind a little intrigue. In fact, at my age I rather like it. Good painters are always such prima donnas, aren't they? So tell him I insist he have someone bring his work to me within the next few days. I'll make it worth his while." She looked back to Harrison and smiled. "Good to see you, my lord. Good evening, Miss Rule."

She was gone as quickly as she'd appeared.

"Is she always so intimidating?" Miss Rule asked, watching the duchess walk away.

"Yes. And that's the way she likes it."

"You've known her a long time?"

"I met her my first year at Eton. She's not friendly to many people. You should feel honored she even spoke to you."

"In that case I am." Miss Rule paused. "What will she do if I don't identify the artist or have the person send her his work?"

"She would have ways of finding him, but why would you not? The artist who painted your fan should be greatly flattered. If the duchess likes what she sees she will probably buy a fan to match every gown she has. If she does, all the ladies in the ton would want one from him."

"You jest."

He queried her with his expression. "Do I seem the kind of person who would tease you about this?"

"If you thought it would shock me, yes."

"I only tease when I have reason to, and in this I don't."

Something caught her attention and he looked in the direction of her gaze. A gentleman dressed in military attire, but by the disappointment he saw in her eyes it was easy to guess not the officer she was looking for.

Suddenly Harrison thought, *No.*

Hell no.

He wasn't going to go through that anguish again. He would bow out now before his feelings for Miss Rule went any further. Yes, he was attracted to her. She wasn't afraid to speak her mind and take him to task. He liked that and he didn't mind her frosty attitude. She was spirited and desirable. Usually he welcomed a bit of unfriendly competition—as long as he won in the end.

But he knew already there was something different about Miss Rule and he had no yearning to fight another man for her heart. He'd been down that road. He didn't want to travel it again no matter how attracted he was to her. It was best this end right now.

"You don't want this marriage, Miss Rule, and neither do I. There's no reason to pretend otherwise for the rest of the evening, is there?"

She blinked rapidly. "I don't understand. I know I've been quite outspoken and objectionable at times."

His jaw clamped down tightly before he released it and said, "You are not objectionable. I find you refreshing."

"Then you must marry me," she said, standing her ground, not seeming the least cowed by his imposing frame.

"I must? I put orders in the same category as rules. I don't like them and I don't follow them."

"I was told you would marry me if I was acceptable. You admitted you found me acceptable."

He gave her a curious look. He could see the turmoil she was going through flash in her face but did nothing to help her. She was the one who had just built the wall between them with her vow that her heart belonged to another. It wasn't a wall he wanted to tear down or climb over.

"That was before I knew your heart belonged to another man," he answered in a tight voice. "Just how desperate do you think I am for a bride?"

Her gaze didn't waver from his eyes. "Desperate enough to consider marrying me in the first place."

Harrison hesitated. Yes, because the threat of prison loomed. He had to rebuild Thornwick. He had to restore his father's and his brothers' legacy and he couldn't do that from Newgate.

He saw uncertainty in her eyes. Still he said, "I did consider it. Now I've reconsidered."

"I know I've been less than pleasant tonight but I do know how to be contrite and amiable. If you don't agree to at least consider marrying me my father will go to debtors' prison. I have no choice but to ask you to give me another chance. The Prince will only pay his debts if you agree to marry me."

What would he want with a contrite and amiable lady? Couldn't she tell he actually liked her strong spirit and boldness? It wasn't her he objected to. It was her proclamation that her heart belonged to another. Did she really think he'd want to take her to his bed and let her bear his children knowing she loved another man?

He saw regret in her deep-blue eyes. He felt it, too.

She didn't want her father to go to prison any more than Harrison wanted to go. He could understand that.

He almost relented.

Almost.

But then he remembered the pain of the past and instead, he said, "You should speak to your army officer about that."

Chapter 6

What do I fear? Myself?
Richard III *5.3.183*

What was she going to do?

The music continued to play, and the dancers twirled with delight. Angelina watched the handsome, tall, and broad-shouldered man walk away from her. She cringed inside.

It took all her willpower not to chase after him and ask once again that he change his mind about marrying her so she could save her father. She realized now that it had never crossed her mind when they were sparring that he might actually reject her.

Her beauty wasn't legendary, but most would consider her pretty. She was intelligent and well-schooled in all the finer things a young lady was supposed to know. She didn't have many vices, or none really, except not knowing when to back away and be quiet. It must have been at the back of her mind that since the Prince had sanctioned the arrangement, it would happen. Otherwise, she surely would have held her tongue and played the part of a young lady whose only goal in life was to be the wife of a titled gentleman.

Why had she been so confrontational with him?

Because he made it so easy.

It was as if he said things deliberately to get her temper up. And he had.

Why had she mentioned Captain Maxwell?

Because Lord Thornwick was so self-confident, so arrogant, and so handsome. I needed to let him know I'm not dying to marry him.

How could she have bungled her meeting with him so badly?

Because he wasn't what I expected him to be.

Most of the time, she was calm, reasonable, and in control, but she'd felt flushed and out of breath just looking at the earl. There was something about him that made her want to challenge him, match wits with him, bandy barbs with him. And it wasn't just what he said, it was how he looked at her, too. When his gaze had swept so lazily up and down her face as if he was trying to memorize her features, her stomach quaked. She experienced something that could only be described as wonderful skimming along her breasts and sailing down into the lower recesses of her abdomen. Just thinking of that feeling brought back the tingling, rippling, enjoyable sensations. The only way she knew to counter the strange reaction to him was to think of Captain Maxwell.

Now her father would be heading to prison—and all because of her inability to just play the part of the quiet, demure young lady men adored and pretend all she'd ever dreamed of was marrying a titled gentleman such as Lord Thornwick. That was all she had to do and she couldn't manage it to save her father.

She sucked in a deep breath and watched Lord Thornwick disappear into the crush in the ballroom. She was furious with herself. Why couldn't she have been the kind of young lady her father expected her to be: dependable, obedient, and pliant?

Even now when she should be lamenting over her father cold, hungry, and wasting away in prison, everything the earl had made her feel was what was in the forefront of her mind. What kind of daughter was she? And what was she going to do now that she had failed her father?

"Angelina, what's wrong?" her grandmother asked, walking up to stand beside her. "You keep staring at the crowd."

"Granna," she whispered softly. "I've made a huge mistake."

"Oh, dear, that doesn't sound good. I knew something was wrong when you and Lord Thornwick never took the dance floor. What happened?"

I was outmaneuvered, she thought, but she said, "I failed Papa."

The dance that Angelina was supposed to have with the earl ended and the chattering and laughing couples started leaving the floor and mixing back in with the crowd. Some of the dancers greeted her and her grandmother; others smiled and nodded as they passed by.

When the bulk of the crowd was gone, her grandmother said, "Let's move to a quieter place where we can talk."

Before Angelina and her grandmother could make their way to a corner, a friend stopped to introduce a shy but nice gentleman to Angelina, whom she promised a dance later in the evening. Finally, she and her grandmother made it to a far wall near a large urn that had been filled with colorful flowers and greenery.

"Now tell me what happened before someone else steps up and interrupts us," Granna said.

Angelina peered down into her grandmother's light-brown eyes and quietly said, "The earl isn't going to marry me."

"Mercy!" she exclaimed. "How do you know this?"

"He told me," Angelina said.

"I don't understand. You have the right heritage. You're beautiful. Intelligent. What could be his problem?"

Angelina hated admitting it but said, "I foolishly told him my heart belonged to another."

"Oh, dear," her grandmother said again as the edges of her mouth dropped.

"He made it clear he has no interest in marrying a young lady who already loves another man."

"I have to admit, Angelina, that was not an appropriate cat to let out of the bag to a possible fiancé—or a suitor, either."

"Oh, Granna, do you think I don't know what a horrible mistake that was? You are not helping me," Angelina said, squeezing her fan tightly into her hand.

"I must be honest with you, dear, or I will be of no help at all. Men, especially titled gentlemen, have extremely high opinions of themselves. And quite frankly, no man wants to play second to another. Especially not in his wife's heart or in her bed."

Angelina felt wretched. "I'm sure you're right. Granna, why couldn't I have just stayed quiet, listened to him, and smiled prettily at him in all the right places? Why do I never know when to just hold my tongue, be quiet and submissive, and leave well enough alone?"

Her grandmother laughed softly. "Because you are just like your mother. Not in looks, of course, but she would argue with a lamppost and would rather chew nails than not have the last word in any conversation with friend or foe."

"Tonight I wish I weren't like her."

"Now, don't say that," her grandmother admonished with no punishment in her tone. "It isn't easy to change who we are. She loved it that you have her fighting spirit."

"It's just that the earl was so sure of himself, and so devilishly handsome that I found myself doing what I usually do and speaking my mind with no thoughts of consequences. What am I going to do? I can't let Papa go to prison."

Her grandmother pursed her lips thoughtfully. "I don't know that there is much of anything either of us can do."

"But I'm the reason Papa ended up in debt in the first place. He wanted to have a larger dowry for me. And I was the one who was supposed to get him out of debt."

"This is not your fault, Angelina. None of it. It's all your father's doing. You would have made a fine match without an impressive dowry. I won't allow you to blame yourself for his bad judgment and his troubles. Now, I suppose there is always the chance that if Captain Maxwell wants to marry you, maybe he has the means to help your father if the Prince won't do it without your marriage to Lord Thornwick."

Captain Maxwell. Angelina had scarcely thought of him since she'd met the earl. When Lord Thornwick was around he took up all the space in her mind. There was no room or time to think of anyone else. "I haven't seen him or his aunt tonight, have you?"

"No. It's been a few weeks since I spoke to her, but last I did she expected her nephew to be home soon and attend the ball with her tonight."

"Perhaps he hasn't made it back from India yet," Angelina said a bit wistfully.

"That's very likely. Sailing from India is a long

voyage, dear, and many things could happen to cause delays."

Angelina looked down at the fan in her hand. She spread it open and stared at the painting. It *was* beautiful. A pond with lily pads, and flower-filled banks, and colorful butterflies. She remembered that the duchess wanted to see more of the artist's work. Angelina should have told Her Grace that she was the artist.

"The duchess wants the artist who painted my fan to send her some of his work," Angelina said.

Her grandmother gave her a curious look. "Which duchess?"

"The Dowager Duchess of Drakestone was passing by and saw my fan when I had it open. She knows Lord Thornwick so she stopped. She wanted to know who painted it because she wants to buy some fans."

Her grandmother's eyebrows rose. "She talked to you?"

"Yes."

"I'm surprised but pleased you caught her eye. What did she say when you told her you painted that fan?"

"I didn't have time to tell her."

Granna gave her a disapproving glare. "Really, Angelina, you should have. Now she thinks she can get one."

"Her Grace interrupts often and talks fast. She even answered the questions she directed at me." Angelina ran her fingertips over the fan as an idea took root and formed in her mind. "Lord Thornwick said she would probably buy a fan for every gown she has."

"Nonsense. I'm sure she already has plenty of fans for every gown and every occasion."

"She could buy some fans from me, Granna."

Her grandmother laughed. "No, she couldn't. She'll have to find her own artist if she wants more fans."

But Angelina continued. "If she buys a fan or two from me, all the ladies she knows will want to buy one, too."

"Angelina," her grandmother said, using a rare warning tone.

"I have several fans already painted, you know."

"Of course I know," she answered cautiously.

"I could paint more."

"Hush that kind of talk."

"No, wait, Granna," Angelina said, eager to spill her idea. "Maybe all is not lost yet. I've very obviously lost the earl, and even if Captain Maxwell were here I have no inkling if he would or could help Papa. If I can find a way to sell my paintings, though, I could make money."

"Angelina, no," her grandmother said emphatically.

"Hear me out."

"No, I will not listen to this preposterous idea," her grandmother said as if that put an end to Angelina's plan before she voiced it.

"You said yourself that the earl would not be a good match for me."

"Yes, he's an outrageous rogue but he's still an earl. You would be a countess. Besides, it's never completely wrong to accept an offer of marriage from an earl."

Suddenly Angelina wasn't convinced that Lord Thornwick was the only way to save her father. "But there's not going to be an offer now. And the only way to keep Papa out of prison is to pay off his debt. I have no money, but I do have things that are worth money. Most of my fans have either silver or gold dust in them, and some both. That should make them worth a lot of money."

"You don't know what you are talking about, dear. You have no knowledge of this sort of thing and it wouldn't be acceptable for you if you did."

"I agree but I'm quite capable of learning and I will. You know yourself that everyone who sees my miniatures says they are far better than what they pay enormous amounts of money for in the shops. I can sell my collection of snuff and mourning boxes that I've painted. I must have at least twenty of those and some other things as well."

Her grandmother looked aghast and was speechless for a few moments.

"A granddaughter of mine selling her paintings in a shop! Going into trade?" As soon as the words left her mouth, she looked around to see if anyone was close enough to have possibly heard as her hand clutched the pearls at the base of her throat. "Merciful heavens, Angelina! Never! And your father would never approve, either. He would happily go to prison before he'd let you do something so common. I don't want to hear mention of it again."

Angelina smiled at a nosy lady who was looking curiously at her while her grandmother ranted. An idea had already popped into her mind: She could borrow her maid's cloak and slip out while her grandmother took her afternoon rest. That was one possibility. Still, would she find a shopkeeper willing to do business with a young lady who wasn't properly chaperoned? Probably not. Her only choice was to talk her grandmother into helping her.

"I can't sit around and do nothing, Granna."

"You will have to," Lady Railbridge answered firmly.

"No. If I can fix this, I must."

"This trouble is your father's making, not yours. He will have to figure his own way out of it. We don't even have an idea of how much he actually owes. It has to be quite a bit more than the cost of a few paintings and a dozen or so fans. He indicated that he's in debt to more than one lender, too."

"Then I must get started right away and paint more. If the duchess likes my fans, other ladies will, too. I will paint day and night to keep up if I must."

Lady Railbridge slowly shook her head. "It's not fair what he has done to you, but you cannot sell your paintings like a common tradesman. You can't fix everything, Angelina. You can't save every stray dog and you can't be responsible for your father's shortcomings."

"Granna, what I can't do is stand by and do nothing while Papa goes to prison. I will find a way to do this with or without your help. You know I will."

"I believe you would." Her grandmother's mouth drooped again and she seemed to be struggling inside herself. "All right," she said, softly. "I never thought I'd say this, but your father has driven me to it. He's not worth it, but yes, dear, I will help you. I have a little money put aside that your father doesn't know about. It's not much but I'll give it to you for him. And I will help you find a way to sell your paintings. Your mother would want me to help you. I must do it for her."

Relief washed over Angelina. "Thank you, Granna. I don't know when it will be, but I promise to repay you one day."

"Nonsense." She shook her head. "Your happiness— whatever that ends up being—the captain or someone else—will be my payment. I know of a man who might be able to help us. An old friend of your grandfather's. I haven't seen him in a long time but tomorrow I'll see if I can locate him and pay him a visit. No one must ever know what we are doing."

"I understand. Between the two of us, we'll come up with enough money to keep Papa out of prison and give me the freedom to choose my own husband. Now excuse me, Granna, but I need to find Lord Thornwick."

"Whatever for?" Angelina heard her grandmother ask, but she was already walking away. The earl might have gotten the best of her and won their first battle, but the war was still going on. She was armed and ready. Another battle was about to start.

Though her heart was racing, Angelina wove slowly through the crowd smiling at first one person and then another. She had just spotted the earl when she was stopped by one of the young ladies who was a member of both her sewing circle and her reading society.

Miss Helen Ramsey grabbed hold of Angelina's hands and held her. The last thing Angelina wanted was to be waylaid and certainly not by Helen.

"Angelina, I saw you talking to the handsome Lord Thornwick earlier. How did you manage to hold his attention so long? I was so envious he talked to you and not to me," she said dramatically as she rolled her shoulders forward and squeezed Angelina's hands tightly while smiling coquettishly. "Didn't you want to just melt into the floor?"

Oh, yes, but not for the reason you think.

"He is handsome but I found him rather arrogant for my taste, Helen."

The green-eyed debutante with flame-red hair dropped Angelina's hands as if they were hot coals. "Then you must have said something most unbecoming of a young lady to have sparked such a response from him."

True.

"What did you say to him?" she demanded.

Angelina didn't want to be drawn into a conversation about the arrogant earl. Helen was probably itching to hear something more about the man from Angelina so she could tell everyone she knew.

"Have you met him?" Angelina asked.

Helen hesitated and pretended to brush a strand of hair from her face. "No, not yet, but I will soon. I haven't only because Papa didn't want just anyone presenting me to the earl. It's very important who you know and who knows you. We are waiting for Viscount Thistlebury to arrive so he can do the honors for me."

"That's an excellent idea, Helen," Angelina said with a smile. "Now, if you'll excuse me I was looking for someone."

"Who? Maybe I can help you find her." She smiled deviously. "Or him?"

Angelina had never been any good at lying so she simply said, "No need. I see who I'm looking for. And perhaps you should go find your father. I see that Lord and Lady Thistlebury just arrived."

"Oh, I'm so glad you saw them. I must go at once," she said and hurried away.

As soon as Helen vanished, Angelina was beset with another young lady from her reading society. She politely chatted even though she was eager to be on her way. When a couple of other young ladies joined them, Angelina excused herself and continued her search for the earl.

He wasn't in the main ballroom, the buffet room, or the vestibule. She was beginning to think he had left the party when she saw him near a set of double doors that led to a garden. He stood with his legs spread just far enough apart to lend a touch of arrogance to his stance. He was talking to a gentleman who was just as tall, handsome, and powerfully built as the earl. A beautiful young lady with golden-blond hair stood with them. She was looking up at Lord Thornwick and smiling.

Angelina debated approaching the earl while he was engrossed in a conversation with others. The rules were clear: It was rude to do so. Be that as it may, Angelina had no choice but to interrupt their conversation. She might have botched her first opportunity with Lord Thornwick, but she wasn't ready to give up on him just yet. Her father's freedom was threatened. She had to stay courageous and fight for him.

Though she didn't realize it, she must have held her breath all the way across the room. She sounded breathless when she stopped beside the earl and said, "Lord Thornwick, I'm sorry for interrupting, but may I have a moment of your time?"

When he turned and looked at her she saw a sparkle of surprise in his eyes. His gaze quickly swept up and down her face. She immediately felt those same wonderful sensations that had simmered through her when they talked before. The earl was an imposing, magnificent man. His chest was broad and his shoulders straight. He was superbly dressed in a black dinner jacket with a tightly fitted beige waistcoat. Surely his handsomeness was the only reason he'd set her heart to fluttering.

"Miss Rule," he said, a half smile forming his well-sculpted lips. "Of course. Was there something you forgot to say to me when we spoke earlier?"

Oh, he is a devil.

Apprehension raced through her, but she hoped she looked calm on the outside as she said, "Yes, if you don't mind." She glanced at the young lady and then the other gentleman, hoping desperately she was showing more confidence than she was feeling. "I do hope you will forgive me for barging in on your conversation."

"Of course," the lady said with a friendly expression. "We don't mind at all, but would you please allow Lord Thornwick to introduce us?"

Angelina's heart gave an uncomfortable lurch when the earl presented her to the Duke and Duchess of Drakestone. She curtsied low, hoping the heat in her cheeks would have lessened by the time she had to look them in the eyes. She never would have interrupted them if she'd known he was talking to a duke and duchess.

Nothing was going right for her concerning the earl. She seemed to be making one blunder after the other.

"It's my pleasure to meet you both," Angelina said, thinking what she really wanted to do was make the floor open up and swallow her. "I was presented to your mother, Your Grace, a short time ago."

"Then you have managed to do something it has taken others several Seasons to do. I hope she behaved herself, Miss Rule, and didn't have you in tears before she parted."

"No, of course not. I'm happy to say we had a lovely chat about the artwork on my fan." Angelina held up the fan and then quickly put it down again.

"Thank you for letting me know she can behave herself at times," the duke said.

"I can see why she noticed your fan," the duchess added. "It's lovely. That sheen on the water is remarkable. And I like the dramatic colors. It looks especially appealing when pastels are all the rage."

"Thank you, that's very kind of you to say," Angelina said and glanced at Lord Thornwick.

He extended a glass to her. "I thought you might like a glass of champagne?"

His expression was soft, caring, and she appreciated his trying to make her feel more comfortable. She wasn't usually the type to be nervous, but she'd be a fool not to be cautious in dealing with the earl. "Yes, thank you," she said and took the glass from him. "I believe I would."

"Is this Season your first, Miss Rule?" the duchess asked.

"Yes," she said, trying not to be upset with herself for making it so obvious.

"Perhaps later I could to introduce you to some other young ladies before the night is over."

"Thank you, Duchess," Angelina said, thankful Her Grace was so friendly. "That's very kind of you. I'll look forward to it."

"Good. If you and Lord Thornwick will excuse us, Bray and I see someone we need to speak to."

"Yes, of course."

Good-byes were said and the duke and duchess walked away. Angelina took a sip from her glass. The champagne was cold, bubbly, and soothing. Getting Lord Thornwick to agree to what she wanted wouldn't be easy. She'd made a muddle of her first conversation with him but was determined to rectify her earlier mistakes.

"Was there something else you wanted to say to me?" he asked.

"I've been thinking over our conversation and I have a favor to ask of you."

"A favor, you say?" He folded his arms across his chest and looked at her from guarded eyes. "This could be very interesting. Tell me what it is."

She lifted her chin and her shoulders. "I understand you not wanting to marry me because of my feelings for another, but I would like to ask you to please consider pretending that we will make a match by the end of the Season."

He didn't move but continued to regard her carefully. There was a calmness about him that made her feel as if he could see inside her and know how desperate she was feeling. It was a position she didn't like being in but she had no other choice.

"If you will agree, it will give me time to come up with another way for me to help my father avoid prison."

Keeping his tone casual and his body relaxed, he asked, "You want me to pretend through the entire Season that you and I will marry at the end of it?"

She knew it was a lot to ask of an earl, a dashing handsome earl who could snap his fingers and have more than a dozen young ladies willing to marry him in an instant. For a moment, she considered fleeing his questioning gaze, but she had to fight against her instinct and stand her ground and persist. "Yes, that's exactly what I'm asking."

"I don't like any kind of pretense, Miss Rule."

One hand tightened on her fan and the other on the glass she held. "It may be difficult for you to believe, my lord, but neither do I. In fact, this is very hard for me to ask of you but I must."

A tempting, roguish grin lifted the corners of his mouth. "I don't find that difficult to believe."

Her breathing became shallow and her heart started fluttering again. Just when she thought he might scowl at her, he smiled, giving her hope. On a rush of words, she continued, "Our engagement wouldn't need to be announced to the ton. In fact, it would be best if it wasn't. As long as my father believes it will happen, he will tell the Prince and that will be enough."

"And that is because you wouldn't want your army officer to think you had eyes for anyone but him, right?"

Was it?

"No. At this point, my lord, I am only thinking about my father. The captain isn't here tonight. I can only assume he hasn't returned from India. My father is in very real danger. I'm not excusing his behavior, but he hasn't quite been the same since my mother died. He shouldn't be in this unsavory position, but he is. I will not run from it; nor will I hide. I will do whatever I must to help him."

Her pulse quickened and her hope soared as he leaned toward her. He lifted his chin a notch and his gaze skimmed over her as he said, "Then my answer is I will think about the favor you request and let you know my answer at a later time."

His words feathered softly across her cheek. A shivery tingle raced up her back, and all her senses went on alert.

"Thank you," she whispered, feeling a little relief. "You are a formidable opponent, my lord."

"I've had much practice."

She drained the glass and held it out to him. "I didn't realize how much I needed that."

He took the glass and asked, "Another?"

She shook her head once. "I'll wait to hear from you, Lord Thornwick."

Angelina turned and walked away, her step much lighter.

Chapter 7

He will give the devil his due.
Henry IV Part 1, *Act I, sc. 2*

Hell's teeth.

Harrison rubbed the back of his neck as he walked out of the stuffy room with Bray. All the probing questioning he'd had to endure just to become a member of the Heirs' Club was ridiculous and beyond his rational thought. Why he had to go through a series of boring conversations just to become a valid member, he had no idea. It wasn't like the three fellows on the panel didn't know he was now the Earl of Thornwick, or that they didn't know *him*. He'd been coming to the club as Bray's guest for close to ten years.

The only reason he was making it official now was because he could. That and so he wouldn't have to depend on Bray getting him inside the smaller, quieter club when he was in town. That is, if the old bats on the review board, in their ceremonial robes and outdated, powdered wigs, decided to put their mark of approval on his request and confirm he was indeed the legitimate eighth Earl of Thornwick.

Harrison followed Bray through the maze of corridors that led them out of the private inner sanctum of the secluded building and into the area where the members drank, played, and occasionally conducted a little business. They bypassed the gaming rooms, where Harrison heard the sound of billiard balls smacking together and rounds of laughter. All was quiet when they passed the reading room, though a glance inside showed several gentlemen seated with newsprint in front of their faces.

The two friends didn't break stride until they entered the large taproom. It was just past midday and only a handful of people were in the darkly appointed room. Harrison and Bray stopped by the highly polished bar and ordered up two tankards of ale. They greeted the gentlemen standing nearby but didn't stay to chat after their drinks arrived. Harrison motioned to a table by the window where a slice of sunshine filtered through and they settled themselves in their chairs.

Bray lifted his tankard and said, "To the latest member of the Heirs' Club."

Harrison acknowledged the toast with a nod and took a drink.

"So," Bray said, "what do you want to talk about first?"

"Why don't we talk about you first?" Harrison answered. "Tell me about married life."

"You are making this very easy, my friend. I am content. Quite happy and finally settled in my larger home with my lovely wife and all four of her sisters."

"That many sisters?" Harrison shifted in his seat. "I didn't remember. How are you handling that?"

"I'm managing. There have been a few instances

when I wished it was only the two of us, but very few. I'm getting used to having sisters."

Harrison gave him a doubtful look. "Really? Ah, but then they are girls. I suppose they are much quieter and nicer than boys."

"There was a time I would have thought that, too," Bray said. "But no. It's maddening at times. They will cry over nothing, squeal to the high heavens when they are happy, stand still, pout, and say nothing when they are angry. But things are better now that I've employed a tutor to keep them busy with learning."

Harrison laughed.

"What is amusing you?"

"You. That you're not just married, but living in a house with five females. You who never had a brother or a cousin. And as of now, your mind still seems to be sound."

Bray laughed, too. "I know. It's unbelievable, isn't it? But I like having sisters," Bray assured him. "Most of the time, anyway. They are all different and I enjoy each one of them. But even if I didn't, I would put up with any amount of aggravation from them to have Louisa in my life because she's worth it."

"I'm sure Louisa appreciates your good nature about them," Harrison said and took another drink. "I suppose that's how Adam felt about his wife, too."

"Damnation, don't remind me of the horror he went through. Better than ever now, I understand why he gave up on life and moved to the cold north to be alone. I can't imagine life without Louisa in—"–Bray paused and seemed to consider his words. "I know it was just as hard on you losing Maddie."

"No," Harrison said and knew it was the truth. "It couldn't have been. I made peace with my feelings for Maddie after she married my brother and had his son. I considered her my sister. It was still difficult losing them all at once."

"I'm sure it was hell," Bray said.

"Let's talk about Adam."

"When do you want to go see him?"

"You let me know a time that works for you," Harrison said, putting the decision on his friend.

"Sometime in the next two or three weeks?" Bray suggested. "Will that be good for you?"

Harrison nodded. "Should I send a post that we're coming?"

"I see no reason to put him on notice. Let's take our chances like we did last year. That seemed to work out all right for us."

"Horses again, since they're faster than a carriage?"

"And a hell of a lot more fun," Harrison said with a laugh.

"It's settled then. I'll have my horse saddled and ready whenever you are." Bray leaned his chair back on the hind legs. "I'd like to stop by Thornwick on the way back. The renovations have started. Every other day I receive updates on the progress but I'd like to take a look for myself."

"I can see why you would. I'm certain it's not a small task. Now tell me why you asked about the Prince."

"He's an interfering blackguard, isn't he?"

"He can be. Why?"

"Do you have any influence with him?"

"Not half a pint. I don't know anyone who does. He seems to live in his own world, and he's very peculiar about who he allows in it."

Harrison could believe that and it wasn't good news. He took a drink of his ale. "Through a man named Mr. Hopscotch, the Prince has given me an ultimatum."

Bray's eyes narrowed. "I'm familiar with Hopscotch. He's the Prince's man. What does he want from you?"

"Not much," Harrison said in a nonchalant manner. "Just that I marry Miss Angelina Rule or I will go to Newgate, and he'll see that I stay there for the foreseeable future."

"What the devil?" The front of Bray's chair legs hit the floor with a thud. "To prison if you don't marry Miss Rule?"

"Keep your voice down," Harrison said, noticing that one of the men at the bar turned to look at them.

Bray's eyes scanned the room, too. He then leaned over the table and said, "The Prince can do a lot of things but I don't think he can put you in prison for not marrying someone. That wouldn't be considered just cause even for him."

"No, not for refusing to marry her. According to Hopscotch the Prince can and will because I shot a man in a duel last winter."

Bray whistled low under his breath. "Yes, I remember that. Who the devil was that man?"

"I don't think I ever knew his name. If I did, I've long forgotten it. Hopscotch says the man I shot and half a dozen others will swear to the duel in court so that I will be charged with attempted murder."

Bray's eyebrows shot up. "Bloody blackguards. Do you think he was serious?"

"He was serious all right," Harrison said, remembering the blunderbusses pointed at his chest. "Hopscotch brought armed guards to Thornwick with him and was prepared to take me straight to prison and keep me there while I contested the charges if I hadn't agreed to be at the ball the other night to meet Miss Rule."

"Miss Rule is lovely."

Without question.

Harrison agreed with a nod.

She was the last young lady he wanted to be thinking about or interested in but for some reason she was the only one he met who kept returning to haunt his thoughts. Three days since he'd seen her and he was still thinking about her, about her request. He knew what he was going to do. He just didn't know when he was going to let her know.

"She seemed intelligent, personable. Even my mother approved of her and you know how unlikely it is for my mother to give anyone a passing glance. Miss Rule is from a good family, I suppose."

Harrison chuckled ruefully. "Her father is a distant relation to the Prince himself."

"Ah, so that is why he is trying to find her a title. He's paying back a family member for a favor."

"It's more like her father is in debt up to his whiskers and in jeopardy of debtors' prison."

Bray took a drink from his tankard and then said, "It might be a bad choice of words, Harrison, but it appears you are the stone that the Prince is using to get rid of two birds at once."

"Perfect analogy," Harrison answered. "And I don't like it."

"At one point last year, the Prince tried to force me to marry Louisa, too."

"I never knew this," Harrison said with keen interest. "What did he have on you?"

"Nothing nearly as scandalous as a duel. And he never threatened me with prison, either."

"But this tactic of trying to manipulate marriages just to please himself or his relatives should be stopped."

"You won't have any luck with that. I'm sure I don't have to tell you that sovereigns have been interested in marriages for their personal gain as well as for political and financial gain since the beginning of time. I think kings somehow think it's their duty to arrange marriages for their family members and peers."

Harrison harrumphed. "The threat of prison is a damned nuisance. I hadn't planned on coming to London. I need to be at Thornwick overseeing the rebuilding of the house, not here going to balls and playing cards."

"I'm sure." Bray took another drink from his tankard. "So what are you going to do?"

"I don't know."

"You're not interested in her."

"No, that's the damned shame of it," Harrison said and pushed his tankard to the side. "I could be. She was challenging, provocative, and sweetly innocent all at the same time."

Confusion wrinkled his brow, and Bray said, "Then I don't understand. What's the problem?"

"Apparently she has her heart set on another gentleman. Her only interest in me is to keep her father out of debtors' prison."

"Hellfire," Bray whispered. "I can see where that would dampen your interest in her. Who is the blade?"

"The only thing I know is that he's an officer who was awarded the rank of captain after Waterloo."

Bray picked up his ale again. "A war hero."

"It appears that way."

"If you have his name, we could have a runner from Bow Street see what he can find out about him."

"No reason to. At the moment, I have no desire to try to win her away from him."

"Are you sure?"

Am I?

"I've been down that hellish road and don't plan to revisit it."

"Maybe you won't have to. You know how fickle young ladies can be. They can get their hearts wrapped up by a man in a uniform one day and be completely in awe of another gentleman the next. I daresay the man can compete with you if you decide you want to make her change her mind."

Harrison had thought about that and was still thinking about it, but he wasn't going to talk about it with Bray. He changed the subject by saying, "Why don't I give you a chance to win back all the money you've lost to me. Billiards or cards. Your choice?"

"We'll have to save the conversation and the cards for another time. I have a meeting with my solicitor." He rose from his chair and looked down at Harrison with a mock-serious expression. "Keep in mind the courts are usually lax in applying the laws when it comes to duels. Most sympathize with the right of a man to defend or restore his honor. However, most cases don't have the Prince's ear."

"If you are trying to end this conversation on a high note you're not doing it," Harrison grumbled.

"Then I'll try again. If you do choose the comforts of Newgate over the comforts of a pair of feminine arms, I'll come visit you."

"You blackguard," Harrison said and they both laughed.

"I know you've met Gwen, but you'll come to dinner soon and meet the rest of Louisa's sisters, won't you?"

"Dinner in your home? That must be a big change for you."

"It is."

"All right, yes, I'll come. Let me know when."

After Bray left, Harrison motioned for another ale, intent on taking it into the gaming room with him. He had no desire to sit alone and spend the rest of the day brooding. He'd already discovered, over the past couple of days, that whenever he was alone, his thoughts drifted to Miss Rule and her earnest request for him to allow her father and the Prince to assume Harrison would wed her at the end of the Season.

He was determined to keep her off his mind, if only for a short time. He just hadn't found out how to do it yet. A game of billiards with the laughing group of gentlemen he'd heard earlier should be a worthy diversion for a couple of hours.

A shadow fell across the table and Harrison looked up, thinking it was the server.

"Good day, my lord. May I join you?"

Harrison glanced up to see Mr. Hopscotch. "I was just leaving," Harrison answered as the servant placed a full tankard in front of him.

"I won't take much of your time. Only a moment please," he said and pulled out the chair Bray had recently vacated.

"Are you a member here?" Harrison asked.

"No, no, I don't qualify, of course." His chest puffed up. "I'm merely a messenger. But the Prince is a member and I am here at his pleasure."

"Then get on with it," Harrison said in an exasperated tone. "Tell me what message you have for me from the Prince today."

"He wants to know if you found favor with Miss Rule as he'd hoped. No one has seen you talk to her the past couple of nights. In fact, no one has seen you at any of the parties."

"I prefer a quiet game of cards to dancing in the evenings so I haven't been to any."

Mr. Hopscotch sat back in his chair. "The Prince will not be happy to hear that."

"The Prince's happiness is not my concern."

A puzzled expression wrinkled the skin around Hopscotch's eyes. "That I appreciate, but what I don't understand is your restrained interest in Miss Rule. She is quite eye-catching, intelligent, and her family is given the highest regards by the Prince."

Harrison scoffed. "Her father is a gambler and risk taker."

"So, Miss Rule told you about his troubles. Or perhaps you looked into the man's habits."

Harrison scoffed again just as quickly as before. "I have no desire to look into anyone's habits."

"Perhaps you should give this suggestion from the Prince more thought. In fact, take your time. His creditors have been notified that a solution is in the making so the situation is under control for the present. You don't need to marry her before the end of the Season so there is no rush."

That was good to hear because Harrison needed more time. The same thing Miss Rule had asked for. More time. If he wanted it, shouldn't he give her the same courtesy?

Hopscotch fiddled with the long ends of his neckcloth. "What you do has always been up to you," Hopscotch continued as he rose from the chair. "I won't bother you again until the end of the Season, but I'll see you then. Whether I bring the guards is up to you."

Harrison picked up his drink and took a sip. Yes, Miss Rule was captivating, intriguing, and sensuous in a way that drew him. If he decided to pursue her, he would do so for one reason and one reason only: because *he* wanted to.

Chapter 8

Have you not heard it said full oft,
a woman's nay doth stand for nought?
The Passionate Pilgrim

Harrison set the brake and then jumped down from his curricle. The small Mayfair home looked well-tended with a tall, neatly trimmed yew hedge lining each side and short, boxed shrubs crowding the front. It was another afternoon of sunshine. Three days in a row of cloudless blue skies at this time of year was rare for London.

The spring air had a bite to it, but warmth from the sun made the chill easy to bear. He shook his head. He would have much rather been at Thornwick than in London, looking for a wife. Hopefully the weather was just as nice at the estate and the laborers were well on the way to rebuilding the house.

All his efforts to get Miss Rule out of his thoughts had failed. She was decidedly more captivating than any of the other young ladies he'd met since returning to London. And no matter how many times he tried to talk himself out of it, he wanted to see her again. Talk to her.

Find out if he was still as attracted to her as his imagination and his body were telling him he was. It was time
he gave her the answer to her request.

Harrison sauntered up the stone walkway. He lifted
the brass knocker and gave it two hard raps. From inside the house barking exploded and, for an instant, Harrison wondered if all the hounds in hell were waiting
for him behind that door.

"Hush up that racket before I get the broom after
you," he heard a woman yell from inside. The barking
quieted to a soft woof or two, but the loud talking continued. "Come on, the lot of you, into the music room.
That's right. You know I'm not going to open the door
so we can see who it is until you're all in there. You too,
Molly. There you go. Now stay quiet or I won't let you
out until you're fed and put to bed."

The door opened and Harrison saw a short, sturdy
woman with a flat face and big brown eyes peering up
at him. "Good afternoon, sir, may I help you?"

The servant's voice was a bit softer when she spoke to
him. He swept his hat off his head and said, "Yes, I'm
the Earl of Thornwick here to see Miss Rule."

"I beg your pardon, my lord," she said with a curtsy.
She stepped aside and added, "Come in. I guess Miss
Rule forgot to tell me she was expecting an important
caller."

"Well, she's not——" As soon as he spoke the dogs
heard his voice and started barking again.

"Quiet, you ill-mannered brood," the housekeeper
yelled over her shoulder. "Can't you hear we have a lord
as a guest in the house?"

From the sound of the dogs, Harrison would guess
there were at least three of them and possibly more. Animals were never allowed in his house when he was
growing up. If Harrison or one of his brothers had

wanted to make a pet out of one of the hunting or herding dogs, his mother would remind them that four boys were enough to have inside the house. She wouldn't allow dogs, too.

"Begging your pardon, your lordship, what were you saying?"

"I would like to see Miss Rule."

"She's in the back garden working on her paintings. I'll show you into the drawing room and then go tell her you're here."

In the house with the noisy dogs or the quiet of the garden? Harrison handed the woman his hat and gloves. "Perhaps I could just join her in the garden. Do you think that would be possible, Mrs.—?"

The woman smiled shyly, clearly flattered he wanted to know her name. "Oh, my name is Bickmore, your lordship. Mrs. Bickmore. And yes, if you say it's all right to visit with her in the garden who am I to say different. It's fine by me. I wouldn't ever question an earl, but I don't think Sam's going to like it."

Sam?

Harrison knew Miss Rule was an only child so it wasn't possible Sam was her brother. Did she have another suitor? Was Sam the army captain? Perhaps he was a relative. But surely the housekeeper wouldn't call a guest by his Christian name. In any case, the polite thing to do would be to stay in the drawing room and wait until the gentleman left, but how often had Harrison ever done the polite thing.

"Is Sam with her now?"

"Yes, my lord."

"Good. I'd like to meet him."

A worried expression twisted her face as she laid his hat and gloves aside. "He's not the friendly sort, if you know what I mean."

No doubt the man was a pompous blade and would not take kindly to an earl intruding on his time with the lovely miss. But that didn't give Harrison a moment's hesitation.

"I do," Harrison acknowledged. "That won't bother me." He wasn't the friendly sort, either, so they would get along very well together.

"I'll take you to her," she said and started lumbering down the corridor.

Harrison followed the woman to the back of the house. She opened the door and moved aside so Harrison could walk past her and out onto the stoop. He caught a glimpse of Miss Rule sitting in a chair looking as if she was bending over something. The next thing Harrison saw was something large, dark, and growling loping toward him.

Miss Rule rose and yelled, "Sam! Stop!"

The brindle-colored dog kept coming and growling.

"Sam," she called again and started toward them.

The dog knew his mistress's voice. He skidded to a stop at the bottom step, giving Harrison a curled-lip, wide-stance warning, a low growl coming out of his strong jaws.

"Sam, sit," Miss Rule added in a strong voice.

Sam immediately rested on his haunches but kept his big black eyes locked on Harrison. By the looks of the animal, he was at least part bull terrier. His shoulders and legs were muscular and sturdy but thankfully he wasn't as large as most of his breed. Harrison knew to be respectful of the dog's territory so he remained perfectly still when he heard Mrs. Bickmore close the door behind him. Bull terriers were faithful to their masters but wouldn't hesitate to threaten a stranger.

Not wanting to appear aggressive to the growling

dog, Harrison didn't look him directly in the eyes but said under his breath, "Don't worry, ol' chap. I promise not to touch her. At least while you're around."

Harrison kept his attention on Miss Rule. She walked toward him with an easy, confident stroll. She wore a paint-stained apron over a pale-gray dress. A brown woolen shawl covered her shoulders and was knotted at her breasts. A narrow green ribbon, tied neatly in a bow underneath her chin, held a wide-brimmed straw hat on her head. Her long golden-brown tresses flowed from beneath the hat and shimmered in the sunlight.

She was dressed nothing like the beautiful, expensively gowned goddess he'd seen three nights before, but for some reason he was even more captivated by the way she looked today. She reminded him of a mountain stream in the first few days of spring. Cool, clear, and refreshing. Her casual, at-home look made her appear chaste, wholesome, and very approachable. The flush on her cheeks was becoming, and he wondered if the pink tint was from his unexpected arrival or from the sun.

She stopped by the dog and patted him on his big head, then rubbed the side of his neck. "You are such a brute, Sam. I will have to apologize for your inhospitable welcome to his lordship."

Inhospitable? That's putting the greeting far nicer than it actually was.

"Go lie down, Sam," she added.

The brindle hesitated. Miss Rule patted him again and lightly shoved his head, urging him to move away. Obviously satisfied, for the time being at least, that Harrison was no threat to his mistress, Sam turned and walked over to where her chair was and lay down.

"He minds well," Harrison offered. "I'm afraid I will have to apologize to Mrs. Bickmore."

Miss Rule gave him a curious look. "Why is that?"

"She told me Sam wasn't the friendly sort. I didn't believe her."

"He's protective of me but he's never failed to obey me."

"I'm not sure that gives me comfort."

She gave him a knowing smile. He could tell she loved it that her dog had caught him off guard.

"I had no idea you were coming today." She looked down at her soiled apron and paint-marked fingers. She quickly put her hands behind her back. "You caught me completely unprepared for guests, my lord. Mrs. Bickmore should have checked with me before she showed you into the garden."

Harrison remembered how the housekeeper had yelled at the dogs. She was obviously not fond of them and probably didn't want to tangle with Sam.

"No need to be harsh with Mrs. Bickmore," he said, descending the two steps to stand in front of her. "I didn't give her much choice in the matter."

"That I can believe," Miss Rule said, untying the sash of her apron. "Why don't we go back inside? I'll have some tea prepared, or something stronger if you wish."

"I had my cook prepare a basket of refreshments. I thought you might enjoy a ride in the park this afternoon."

He liked the surprise he saw in her eyes. "Does this mean you have an answer for me?"

He smiled. No reason to hurry the afternoon. "Perhaps. Let's take a ride and you will find out."

She turned loose of the apron sash and started untying her shawl. "And a ride with me would help you make up your mind?"

He tilted his head and gave her a small grin but committed to nothing.

"The ride would have been nice on such a lovely day, but my father isn't home to give approval so I couldn't possibly accept."

"What about Lady Railbridge, your grandmother?"

"She's isn't available to consent, either. Every Thursday afternoon she goes to visit a friend who is ill."

Harrison had thoughts that had no business being in his mind. What were the odds he'd arrive when Miss Rule's only chaperones were a housekeeper and a snarling dog?

"Then I suggest we stay in the garden and save the ride for another afternoon."

"I'm sure my grandmother wouldn't approve of us being out here alone, but I suppose it will be all right if you don't stay too long."

He watched as she untied the knots at the ends of her shawl. Her fingers were slender, nimble, and marked with various colors of paint.

"Would you like for me to hold your shawl while you remove your apron?" he asked.

"Yes, thank you," she said, seeming pleased that he'd offer. "If you don't mind."

She extended it to him and as she did she noticed the paint on her fingers and quickly closed her hands into fists. Harrison chuckled softly. "Too late to hide them now. I've already seen them. Nice colors by the way." He took hold of the shawl and slipped it through her fingers.

She laughed, too. "I'm glad you approve, but again, my grandmother would not."

A soft smile lifted just one corner of her lips and Harrison felt warmth and tightness surge through his loins. She was more than fetching. She was downright desirable.

He watched as she untied the ribbon under her chin

and swept off her hat. He reached for it and she handed it to him. She was naturally sensual and didn't even know it. Another twinge of desire shuddered through him. He had undressed many ladies over the years but he was certain he'd never before acted the servant's role for one. He didn't realize how stimulating it could be. He found her every move tremendously seductive.

She pulled the apron over her head. She wore a simple pale-gray dress with a round neckline that laced up the front of the bodice. The thought of untying those laces gave him ideas he didn't need to explore when he was alone with her in a garden. It would be too easy to pull her to him and see if her lips were as soft and tasty as they looked.

"Excuse me, my lord," she said, looking behind her. "I forgot to cover my work."

Harrison followed her over to a table where her painting supplies were scattered. "What did I interrupt?" he asked, catching a glimpse of a fan with columns and a chandelier painted on it before she covered it with a tin dome.

"Nothing important," she said, averting her eyes from his and laying her apron on top of the dome. "I don't like to leave my paints unprotected. Insects have been known to land in them and create quite a mess."

It surprised him that she hid her work so quickly. Most young ladies were eager to show him their stitchery or paintings, or read him their poetry. Miss Rule shielded hers as if it wasn't very good, or she didn't want him to see it. That was refreshing.

"What were you painting?" he asked.

"I paint different scenes," she said, rubbing some of the pigment from her hand with her thumb. "On lids to snuff and mourning boxes, fans, and miniatures. The usual things." Then, as if realizing the paint wasn't going to come off, she reached for her hat and he gave it to her.

While Harrison was thinking it was a sin to cover her glorious long curls with that brown straw, he felt something wet and cold on the tips of his fingers and realized that Sam had decided it was time to walk over and sniff him. It took all his willpower but Harrison forced himself to keep his arm hanging still at his side and let the big animal sniff him wherever he wished so the dog would become comfortable with him.

"Your father obviously likes dogs," he said.

She laughed lightly as she loosely tied the ribbon under her chin.

"Why does that amuse you?" Harrison asked.

"Sam, leave Lord Thornwick alone and go lie down. Now," she ordered, giving him a firm stare. The dog obeyed and wandered away. She continued. "My father doesn't like animals of any kind. He indulges me from time to time and allows me to keep a stray who happens by our house, but not often."

"Sam was a stray?"

"Yes, he was wounded and starving when I found him. I nursed him back to health."

"No wonder he is so protective of you."

"I think it's natural for his breed to be that way. He has some bull terrier in him I'm sure, though what the other breeds mixed in might be I have no idea. He gets along well with the other dogs and that's what matters."

Harrison knew another woman who liked to take in strays and wounded animals. But she wasn't a woman he could introduce to Miss Rule. In her time, Mrs. Olivia Vaughan was legendary as the highest-paid mistress in London, and she loved dogs, too.

"How many do you have?"

"Three."

"All strays?"

"Yes. Rascal was the first and is the oldest and part hound. The newest addition is Mr. Pete. He's a puppy and I think he might be part beagle." She paused. "Well, we really have four dogs as my father often reminds me. My grandmother has a Maltese but she is so small she hardly counts. And she wasn't a stray. It's always important to my grandmother that people know Molly is the only purebred dog in the house."

His gaze swept easily down her face and then back up to her eyes. So Miss Rule was not only very loyal to a father who would force her to marry a man she didn't love in order to save his hide, she also had a love for wounded animals. Somehow that didn't surprise him. He didn't need one more thing to like about her—but how could he not be drawn to the fact she took in strays and cared for them?

"The wind is picking up. You should put this back on," he said, holding out her shawl. She reached for it and he said, "Allow me."

She hesitated only a moment before turning her back to him. He placed it on her shoulders and before she had time to turn around he lifted her long hair from beneath the shawl. It was warm and soft in his hands, and smelled heavenly. He was tempted to lift its weight and bury his face in it.

Everything about her was intoxicating. There was something exciting about her, and something elusive, too. He couldn't fool himself. He knew what it was. She said her heart belonged to another and as much as he didn't want it to be so, the fact was, it presented a challenge for him to woo her, and to win her.

Damnation, he didn't want to pick up that gauntlet. There were too many ladies willing to share his bed, and his life for that matter, to worry with fighting for one who had already made it clear her heart was taken.

But Miss Rule was different from all the others. That was as evident and simple as night and day. And even though she claimed to love someone else, she wasn't completely uninterested in Harrison, either. He'd watched her look him over with a discerning eye and appreciate what she saw. He was sure of that.

So how hard would it be to win her away from a soldier if he decided he wanted to?

He liked that she was passionate about trying to help her father. Loyalty was an admirable quality in anyone. She was obviously passionate about helping others or she wouldn't take in the wounded strays. Something told him she'd bring that same spirited passion to her wedding bed.

When she faced him, she looked directly into his eyes and said, "So tell me, my lord, have you decided whether you will help me save my father? Or are you still thinking?"

That was the furthest thing from his mind presently. "I am thinking, Miss Rule, but not about that."

Her brow wrinkled. "Then what?"

He stepped closer, deliberately towering over her so she would know he was the one in control, and said, "I'm thinking about kissing you."

She went very still. He watched a flush creep up her pretty neck and into her lovely face. He wanted to kiss her. He wanted her, and he no longer wanted to ignore what she was making him feel.

"That wouldn't be wise, my lord," she said.

She didn't tell him no. Encouraged, he said, "Probably not, but I have done many unwise things in my lifetime. What will it hurt to do one more?"

He lifted his hand and skimmed the backs of his

fingers down her soft cheek, brushing aside a wispy strand of hair that hadn't been caught back by her hat. She didn't flinch from his touch. He took that as a good sign, but asked, "Will you slap me if I kiss you?"

Astonishment flickered in her eyes but there was no panic. Another good sign that there was a possibility this conversation would end in a kiss. "What? No. I mean, I don't know. I've never thought about it."

"You've never thought about being kissed?" he asked, deliberately misunderstanding her.

She hesitated, seeming to study what to say. "No, of course, I have," she conceded. "I meant I've never thought about the possibility of slapping a gentleman for kissing me."

"So you've been kissed?"

"Definitely not," she assured him and wrapped her shawl tighter about her arms as if the woolen garment would protect her from his probing words.

It was another good sign that she hadn't moved away from him. If she hadn't been considering letting him kiss her she would have already been backing up, showing him the door, or calling Sam over to intimidate him.

"Not even by the captain?" Harrison asked.

She looked aghast. "He is a gentleman, my lord. I haven't even seen him in over a year. Besides, I wasn't old enough to be kissed the last I saw him."

Never been kissed.

That pleased Harrison and motivated him.

He wanted to be the first to kiss her. He would be. Why should the captain have that right just because she'd given her heart to him? She wouldn't be the first young miss to receive her first kiss from Harrison, but he couldn't remember wanting to kiss one more than he wanted to kiss her right now.

The sun was warm, the breeze was cool, and the garden was empty of chaperones save Sam—and he couldn't talk. The timing was perfect. Yes, the more he thought about it the more he wanted to do it. He wanted to feel her in his arms. He wanted to know how those pink-tinted lips would feel beneath his.

"You are of age now," he said in a low tone as he inched even closer to her.

"Yes, I'll be nineteen by early summer."

Oh, yes, plenty old enough for a first kiss.

He noticed the words in her last sentence were softer and she sounded breathless. She was already contemplating his kiss. That made his breathing a little ragged, too.

Maybe, just maybe he did want to pursue her and win her from the captain.

"Kissing is against the rules of Society for young ladies," she warned him.

He moved closer to her. Again she didn't flinch. Did she know that was as good as an invitation for him to continue? "But surely you know that some rules are made to be broken."

She remained quiet. Pensive.

"And this is one of them," he added. "So don't blink."

"Don't blink," she questioned with an uncertain expression on her face. "Why?"

I want you to see me and no one else.

"Because I'm going to kiss you and you'll want to witness your first kiss."

"Telling me not to blink makes me want to."

He gave her a hint of a smile, thinking how much he would like to do more to her than just kiss her tempting lips. "Then it will be your fault if you miss this."

He lowered his head to hers and let his lips graze across hers with the merest amount of pressure. The contact was sweet, enticing, and undemanding. It sent a quick, hard throb of pulsating heat directly to his manhood, causing an unexpected rush of intense desire to shudder through him.

Harrison only meant to give her a proper, innocent first kiss but his body was demanding much more. He hesitated before deepening the kiss, slanting his lips seductively over hers, seeking more of a response from her until he realized she was too in awe of the kiss to answer the instant passion that had erupted in him.

He hadn't expected the kiss to be so powerful, or to feel such satisfaction that she'd obeyed. To her credit, her wide-eyed blue gaze stayed on his eyes for the entire kiss. He wanted to abandon his reserve and show her just how quickly she'd made him want her, but not wanting to frighten her he refrained.

When he heard a soft sigh from her, he lifted his mouth an inch or two and whispered, "You just witnessed your first kiss."

Chapter 9

Careless lust stirs up a desperate courage.
Venus and Adonis *556–57*

Angelina blinked and bobbed her head slightly.

"You're blinking," he said huskily.

Of course she was, and her stomach felt like it had a thousand butterflies in it, too. He was so close she felt his breath on her cheek, the heat radiating from his body. A shivery prickle of something wonderful sailed across her breasts, tightening them before it raced to the deepest of her most womanly part and settled there. Lord Thornwick was a scandalously presumptuous man and for reasons she didn't want to think about, it thrilled her.

As much as she wanted to speak, she was too stunned to say a word. She was still reeling from the fact that she'd just received her first kiss and the new marvelous awareness it had created inside her. The only thing she could do was moisten her lips and swallow.

"I'll take that as an invitation for another kiss," the earl said.

Was it?

No. No.

Yet the word wouldn't form on her tongue.

"Close your eyes this time," he whispered, and without giving her a moment to object, his head dipped low and his lips found hers once again.

God help her, her lids fluttered down. She obeyed him without a hint of reluctance and closed her eyes.

Angelina felt his strong hands circle her waist and slide to her back. She knew she should spin, shove, or twist away from him but she had no desire to miss what his touch was promising. Instead, she went willingly into his embrace and was caught up in his powerful arms and pressed to his hard chest. Something compelling stirred inside her and despite a lone stray thought to recoil, she melted against him. The strength behind his hold on her was exhilarating. Warmth from his body was more pleasing than sunshine on a bitter-cold day. She had no idea just how heavenly it would feel to be engulfed in such muscular arms and have a man's lips moving so sensuously over hers.

She gave herself over to the undeniably pleasurable sensations and without forethought lifted her arms and wound them around his neck. Her action made him hug her tighter, press her closer. His hands tangled in the length of her hair. Her shawl fell away from her shoulders. A shiver made her tremble but she'd never felt warmer in her life.

His lips were soft and moist. The kiss was long and generous. Instinctively, her lips parted, her mouth opened. His tongue slipped inside with a warm, slow probing. She trembled and swallowed a gasp of wonder. He made a languorous exploration of her mouth. Their tongues touched, played, and explored. Their breaths mingled. Her hands skimmed down his wide shoulders to examine the broad width of his firm, muscular back before sliding down to his tapered waist, leaving no doubt there was a fine cut of a man beneath the clothing.

He broke the kiss and lifted his head. Her eyes opened to stare into his. She felt weightless, breathless, and wonderful.

"I've wanted to know how you would taste since I saw you standing at the entrance to the ballroom," he said.

"Tea," she said without thinking and without blinking.

He quirked his head a bit to question her.

"I had tea a little while ago," she explained. "Do I taste of tea?"

A soft chuckle whispered from his throat, and he said, "Very sweet tea," before his lips came down to hers again with confident, commanding pressure that made her body eager for more of his touch.

He kissed her deeply, hungrily, and she didn't resist. To her amazement, she kissed him back with equal fervor. His lips were lush, his embrace was powerful. He kissed his way over her chin and down her neck to the braided piping trim on her bodice and then started back up again. Her hands slipped into the back of his hair and she crushed its softness between her fingers.

A small sigh escaped her lips. She wanted to enjoy the luxury of all the new sensations that rippled, drifted, and curled throughout her body before settling in intimate places.

It was a heady experience, but all too soon his lips left hers again. He lifted his head and his arms relaxed around her. He let her go and slowly stepped away. To her chagrin, she was disappointed by his withdrawal. She inhaled a deep breath and backed away, putting even more distance between them. Her gaze flew to the back

of the house to see if Mrs. Bickmore might have been
watching from the window or the door, but Angelina
saw no one.

When their gazes met again, he said, "Now it's your
turn to tell me what you're thinking."

There was no command in his voice. There didn't
have to be. His intent showed in the way his eyes took
in every detail of her face. He knew she enjoyed the
kiss but he wanted to hear her say it. It seemed his
breathing was a little unsteady, too, and she wondered
if he had felt all the amazing things that had swirled
inside her.

"That it was inevitable I would eventually have my
first kiss."

He nodded. "Was it pleasurable?"

Oh, yes!

The intensity of his gaze continued to do confound-
ing things to her heart rate. She thought about evading
the truth, possibly even prevaricating, but knowing she'd
never been any good at hiding her true emotions in the
end she simply said, "Yes, and for you?"

His brow rose as if her question surprised him. "Very
much."

"Tell me, my lord, did you come here today just to
kiss me?"

"No."

"Then why did you kiss me?" '

"You asked me to."

"What? Don't be ridiculous," she said firmly. "You
know I did no such thing."

"I beg to differ, Miss Rule. When I looked at you,
your eyes were asking me to kiss you. They were saying, *Kiss me, Harrison.*"

The glowing light of humor shone in his eyes and she
realized he was teasing her. That helped her relax. It was

best to make light of the kiss since it never should have happened. And maybe that would make it seem less powerful than it actually was.

She brushed a strand of hair away from her face. "That's the oddest thing I've heard you say," she replied pleasantly. "Besides the fact that it's not true."

"How do you know? You can't see your eyes."

"But they are my eyes, and I know because they wouldn't have called you Harrison. They would have said *my lord*."

The corner of one side of his mouth lifted attractively. "Your eyes know me better than your mind. They call me Harrison."

She appreciated that he was still trying to put her at ease about the very intimate kiss. Even so, she said, "I can't believe we are having this conversation."

"I can. We also had one about a horse a few nights ago. I believe I won that round as well."

That made her smile. "We will not revisit the discussion of me and the horse."

"I agree, and just in case you want to know, I'm reading your eyes again right now, Miss Rule, and right now they are saying, *Kiss me again, Harrison*."

His confidence, his audacity amazed her. The low husky way he said the words made her abdomen tighten, and she wanted to step back into the circle of his arms.

"No," she said, putting more distance between them for fear her resolve not to kiss him again might weaken. "No, they are saying it's time for you to go. I understand that you haven't decided whether you will help me save my father from prison. That's fine. The kiss is the only other thing you have accomplished since arriving and my education in that area is now completed. I need no further instruction."

A hint of a smile curved the corner of his mouth again. "Then perhaps I should put your mind at ease, Miss Rule. As far as your father is concerned, I will pretend that we will be wed at the end of the Season, and your father can lead his creditors to believe the same. You will have the time you asked for to come up with another way to keep your father out of prison."

On a rush of excited breath, she whispered, "Thank you, Lord Thornwick. Though I'm sure you don't want my gratitude, I give it. This indeed puts my mind to rest."

He reached down, picked up her shawl, and held it out for her. This time instead of turning so he could place it on her shoulders, she pulled it from his grasp.

He gave her a roguish grin and asked, "Aren't you going to ask me what I want from you for doing this noble deed?"

Oh, my. She should have known there would be something.

"Yes, of course." She looked at the tall, broad-shouldered man poised commandingly in front of her and asked, "Do you want more kisses from me?"

He laughed and folded his arms across his chest in a casual manner. "As tempting an offer as that is, kisses are not something I have ever had to bargain for."

Angelina cringed inside over that mistake. "Of course you haven't. I don't know what I was thinking. Surely a man like you doesn't actually need anything and that includes kisses."

"But I do occasionally want things. I'm sure I will come up with something, and I'll let you know when I do."

"Something reasonable," she added.

He lifted a brow. "That I can't promise. Tell me, did

you and the officer you mentioned have an understanding that you would wait for him and marry him when he returned?"

"No. We never spoke of marriage. It was, it was—"

"What?"

She felt her eyes and face soften. Her shoulders relaxed. "More in the way we looked at each other."

"Ah," he said.

"Ah? What does that mean?" she asked.

"It means I understand it was a feeling that happened between the two of you rather than a promise given."

"Yes, that's right," she agreed. "I told you, we only spoke briefly for a few times. It wouldn't have been proper for us to spend any time together. The last time I saw him, he asked me to save him a dance and I told him I would."

Lord Thornwick seemed to study on that for a moment and then nodded. "Will you be attending the parties tonight?"

"Yes. We'll end the night at the Great Hall."

"Then I'll see you there and we'll dance."

"But you don't like to dance."

"There are times we all must do things we would rather not do. Dancing, rides in the park, and afternoon walks in your garden should satisfy your father—" He paused. "—and other interested people that I'm actively pursuing you in the hope of making a match by Season's end."

The earl looked around, whistled and called, "Sam," then whistled again.

The dog came running out from under a bush near the back gate. He stopped at Lord Thornwick's feet, looked up at him, and barked once.

"Good job taking care of your mistress," he said,

reaching down to pat the dog's shoulder. "I'll see my-self out the back gate. Until tonight, Miss Rule."

Angelina watched the earl leave.

He'd kissed her. She'd kissed him and enjoyed it tremendously.

Her first kiss? An unexpected glorious experience. How could that be when she loved Captain Maxwell?

Lord Thornwick had arrived at her home with no advance notice, for no particular reason, and suddenly he was kissing her. Kissing her ever so gently with such slow tenderness it was heavenly, and then with such deliberate, intimate passion it stole her breath. She had always thought a devilish rogue's kiss would be harsh, horrible, and demanding. How could she have been so wrong about that? Lord Thornwick had taken his time and gently coaxed and then encouraged her to respond to him, and she had.

With eagerness!

And merciful heavens, she hadn't wanted it to end!

She knew he was known far and wide for being a scoundrel of the highest order. And now she knew why. What kind of gentleman kissed a young lady with so much feeling she thought she would melt? What kind of lady allowed him to do it! Especially after she'd already told him her heart belonged to another.

"Heaven help me," she groaned out loud. "Evidently I am that kind of lady."

As much as she wished she could deny the earl's effect on her, she had to admit she had enjoyed his embrace from beginning to end. He had an easy charm about him that was infectious and irresistible. Everything he'd made her feel was inappropriate. She should have felt defenseless, coerced, or maybe even used, but all she felt was wondrous pleasure. She had loved the feel of being in his arms, his lips on hers. The soft silky sounds of pleasure they made had wafted past her ears. The clean smell of shaving soap that clung to his face was inviting. He had touched her deeply and awakened her senses even more than Captain Maxwell had when she'd first seen him look up at her with his dreamy eyes and smile.

Angelina shook her head and returned to the chair in front of her paints. She had to put the earl out of her mind and get back to the scene. She removed the dome and picked up her paintbrush but before she'd remembered where she'd left off, Lord Thornwick had invaded her thoughts once again. He was a handsome rake, but that was the only compliment Angelina was willing to give him right now. Except, maybe, she did find his roguish smile attractive at times, and she did like it that he hadn't seemed in the least daunted by Sam, but that was as far as it went. Well, except, he certainly knew how to get the most out of a kiss. She would give him that as well. But surely Captain Maxwell's kisses would be even better.

Merciful heavens! She would melt into a puddle if Captain Maxwell's kisses were any better than the earl's.

Lord Thornwick's kiss had shocked her, stimulated her, and vexed her. What a devil he was to walk into her garden and deliberately take control of her senses, take her in his arms and kiss her as if she belonged to him. Yes, that was how it felt to be wrapped in his arms. It was as if she were his. He made her forget her sensible self; more than that, he made her forget all about Captain Maxwell.

And what would Captain Maxwell say if he knew she had been so thoroughly kissed?

She'd often dreamed of being held in a gentleman's strong arms, her breasts flattened against his wide chest, but she'd always thought the man would be the Army captain.

When he returned, would he want to kiss her? If he did, would he know that she had already been kissed? If not, would he ask her?

And if he did, would she tell him the truth?

Chapter 10

*As many arrows, loosed several ways, come to one
mark . . . so may a thousand actions, once afoot,
end in one purpose.*
Henry V, *Act I, sc. 2*

Angelina shivered.

The wind had kicked up and the bright sun and blue
sky had faded to gray, reducing her light. It was time to
put her painting away and go inside. She'd done all she
could for one day.

She looked at the fan she'd just finished and smiled
with pride as she carefully placed it in a small wooden
box so it wouldn't get bumped and smudge the paint before it completely dried. Without knowing it, the Dowager Duchess of Drakestone had given Angelina the idea
of painting a portion of the ballroom at the Great Hall.
The white columns and sparkling chandeliers looked
beautiful against the dark-blue silk of the fan.

Angelina knew it wouldn't matter how many times
she walked into that room; she would always be staggered by its opulence. The gilt fretwork and carved mold-
ings were extraordinary. She'd never seen anything to
rival the ceiling. It was painted sky blue and littered with

heavenly creatures shooting arrows and playing harps. She hadn't bothered to count them but there had to be more than a dozen of the huge Corinthian columns gracing the floor.

It had been difficult but by using the gold and silver dust, she'd captured the look of the sparkling chandeliers throwing golden streams of light across the elegant room. At the bottom of the fan, she'd painted swirls of bright colors to represent the gowns, headpieces, and waistcoats of the attendees. The dowager would love it.

It had probably taken Angelina close to half an hour after Lord Thornwick had left to get her hands steady enough to return to painting. She didn't know how she'd done it but she'd managed to finish the fan and think about Lord Thornwick, too. Think about his kisses and strong, warm embrace.

Angelina didn't want to be infatuated by him. But how could she not be? His kisses had been delicious, inviting, and—strangest of all——possessive. Surely when Captain Maxwell returned and kissed her she would have the same marvelous feelings. No, the captain's kisses would be even better because he was the man of her dreams. She was in love with him. Yes, his kisses would make her forget all about Lord Thornwick's.

Oh, she hoped Captain Maxwell returned soon so she could get the earl off her mind.

She heard the back door open and spun around. Her grandmother stepped out onto the stoop. Angelina smiled to herself. She was being silly. For an instant she thought the earl had returned.

"I've found him," Granna called with a smile as she waved a piece of foolscap in her hand. "The gentleman I was looking for. Do you want to go with me to see him?"

Angelina's breath leaped. "Yes, that's wonderful news. You know I want to go," she answered, covering her paints. "But I need a minute to put these away."

"No, I'll send your maid out to bring your things inside and put them in your painting room. You hurry inside and wash up, change, and get some of your best paintings together. Meet me by the front door as soon as you can."

"I'll hurry and then get my coat and bonnet and be right there."

Angelina didn't think she had ever changed and put her hair in a chignon so quickly. In less than twenty minutes, she and her grandmother were settled in the carriage rumbling down the bumpy road.

"Now can you tell me where we're going and who we will see?" Angelina asked, clutching in her lap a satchel that held two fans, two mourning boxes, a snuffbox, and a painting of a ship being tossed at sea on a piece of ivory.

"We're going to see an old friend of your grandfather's. I know it's not proper to arrive at anyone's door unannounced but what we'll be asking him to do for us is an even worse offense. So we're already beyond the pale. If he's unavailable, I'll leave my card and ask him to pay me a visit tomorrow. We're already almost a week into the Season and if we are going to help your father there is no time to waste."

Angelina felt an overwhelming love for her grandmother. She didn't approve of what Angelina was doing, yet she was willing to put aside her own beliefs of what was right and proper to help Angelina. She patted her grandmother's gloved hand. "My appreciation runs deep, Granna. I know participating in this unsavory arrangement is not something you would choose to do."

"No, my dear, it is not," Granna said with a smile. "However, when duty calls I will answer. I do this only because I know my daughter would want me to help you." She sighed. "And loving heart that she had, she'd want me to help your father, too, so I must."

Angelina's throat tightened and she was quiet for a time. She often missed her mother, and at times wondered if her life would have been any different if her mother had lived.

"Since we'll soon meet this man, Granna, can you tell me his name now and something about him?"

"I'm sorry I sounded so cautious and didn't tell you anything before I went about finding him. I didn't want to get your hopes up if the man I was thinking about was no longer living in London. I really didn't know if he was still alive. I had to go to the church to find out."

"The church?"

"Yes," she replied. "An odd place to be sure. I knew the vicar would know how to get in touch with him. I'd heard they had remained friends. The vicar said he'd find Bishop Worsley's address and send it to me. It was waiting for me when I returned today."

That bit of information took Angelina aback. "A bishop in the church is going to help us?"

"Well . . ." She hesitated and averted her eyes. "Not exactly. That is, he was a bishop in the church a few years ago, and a very fine one from what your grandfather told me. They'd been friends since they were boys."

"I heard a *but* about him in there, Granna."

Her grandmother sighed. "Unfortunately, there usually is. Some things happened, and, well, he's no longer a part of the clergy, but he refused to give up his title."

"That's curious. Do you know what things happened?"

"Yes, of course, your grandfather was still living at the time and he confided in me all the things that didn't make the newsprint."

Now Angelina was even more interested in this man they were to meet. "Can you tell me?"

"I suppose it will be all right to share it with you. It was so long ago, I'm sure no one talks about his downfall anymore, and it's really no secret. Apparently, the vicar at the time found out Bishop Worsley liked to gamble."

"That doesn't sound so bad to me," Angelina said with a smile. "From what I've heard, most men enjoy their games and wagers. But now that I think about it, I suppose the church wouldn't want men on their staff to be regulars in such behavior."

"Especially if the man was using the church's money to gamble with and then pay his debts."

"Oh, my," Angelina said. "Granna, if that's the case, are you sure he will be trustworthy for what we want him to do?"

"Yes," her grandmother said emphatically. "According to the vicar, he's completely reformed now and has mended his ways. The vicar told me the two of them stay in touch from time to time and that Bishop Worsley has stayed on the straight road regarding his gambling inclinations."

"And because of his past experience with gaming you think he'll know how to help us."

"Well, he'll certainly know more than we do."

Angelina liked her grandmother's attitude about this entire situation. "That's for certain."

"No one will think twice about a man going into the shops to see if they will buy your paintings. And I know we can trust him not to ever divulge to anyone that you are the artist."

Angelina believed her grandmother but asked, "How can you be sure he'll keep our secret about this?"

She gave Angelina a pointed look. "All I can say is he'd better. Your grandfather always liked him and helped him a time or two when he was in need. Including replacing the all the money he took from the church so they wouldn't press charges against him. I'm sure Bishop Worsley still feels quite indebted to your grandfather and will be only too glad to help his only granddaughter if possible."

Angelina relaxed against the black velvet cushion, feeling as if this wild idea she'd had a few days ago might actually work. "I'm glad you thought about him, Granna. I'm sure between the two of us we can talk him into helping."

A few minutes later Angelina and her grandmother were waiting in Bishop Worsley's sparsely decorated drawing room. The settee where they sat and two matching chairs were tasteful but worn. A large but simply framed mirror hung over the fireplace, and a large gold harp stood in one corner of the room. Somehow she thought it fitting that the bishop had a harp in his drawing room. There wasn't much else, other than the small fire in the fireplace to give the room warmth.

"Lady Railbridge, how lovely to see you again after all these years."

Angelina watched an impeccably dressed gentleman walk into the room with a beaming smile. He was average in height but carried himself with the confident stride of a much taller man. He had narrow dark-brown eyes and a full head of hair that was more gray than brown and tied in a queue, making him appear very distinguished. She believed him to be somewhere near the age of her grandmother. He took both her hands in his and kissed them. His smile was charming and his happiness at seeing her grandmother genuine, giving Angelina hope this would not turn out to be a bigger mistake than just staying the obedient daughter and marrying the earl of Thornwick.

"And this must be your granddaughter Miss Rule." He kissed her hand as well. "Sit down, sit down. I've asked that tea be prepared and brought in."

"Thank you for seeing us without previous notice," her grandmother said as they returned to the settee.

"Not at all, my lady. You are always welcome in my home." He looked at Angelina. "You too, Miss Rule."

"Thank you. I'll get right to the reason we are here and not take up more of your time than necessary," her grandmother said, suddenly looking uncomfortable. "Angelina is looking for someone–to help her—er, ah, with her paintings."

He chuckled. "I'm flattered you thought of me, Lady Railbridge, but I have no talent or skill with painting. I couldn't possibly help her perfect her talent."

"No, no." She shook her head. "Not that kind of help. You misunderstood or perhaps I didn't explain myself well. In any case, we need someone who will——be discreet and keep her name out of it at all costs."

His eyes narrowed and his gaze strayed to Angelina again. "What exactly do you want me to keep her name out of, Lady Railbridge?"

Angelina could see her grandmother was struggling with exactly what to say so she said, "Granna, do you mind if I take over and talk with Bishop Worsley about this?"

Granna gave her a grateful smile. "I would appreciate it, dear. I'm quite flabbergasted by the mere thought of explaining what it is we want to accomplish."

Angelina opened the satchel beside her and one by one laid out the paintings she'd brought with her on the small table between her and Bishop Worsley. "This is only a sample of what I have available. I'm hoping you can sell these for me."

He leaned over and inspected each piece. His troubled gaze darted from Angelina to her grandmother. He sighed before saying, "These are truly lovely pieces and quite well done, but I'm afraid I can't sell them to any of the shops here in London."

That dashed Angelina's hopes instantly. "Why not?" she asked.

"Let me be blunt. Whoever you took them from might walk into a shop and see them."

Angelina and her grandmother gasped at the same time.

"She didn't steal them," her grandmother answered indignantly.

"I painted them," Angelina whispered.

"My apologies," Bishop Worsley said quickly, his eyes looking Angelina over more carefully.

Her grandmother picked up one of the fans, opened it, and started fanning herself. "I'm appalled you thought she had stolen these. As if she would!"

Bishop Worsley's eyes widened and he sat back in his chair. "I mistook your meaning when you said——never mind, it's not important. I think I understand now what you are trying to do."

"Well, I should hope so." Her grandmother leaned forward. "We must keep this quiet so no one will ever know Angelina is selling her paintings. We'd never be able to show our faces in Society again if anyone found out she'd gone into trade."

"So you want me to do it for you?"

"Yes," Angelina said, taking over the conversation again. "The truth of it is that we are in need of money. As much as we can get. This idea came to me when the

Dowager Duchess of Drakestone was interested in my fans. She asked me to have the artist who had painted it send over some of *his* work. But of course I am the artist and didn't want to tell her. We need someone who can take the fans to the duchess for her consideration and then take"—she motioned to the bounty on the table before him—"what she doesn't want, along with the miniatures to a shop and sell them without anyone ever knowing I am the artist."

"It's most important that no one ever know these are from Angelina," her grandmother emphasized again.

He pursed his lips tightly for a moment and let his gaze stray over the paintings again. Seeming satisfied, he said, "I can do this for you and keep your name out of it. I think fifty percent of the price would be fair remuneration to me for taking care of this project for you."

"Fifty percent!" Angelina scoffed. "That is outrageous. You might as well be a highwayman robbing me."

"Angelina!"

"No, Granna," she said, firmly. "What good will it do me to risk my reputation to do this if we only get half of what we will earn? Ten percent for you would be fair, Bishop Worsley. All you are doing is selling them. I do all the work."

"Perhaps you don't know what this will entail, Miss Rule. I will have to ask around to find out who is buying. If things don't go well at first, it might even include taking the lot of them from shop to shop and possibly back again to find interest and then to negotiate the best price."

Angelina thought over what he'd said. She supposed some money was better than none. "All right, twenty percent."

"Forty and not a pence less," he said sternly.

Angelina rose. "Thirty percent is as high as I will go. You will either agree to that or I'm walking out that door and will take my chances on finding someone else who is willing to make a fair agreement with me."

Bishop Worsley rose, too. His eyes penetrated Angelina with admiration. "You drive a hard bargain, Miss Rule."

"I am desperate, Bishop Worsley, but I am not stupid."

"I never thought that for a moment. You are also very talented. These will sell. Thirty percent it is. I will see that you will be paid very well for your work, but I must be paid well for my services, too." ·

"Then we are in agreement. Thank you and thank you for the compliment," she said and took her seat by her grandmother, who was looking quite pale. "It would be a godsend if I were paid well. But there is another wrinkle we have to deal with. I'm afraid I am also limited in the amount of time I can wait. I need them sold as soon as possible."

"I'll see what I can do, but some things can't be hurried." Bishop Worsley settled back into his chair. "What do you need the money for, if you don't mind me asking?"

Angelina looked at her grandmother, who gave her a slight nod. "I suppose it will be all right to tell you since we are now partners. I am trying to keep my father out of debtors' prison. We may not be able to pay all his debts, but I hope to have enough so that they will see that if we are given more time, we can eventually fully repay everything."

"You're a good daughter, Miss Rule."

She wanted to be, though at times she had her doubts as to how good she was. And she was sure her father wouldn't think so if he knew she was going behind his back to make money.

"Now I know Lady Railbridge wants to keep you out of these transactions, but that will be impossible. I'm afraid that once I have identified a buyer you will need to go with me."

"Why?" Granna asked shaking her head. "I'm sure I can't allow that. It's too risky."

"No reputable shop owners or art dealers are going to be interested in these paintings unless they are certain they aren't stolen."

"I understand," Angelina said. "It's not a problem. We will go, won't we, Grandmother?"

She threw up her hands, sighed, and said, "Why stop now? Of course we will do whatever you think is necessary to make this a success. Just let us know when, where, and what we need to do. I fear we are already in too deep to turn back now."

"Can you leave these with me?" he asked Angelina.

"Of course. I have more. This is just a sample of my work. I can have the rest of them delivered to you tomorrow morning."

"Good. Then there is only one more thing I need and I can get started."

"What's that?"

"A name. It's a shame, but I agree with your grandmother. You can't be Angelina Rule, so who would you like to be?"

Chapter 11

What bloody man is that?
Macbeth *1.2.1*

Harrison kept watching the door.

Most unusual for him. He didn't like it but couldn't seem to keep his gaze from straying to the landing at the entrance to the ballroom. He wanted to see Angelina again.

He never should have kissed her. He knew better but his need to taste her lips wouldn't be tamped down no matter how hard he tried. Desire for her had settled in his loins and it wouldn't ease. She didn't believe him, but he was truthful when he said her eyes were asking him to do it. Everything about her called out to him. His body kept urging him to do much more, and thankfully he had restrained himself.

Harrison stood in the ballroom with two other gentlemen and feigned interest in their conversation. Every once in a while he'd add something to the subject they were covering but thankfully they were content to do most of the talking. That suited Harrison.

He'd kissed Angelina without much forethought. Surely if he had thought about it, and thought about it intelligently, he wouldn't have done it. Now he wanted to kiss her again. And next time he wanted to linger even longer over their kisses. He wanted to take his time tasting her sweetness, feeling her softness, and hearing her breathless sighs of pleasure. He wanted to hold her tightly to his chest, experience the warmth of her pliable body in his arms, and drink in her womanly scent once more.

It was remarkable that she hadn't been angry he'd kissed her, though she had been surprised. That was understandable. He had been surprised, too. He hadn't gone there with the idea that he would kiss her. He hadn't even gone there with the idea that he might see her alone. The best he'd hoped for was to get close enough to her to whisper that he would agree that her father could assume they would be married at the end of the Season.

But thanks to the housekeeper giving them the time alone, he had kissed her and now he was reconsidering his vow to never again pursue a lady who had her sights on another man. Harrison was pleased to hear her say there hadn't actually been a promise to marry made between them. There was the possibility that what she felt for the officer was a girlish infatuation and not the undying love poets were so fond of writing about.

The only thing that would answer that for sure was when the captain returned to London. Sometimes those blossoming feelings of young love and desire were the hardest to shake. He'd had two years of personal experience with that.

There had been a time he didn't think he'd ever stop wanting Maddie to be his and not his brother's. Now that both of them were gone, Harrison was glad he'd made his peace with his feelings for her after she had become his brother's wife. It didn't matter that it had taken the better part of a trip around the world to do it. Some things were worth the price you had to pay.

Concerning what he was feeling for Angelina, he didn't know if fate was blessing him or cursing him again. A curse, he decided. A curse that had obviously decided to haunt him. Was he destined to only truly desire a lady who had already given her heart to another?

Harrison's surveillance of the entrance finally paid off when he watched Lady Railbridge, Angelina, and her father walk into the ballroom. Angelina wore a flowing gown of a light coppery color that suited her pale alabaster-colored skin and golden-brown hair. He was about to excuse himself from the gentlemen he was standing with when he saw a young blade approach her. Harrison waited while they chatted, and then finally he watched the two of them walk off toward the dance floor.

Impatiently, he waited through two more gentlemen and long dances, but as soon as the third bachelor escorted her back to her grandmother, Harrison eased up beside Angelina and said, "Lady Railbridge, Miss Rule, Mr. Rule, good evening."

After pleasantries were exchanged among the four of them, Harrison said, "I've noticed that you've already had several dances with no time to catch your breath, Miss Rule. Would you like to walk with me and get a cup of punch, or perhaps a glass of champagne, if you prefer?"

"Must you hurry off at this moment, my lord?" her father asked. "I wanted to get your opinion of John Keats' *Endymion* that has just been published."

Harrison didn't know if he'd ever respect a man who gambled away his daughter's future, but he had promised Angelina that he would lead her father to believe a match between them would be inevitable so he couldn't avoid the man.

"I haven't read it," Harrison answered without bothering to mention he hadn't even heard of it. Whenever he wanted to read, poetry wasn't his first choice. "What do you think of it? Should I pick up a copy or pass on it?"

"It received a ferocious review from *Blackwood's Magazine*. But I rather like Keats' work. I mean, he's a young fellow and deserves to be given a second chance, doesn't he?"

Mr. Rule's blue gaze held steady on Harrison's face, showing no signs that the man was referring to Harrison, himself, or anyone other than Keats when he spoke of second chances. Still, it reminded Harrison that he'd had a chance to redeem himself and the rebuilding of Thornwick would do that for him.

"I don't think there is a man around who wouldn't want to be given one. If his poetry isn't well received, I doubt it will force him to give up writing. Poets love to put their musings down for others to talk about."

"Very true," Mr. Rule answered. "I've given poetry a try myself a time or two, but I'm no good at it. I've heard Keats is already working on his next poem."

"Do you know a lot about books, Mr. Rule?" Harrison asked.

"I daresay as much as most," he answered.

That was good to know. Harrison hadn't read many books since he'd left Oxford. Mr. Rule might be just the man to help him buy books for Thornwick once the library was rebuilt. He'd keep that in mind.

A few minutes later Harrison and Angelina left her father and headed toward the champagne table. As they made their way through the crowd, he leaned in close to her and said, "By the way, you look absolutely stunning tonight, Angelina."

"Thank you. I—did you call me Angelina?"

He smiled and nodded.

She looked aghast. "You can't call me by my name."

"Not in front of your father or when others are present. But when we are alone, I will."

"It's not proper," she argued.

"I do a lot of things that aren't proper, Angelina, including kissing you."

"I had a feeling you would get around to reminding me of that before the evening was over."

He chuckled softly. "I've given up drinking and gambling for days at a time, but there are a few vices I refuse to part with. I think of you as Angelina and that is what I want to call you when we are alone."

"You delight in troubling me, don't you, my lord?"

"No, but there have always been some rules I have trouble following."

"My thoughts would be that you break more than you follow."

"Unfortunately, that would be true."

"What if you should forget and say my name . . ." Her voice trailed off. Suddenly her steps faltered and she stopped. Her gaze was looking past him.

Harrison turned to see what had caught her attention. A gentleman dressed in a military officer's uniform stood near the entrance to the ballroom. His back was to them, but Harrison knew by the faraway look in her eyes that he was the gentleman she had been searching for since the Season began. Her entire countenance softened.

A knot tightened Harrison's stomach.

"Excuse me," she said without looking at him. "I see someone I must speak to."

She never looked back at him, but started toward the soldier, weaving between the people, knocking their arms, bumping their shoulders, ignoring their greetings. Harrison stayed right behind her. He wanted to see the man, too.

The captain was tall, with light-brown hair that fell to his collar. He was slim, almost too slim. His coat looked as if it had been made for a larger person. As they neared the soldier, a tingle of awareness prickled Harrison's skin. Something wasn't quite right.

Harrison gave him another once-over and saw what had bothered him. There was a narrow black string tied around the back of his head. A thread of recognition wove through Harrison and with it a twitch of dread for Angelina. He knew what the narrow band meant.

Angelina stopped and said, "Captain Maxwell."

The gentleman turned.

She expelled a loud breath of shock and then quickly sucked in a deep gasp.

"Damnation," Harrison whispered to himself as he came up to stand beside her.

Harrison was right.

The man wore a patch over one eye. Beneath the small swatch of black fabric the reddened and discolored skin puckered with welts and indentions of scarring that looked very much like the healing from a wound that had destroyed the muscle and bone beneath the skin. The battle at Waterloo was over two years ago. This injury was new and still healing, so it had to have happened recently.

The shock on Angelina's face dimmed the light of gladness in the captain's eye at seeing her. And it was slight, but Harrison saw him stiffen.

"Miss Rule," he said, and then almost immediately

glanced past her to Harrison. He nodded to Harrison and said, "Sir."

Harrison had to give the man credit. He hadn't missed the fact that Harrison was shadowing Miss Rule. A good soldier was always aware of his surroundings, and he could quickly size up who was friend and who was foe. And it didn't take Harrison more than an instant to size up the captain, either. The man was smitten with Miss Rule.

An unnatural hush settled over the three of them before Angelina spoke up and said, "Forgive my manners. Lord Thornwick, please allow me to present Captain Nicolas Maxwell."

The man was older than Harrison had thought he would be. He'd assumed the captain was close to his age of thirty, not nearing forty. The graying hair at his temples and lines around his eye were a telling sign. And perhaps being laid up from the injury was the reason he didn't fill out his coat. The man had probably spent months recovering from his wounds.

"My apologies, Lord Thornwick," the army captain said with a bow.

"Captain," Harrison greeted.

"Welcome home," Angelina said with a little smile.

"Thank you," he said, keeping his expression cautious. "It was a long journey."

"I'm sure. You were injured while away."

"It was several months ago."

Her eyes took note of the scarring. "It looks well healed," she said, and by the expression on her face, Harrison knew she believed that.

Angelina's tone was soft, her words slow and guarded. She never took her eyes off the captain's face. She was behaving the way any man in similar circumstances would want her to—concerned and accepting, not aghast or glib.

Harrison wondered how many people tonight had thought to say the simple words *welcome home*. He'd known the afternoon he'd talked to Angelina about rescuing strays that she had a deep capacity to care. She could also offer comfort and kindness in a way that wasn't distasteful to the recipient.

There was no doubt she'd been shocked to her core when she first saw him, but she had recovered quickly and immediately started soothing the captain. Harrison had a feeling that because of the dogs she rescued and fed, Angelina was at her best when she was tending to and reassuring the wounded.

"Does it hurt?" she asked.

Captain Maxwell gave her a cautious smile before glancing at Harrison again. "Not anymore."

"How long have you been home?"

Maxwell continued to regard her with uncertainty in his expression. "A couple of weeks."

"My grandmother wrote a note to your aunt about your return but didn't receive an answer."

"I asked her not to."

"Oh, I see."

"I wasn't sure I wanted to attend any of the parties this Season. I had to give it a lot of thought. I didn't want my appearance to offend anyone."

Harrison thought he caught an edge of bitterness in Maxwell's voice as his gaze cut around to Harrison's once again. He couldn't blame the man if acrimony had seeped into his soul.

"Nonsense, Captain, you could never offend anyone," she said earnestly. "I'm glad you decided to attend."

"That's kind of you to say, but I will not deny the

obvious. My face does require some getting used to, Miss Rule. Even I wasn't sure I wanted to look at me again after the first time."

She stepped closer to the captain. "You have no cause to be so unkind to yourself. Everyone will feel as I do."

His gaze turned intense. "And how is that, Miss Rule?"

"Grateful that you lost only an eye and not your life."

"Are you truly?"

Harrison remained quiet and listened to their exchange. He watched her gentle, caring gaze skim up and down Maxwell's face until it settled on his cheek that was tattered with scarring. She was pouring her sympathy out to him for the hurt and pain he had been through. It was natural and unhurried. Harrison could tell she wanted to soothe the wounded soldier much in the way he imagined that she soothed her father after his wife's death, and all the wounded strays who passed by her house. She wanted to help shoulder his hurt and his sorrow and if possible make it easier for him to bear.

"Of course," she continued. "I don't know what brave act caused your injury, but I'm thankful it wasn't worse."

Maxwell glanced at Harrison for the third time. He got the feeling the captain was wondering what Harrison's relationship was to Angelina: a friend, an acquaintance, or a beau? The man had been gone over a year. And now he was wounded and scarred. He had to have a mountain of fears and doubts about Angelina swirling and racing through his mind.

Especially since there had been no formal promise between them before he left.

Harrison couldn't help but think of all the foolish things he'd done in his life and had never gotten seriously injured. There were so many times he could have lost a tooth, an eye, or a limb. Hell, he could have lost his life when he, Adam, and Bray had shot buckets and bottles off one another's heads, raced their curricles over rocky terrain, and jumped from high peaks into rocky waters. They'd only wanted the thrill; most of the time they were too drunk to give a damn about the danger.

"The loss of my eye doesn't keep me from dancing, Miss Rule, and I believe I asked you to save a dance for me when I returned. Perhaps later this evening, if you're available."

"Yes, yes, of course I remember. I've been waiting for you to return and claim that dance. Yes, thank you, Captain, I would very much like that."

She was overdoing it with her acceptance. Harrison knew it. The captain knew it, and Angelina knew it. They all understood why.

"Good. I'll see you later in the evening." He glanced at Harrison, nodded, and walked away.

Harrison could venture a good guess about all the thoughts jumbling together in Angelina's mind. He heard the last call for a quadrille, and without thinking said, "The music is just starting, Angelina. Let's dance."

"No." She shook her head.

"It will do you good to have something to do right now."

"But I—"

"No buts. Let's dance."

Catching hold of her wrist, he led her onto the dance floor where they joined the others who were already twirling, hopping, and clapping to the music. It was Harrison's least favorite of all the dances, but he was certain it was just what Angelina needed. It was fast, easy, and noisy. It wouldn't give her time to think. She didn't need to right now. Later when she was in the quiet of her home, she could think about the captain and his injuries.

The dance ended after they sashayed under the umbrella of arms and he led Angelina off the dance floor.

"Why don't I get you a glass of champagne before I take you back to your father?"

She stopped and looked up at him. "I really don't want a glass. I didn't want to dance."

"What do you want to do?"

She shook her head. "I don't know. I—I'm so ashamed of myself for gasping and recoiling when I first saw him," she whispered earnestly and lowered her lashes over her eyes.

Harrison ushered her away from the middle of the room to the wall. He wished he could take her in his arms and hold her. He didn't know much about consoling anyone but she needed comfort. She needed to be told that everything was going to be all right even if it wasn't.

"He expected you to. He knew you would be shocked."

"No," she whispered and shook her head again. "He didn't deserve that. I was mortified I behaved so badly."

Harrison had no doubt of that.

"You didn't behave badly, Angelina. You were human. That's all. And it's easy to forgive people for having human emotions and reactions. You more than made it up to him by saying all the right things afterward."

She looked up at him with a distressed expression, her blue eyes watering, and said, "He lost an eye."

Her heart was breaking for what the captain had been through, for what he'd lost. Harrison could understand that and he hoped to hell the Army officer could too. She was looking for solace and Harrison wanted to give it. He wanted to pull her into the circle of his arms. He wanted to stroke her back, kiss the top of her head, and whisper her name softly. Those pesky rules of Society prevented that.

"Don't think about what he's lost or what happened to him, Angelina. Look how he's handling his life now. Only a brave man could have walked into the ballroom tonight in his situation."

Her gaze swept up and down his face. "Do you really believe that?"

"That he's a brave man? Yes. Everyone in this room does."

She breathed in deeply and on exhale said, "I just feel so sorry for him. He must have felt so alone, so far from home. I wish I could have been there and done something for him when it happened. I wish I could have helped him in some way."

"He wouldn't have wanted you there."

"What?" She gave him a curious look. "Of course he would have. I should have been there. From the scars, I can tell that he must have been in excruciating pain."

"Which is exactly why he was glad you weren't there to witness it."

Why the devil was he trying to help Angelina deal with the captain's scars? Why was he defending the man?

"But he needed comfort. He deserved it."

Harrison had little doubt about that. "Don't dwell on any of that. I'm sure it was traumatic for him, but it's over now. As you've already pointed out, he didn't lose his life."

"You aren't sounding very sympathetic."

Harrison remembered how Captain Maxwell had looked at him. The captain was thinking that Harrison was a rival for Angelina's attention whether or not she was aware of it. And Harrison had a hunch the man was feeling quite inadequate at the moment. But Harrison had no doubts Maxwell would get over that feeling in time, rediscover his courage, and pursue Angelina with all haste. He was a soldier and used to fighting. He would fight for Angelina with the same dedication he fought for his country.

"But I do feel compassion. He deserves it. No one wants to be disfigured like that. And take my word for it, I am the last man he wants sympathy from, and he doesn't want yours, either, Angelina."

"Rubbish. Of course he does."

"No, he doesn't. No man wants anyone feeling sorry for him. He doesn't want your pity. That is the last thing he would want from you."

"How dare you think that I pity him?" she said indignantly. "I don't."

"Yes, you do. I do. There isn't a person in this room right now who doesn't. It's human nature."

"No." She shook her head, as if that would give strength to her denial.

"Disavow it to yourself and to him all you want, but don't try to deny it to me. I know better. And quite frankly, Angelina, Captain Maxwell knows better, too."

Her angry glare softened. "You're wrong. I will not let myself pity him."

"Good, if you can accomplish that," Harrison said quietly and ran his hand through his hair, feeling a stab of impatience. Why was he trying to help the captain? *Because I do have compassion for the injury he suffered and how it left him.* "He obviously isn't letting his misfortune affect him. He came to the ball holding his head high and asked the most beautiful lady at the ball for a dance."

"As he should have."

At that moment, Harrison knew he would never let Angelina go into the captain's arms without a fight. Competing for her was the last thing he wanted. If it wasn't so outrageous, it would be laughable. He'd vowed to never be vulnerable to love again, never fight for a lady's love again, and here he was admitting what he thought the moment he saw her standing at the entrance to the ballroom, what he knew after he'd kissed her. He wanted her to be his. She might claim to love the captain, but they weren't married yet. Not even betrothed. Harrison had time to win her heart.

But for tonight, it was time for him to go. Angelina had a heart as big as England for the wounded in body as well as spirit. That was one of the things that drew him to her. And why it was now time for him to take his leave. He'd heard all he wanted to about the courageous Captain Maxwell.

"I see your grandmother walking this way. If she hasn't already seen the captain I know you'll want to tell her. I'll leave the two of you to talk and say good night, Angelina."

Harrison walked away, wondering how in sweet heaven he was going to fight Captain Maxwell for Angelina's love.

A wounded soldier!

With probably close to twenty years of military service behind him. Those were damned hard standards to measure up to and they put Harrison in an almost impossible position. Especially considering he'd never done a bloody worthwhile thing in his life. He'd never had to. No one had ever expected him to.

Being the youngest son of an elderly earl, Harrison never had to mind anyone until he arrived at Eton, where he quickly teamed up with Bray Drakestone and Adam

Greyhawke. As they grew up they became a formidable trio who didn't follow anyone's rules but their own.

While Captain Maxwell had served his country, Harrison had served himself—to anything and everything
he wanted. The captain had fought for his country and
left a part of himself on some foreign battlefield. Harrison had fought more fights than he could remember.
He'd had fistfights, sword fights, and duels, but he'd
never faced a barrage of bullets or cannon fire as he was
sure Maxwell had when he fought at Waterloo and whatever battle took his eye.

Harrison hadn't lost an eye, but he'd lost his brother,
Maddie, and their children. Though his wounds weren't
visible, he had them. They were as raw as a blade's
cut. His brother had asked him to come for a visit, but he
hadn't taken the time. Perhaps self-inflicted wounds were
the worst kind. Those days were behind him now. Harrison didn't plan on losing Angelina—not even to a man
who deserved her much more than he did.

Captain Maxwell was no stranger to battles but neither was Harrison. Fighting for Angelina would be just
one more for both of them. And the captain should plan
to use every weapon available to him, because Harrison would.

Backing away wasn't in Harrison's nature, but his
sense of brotherly love had led him not to pursue Maddie. He owed no loyalty to the Army officer and would
show him none. Besides, Maxwell was well equipped.
He had a weapon Harrison didn't have and he expected
the man to use it to his advantage. Angelina already
fancied herself in love with the soldier. It would be one
hard battle to prove to her she wasn't, but Harrison could
do it.

He had learned early to do whatever pleased him, to
do only what he wanted, and to shake off any who tried

to restrain or coax him to do otherwise. Maybe Angelina was fate's way of paying him back.

Harrison turned to look back at the ballroom before he left. He caught sight of Captain Maxwell watching Angelina. Harrison had faith he could woo her and win her.

He would give the soldier only one concession. Harrison would do his best to fight fairly.

Chapter 12

I saw his heart in's face.
Winter's Tale *1.2.446–47*

Her heart was still in her throat. The shock of Captain Maxwell's injuries was so acute, it hurt to breathe.

Angelina turned away from Lord Thornwick, not wanting to watch him walk away. What was wrong with her? She just kept wishing he would take her in his arms and hold her, comfort her. For reasons she didn't understand, she desperately wanted to feel his strength. She needed reassurance from him, from someone, that all she'd believed for the past three years concerning Captain Maxwell was still possible. But why would she want solace in the earl's embrace? It didn't make sense to her.

She needed some time to think, but that wasn't going to happen right now. The earl was right. Her short, dainty grandmother was plowing her way through the throng of people with the ease of a much larger person determined to get where she was going. Angelina thought about pretending she hadn't seen her and quickly hightailing it to the retiring room, but she knew Granna would follow her there.

Lord Thornwick was wrong about one thing. Somehow she would prove to him that it was loving concern she felt for Captain Maxwell and not pity. He was still a handsome man, even with the patch and the scarring beneath it.

Her hands made fists. She closed her eyes and grimaced as she remembered her reaction to him. She could only hope that he hadn't taken her shock and concern when she first saw him for anything other than what it was. *Shock and concern.* But if he had, surely he could forgive her for being human and reacting with a gasp when she first saw him.

After she'd had time to adjust to his appearance, his face hadn't seemed as bad as she'd first thought. And now she was even thinking maybe the black patch made him look a bit like the dashing pirates she'd seen in drawings and paintings.

"There you are, Angelina," her grandmother said, sporting an expression filled with worry. "I've been looking for you."

Angelina could tell by the crease in her grandmother's brow that she already knew about Captain Maxwell's appearance. In fact, it was clear almost everyone in the room had heard by now. The music was playing softer, fewer people were dancing, and more ladies were huddled together in little groups, talking in hushed tones, and whispering behind their hands and fans. Angelina's heart felt full. Her admiration grew for Captain Maxwell for being brave enough to face such a daunting crowd. He must have known everyone would be talking about him.

"I've seen him, Granna," Angelina said to spare her grandmother having to say more.

She flattened her hand on her chest and slowly shook her head. "Oh, dear, is it as horrifying as I've heard? Never mind, you don't have to talk about it."

"Yes, his scars are still new and need more time to heal and fade, but no, I'm not horrified by them and no one else should be, either."

"You are very brave, my dear. I know it's devastating. I'm so sorry for you."

"Me, brave?" It took several seconds for her grandmother's meaning to be clear. "Don't feel sorry for me, Granna. I have lost nothing. I haven't been hurt."

Her grandmother looked at her curiously. "But of course you have, Angelina. You've lost a dream. The dream of the handsome soldier coming home to sweep you off your feet and take you away to wedded bliss. That dream is gone."

Her grandmother's answer caught Angelina off guard. Was that true? No. No, she couldn't let her dream die just because of his injury. What kind of person would she be if she did that?

"I'm not giving up on that dream," Angelina defiantly assured her grandmother. "It can still happen. It will happen. We have Bishop Worsley working for us so that we can help Papa replace the money he borrowed, and that in turn will free me to marry the man of my choice. And it just so happens, I'm waiting now for Captain Maxwell to come claim his dance with me."

"That's quite noble of you, dear."

"It's nothing of the kind," she said, feeling strength in her courage. "I'm convinced Captain Maxwell is the same gentleman he's always been. He just looks a little different, but I will not treat him any differently and neither should you, nor anyone else."

"A little different, Angelina?" her grandmother questioned, and then gave her an easy smile. "Well, I suppose that's why they say love is blind. I should have known this would not daunt your spirit. More and more you remind me of your mother, but quiet, dear, quiet. I see Captain Maxwell coming this way, and we don't want him to hear us talking about him. And Lady Harcourt has on the most glorious gown I've seen all Season. I can't believe our modiste didn't show us that fabric first. I will definitely speak to her about that the next time we are in her shop."

Captain Maxwell smiled at Angelina as he stopped beside her grandmother and said, "Good evening, Lady Railbridge."

Her grandmother smiled beautifully, turned, and extended her hand to him. To her credit, she never blinked or showed any signs that she noticed a change in his appearance. Her earlier fretfulness about him was completely gone.

"Captain Maxwell, it's so good to see you again."

He kissed her hand and then said, "It was a long journey, my lady. I'm happy to be home."

"I would think so. I don't believe I'd have the stamina to travel that far. Tell me, did you enjoy India?" Her eyes widened in panic as soon as the words were out. "Oh, good heavens! Of course you didn't."

"I did enjoy most of my time in India," Captain Maxwell said, ignoring her blunder but giving her a humorless grin just the same. "My time there wasn't all bad." He then looked at Angelina and said, "I was hoping this would be a good time for our dance."

"Yes, it is. Would you excuse us, Granna?"

"Of course. Enjoy the dance."

Angelina had always thought of Captain Maxwell as a very tall and broad-shouldered man, but as they made their way to the dance floor, she realized he was shorter and thinner than Lord Thornwick. That surprised her.

In her dreams of him, she always imagined him to be more the height and width of the earl.

She looked at no one in particular as they walked, but knew small clusters of people were watching them. *Good*, she thought. Let them stare and gossip to their hearts' content. Soon enough they would get used to seeing them together and move on to someone else to gossip about.

Angelina didn't know the dance was a waltz until they stepped onto the dance floor and took the position. Captain Maxwell's hand clasped hers. It was warm, but his grip wasn't firm. She hardly felt his hand, which rested on her back to guide her through the difficult steps. It was almost as if he was afraid to touch her. But most of all, she realized there were none of the tingles, sizzles, and shivers that she expected racing through her body at his nearness.

They were quiet for the first few seconds while they waited for the music to begin. The silence became awkward so Angelina looked up at him and said, "Did you attend many dances in India before you were wounded?"

He glanced down into her eyes for only a second before lifting his head. His expression remained emotionless. "A few," he answered and then asked, "Have you been enjoying the Season?"

"Mostly. It's been very hectic," she answered, sensing that looking at him was making him uncomfortable. It had been so long since she'd seen him, she wanted to look at him. He seemed older now. She didn't remember the gray in his hair or the pronounced lines around his eyes. In truth, this was the closest she'd ever been to him.

"It always is."

"I knew what to expect but I've been to at least three parties every evening for almost a week. I've declined all the tea and card parties that are held in the afternoons."

"I hope you have a good reason for denying yourself such pleasure."

Yes, I must paint during the day.

"I find it difficult to dance most nights and then continue to attend parties during the day," she said, knowing it was only partly a fib.

The music started and so did the dance. Captain Maxwell knew the steps well and was light on his feet, but she kept thinking there was no strength in his arms. She wanted him to hold her closer and tighter. She wanted him to take command of her. She wanted to experience the unleashed power she had felt when she was in Lord Thornwick's arms, when they had danced, when they had kissed.

The waltz was long and she could tell the captain was winded before it was over. Her heart went out to him. How selfish of her to want him to hold her as the earl had. His injury had probably taken most of his strength for weeks, and yet he had wanted to dance with her. She shouldn't have expected he'd have the strength of Lord Thornwick.

"You dance very well," she said as the dance ended and they stopped to clap for the musicians before leaving the floor.

"Thank you for telling me," he said. "Quite frankly, I wasn't sure I could still do it. I've, well——"

She smiled at him. "You never faltered and you never stepped on my toes. There are other gentlemen I've danced with who have done both, so pat yourself on the back."

He looked into her eyes and said, "Perhaps you'll let me call on you, Miss Rule."

She thought she heard a quaver in his voice. She

couldn't fault him for being unsure of himself under the circumstances but she didn't want him to be. She wanted him to believe in her and her love for him. This was the man whose return she'd been waiting for. He should have no doubts about her feelings for him.

"Yes," she said, meeting his gaze confidently.

"Tomorrow afternoon?" he asked hopefully.

Angelina hesitated. She wanted to, but she had three fans started that she needed to finish so Bishop Worsley could take them to the duchess. If she didn't sell her paintings, none of her plans for the future would be possible.

"I'm afraid tomorrow afternoon isn't good for me, but perhaps another day."

He stiffened and stepped away from her. "Of course. I understand."

No, he didn't. The coldness of his words surprised her, even though she knew he thought she was rebuffing him. She quickly added, "I'm available on Sunday. Are you?"

At first he looked as if he didn't know whether he could trust her, but then the lines around his mouth relaxed and he said, "I am. Would you enjoy a ride in Hyde Park if it's not raining?"

"That would be lovely."

Angelina wanted to say more but was at a loss for words. Did the captain want to hear that she had a deep ache in her soul for what he had lost and the pain he'd been through? Or was Lord Thornwick right that he wouldn't want to hear how sorry she was for what had happened to him? Should she tell him she was happy to see him? What did he want to hear from her? She didn't know what to say so she remained quiet and so did the captain.

"I see Granna waiting for me. Thank you for the dance, Captain."

He smiled and for a fleeting instant she saw traces of the gentleman she'd first seen from the stairway. Her stomach tumbled, and her heart fluttered.

"Perhaps we can have another tomorrow night?"

"Yes." She smiled, suddenly hopeful that if she could free her father of his debts there might be a future for her and Captain Maxwell. "I'd like that."

"Until then."

She nodded and walked away feeling lighter of foot. She was eager to spend time with Captain Maxwell and get to know him. She wanted to renew those tender, wonderful feelings she had for him when she was sitting on the stairs in her home and he had looked up at her and smiled. She wanted to experience with him the exciting, breathless sensations that she'd felt when she was with Lord Thornwick.

They would come for her and the captain. She had to be patient. Tonight, seeing him for the first time had been awkward and unsettling for both of them. Too, there were so many people around. Including the earl with all his comments about the officer and how she should feel. Everything would be better once she and the captain were alone and not on display as they were tonight.

Yes, she would prove to Lord Thornwick that she didn't pity Captain Maxwell. What she felt for him was love.

"Angelina."

She stopped and turned at the sound of her father's voice. "Yes, Papa."

"I saw you dancing with Captain Maxwell just now."

"Yes," she said cautiously. "And did you also see me dancing with Lord Thornwick a few minutes earlier?"

"I did and I must say I was quite pleased."

"Good." Angelina started walking toward her grandmother again and her father fell in step beside her. "Have you had the opportunity to welcome Captain Maxwell home?"

"No, though I've heard what happened to him. It's a shame. He was always on the handsome side."

"He still is, Papa."

He gave her a look of doubt, but said, "Well, it's good to know his scarring isn't as bad as I've been told."

It wasn't surprising that the captain had been at the ball hardly an hour before the ton was gossiping about his looks, but she didn't have to like it. "I don't know what you've heard but he's coping well with the effects of his injury."

"I'd say very well. I don't know that I would have had the courage to be seen at public events so soon after such a devastating injury."

Angelina stopped quickly and a lady who was following close behind bumped into her. After apologies were said, she turned back to her father and said, "Coming tonight was the best thing he could have done for himself. You know what they say about falling off a horse. You immediately get back on. He must get back in Society and the sooner the better. He lost an eye, not his brain nor his chivalry. He was a perfect gentleman tonight."

Unlike Lord Thornwick who made up his own rules when he felt like it and chose to ignore any rule in Society he disagreed with. He had nerve kissing her so soon after their acquaintance and calling her Angelina.

"I hope you did nothing to encourage the captain, Angelina."

Not exactly.

"I saw nothing wrong with agreeing he could call on me for a ride in the park."

"Angelina."

She met her father's stern look of disapproval. "Because, Papa, I agreed that Lord Thornwick could call on me as well."

"You always have to do things your way, don't you?"

"Not always," she answered, feeling a little contrite.

Her father's light-blue eyes pierced hers. "Do I need to remind you what will happen if you don't marry Lord Thornwick at the end of the Season?"

"No, Papa," she conceded. "I know what I must do. But what is the harm in enjoying the Season and the attention of all the gentlemen who want to dance with me and call on me before I marry?"

"I suppose none, my dear, none," he said and hooked his hand around her elbow. "Dance with all the gentlemen, smile at everyone, and drink all the champagne you want. Enjoy yourself fully. As long as you remember your duty."

Angelina wasn't likely to forget as long as she was spending her days painting.

Chapter 13

How bitter a thing it is to look into happiness through another man's eyes!
As You Like It, *Act V, sc. 2*

Harrison left the ball. It didn't bother him that Angelina was defending Captain Maxwell. He assumed she would, but he hadn't expected he would do it, too. He couldn't stay and watch her dance with the man, however. He had no desire to watch her looking at him with adoring, sympathetic blue eyes.

Harrison leaned against a back wall in the dimly lit game room at White's waiting for a place to open up at one of the card tables. Heavy smells of liquor and burnt wood hung in the air. He heard the clamor of voices and raucous laughter from the taproom and billiard balls smacking together farther down the corridor. The aged brandy was taking the edge off his whirring thoughts, and he was getting ready for a serious game of cards—or for that matter anything that would help him forget about Angelina and the disfigured Captain Maxwell.

He supposed some would think he should be a gen-

tleman and just back away and let the wounded soldier have Angelina. And a few days ago, maybe he
would have done just that, but not now. Not since he
had held her in his arms and kissed her. He didn't
need Hopscotch or the Prince telling him to pursue
Angelina and make her his. He was telling himself that.

Harrison knew the moment he saw her that she was
the lady for him, but he'd denied those feelings when
she'd told him her heart belonged to another. At the time,
what else could he have done? He'd thought he could
walk away from her that night and never give her a
thought again, but that hadn't lasted twenty-four hours.
He had to see her. And what had he done when he'd seen
her? He had tasted Angelina's sweet mouth, smelled her
warm skin, and felt her soft body melt against his. And
now he was aching to hold her and kiss her again.

He'd walked away from love once before and no
matter how many times over the years he'd told himself
it would be easier the second time, it wasn't true. He
didn't want anyone else touching Angelina intimately or
kissing her. And he damned sure wouldn't listen if anyone had the nerve to ask him to back off and let the captain have her. No, Angelina was his to win, and win her
he would. He just wasn't sure how he would do that. Yet.

"I thought I'd find you here."

Harrison turned and saw Bray leaning against the
wall beside him. Damn, he must have been deep in
thought not to have noticed him walk up.

Harrison sipped his drink and eyed his friend over
his glass. "How long have you been here?"

"Long enough" came the answer. "I thought it might
be a good idea to come find you."

Harrison looked at him curiously. "You were looking
for me?"

Bray nodded once.

"Want to tell me why?"

"I thought you might want some company."

Harrison grunted. "And you thought I couldn't find any at White's."

Bray smiled.

Harrison chuckled. "I have to admit you are the last person I'd expect to be looking for me at this time of night. I thought you'd still be dancing with your lovely wife."

"I did, and afterward I scoured the ballroom for you."

"I left early," Harrison said and turned his attention back to the card games in progress.

"I'm not surprised. We heard the news about the wounded soldier that had come home as soon as we arrived. Is he the man?"

Harrison sipped his drink. "You wouldn't be here if you didn't already know the answer to that, my friend."

"I suspected. I had three people tell me about him before I could get Louisa's wrap off her shoulders. It didn't take me long to figure out that Captain Maxwell was the gentleman we were talking about at the Heirs' Club the other day when I saw Miss Rule dancing with him."

"It didn't take me long to figure that out, either," Harrison said and took another drink. "Did you see him?"

"Only from a distance," Bray answered. "The scuttlebutt is that the scarring is quite difficult to look at but will probably get better with time."

"Those were my thoughts, too."

"From where I stood the black patch would have made him look quite the dashing pirate if he hadn't been in a military uniform. He must have stunned everyone and Miss Rule more than most when he entered the ballroom."

Harrison looked down into his brandy and swirled it in his glass. "You could say that."

"So you talked with her after she saw him?"

"I was with her when she saw him."

"Whew." Bray blew out a short breath. "That must have caused a few awkward glances among the three of you."

"And more than a few heated words between me and Angelina later, too."

"I don't see that as a good thing."

Harrison's jaw hardened. "It wasn't."

"Did you hear what happened to him to cause the injury?" Bray asked calmly.

Harrison took his gaze off the crowded card room and looked at Bray again. "No, did you?"

Bray shook his head. "I was curious so I asked. No one seemed to know. I assume the scuttlebutt will get around soon enough."

"Was she still there when you left?" Harrison questioned.

"Both of them."

Harrison's stomach clenched but he said nothing.

"Do you want to tell me about what was said between you and Miss Rule?"

Hell no.

Harrison didn't want to go through all the emotions that conversation evoked again. He grinned and answered, "I want to know what the hell you are doing here. It's not like you to leave your beautiful Louisa at the mercy of all the stuffy old gentlemen who will be asking her to dance in your absence. That's cruel, Bray."

"I'm glad you still have your good humor about you."
It's hard.

"Besides," Bray continued, "I'm not foolish enough to do that to her. Nor would she let me. I took her home before coming here. She understood why I wanted to find you. We'd already made appearances at two other parties. Believe me, she was quite happy to get home early for a change and check on her younger sisters."

"And you should do the same. Though I appreciate the offer, I am not in need of a nursemaid tonight, Bray."

"So you just enjoy standing here holding up this wall because you've nothing better to do for the rest of the evening."

Harrison blew out a laugh. "You blackguard. I'm waiting for an opening to come up at one of the tables so I can join a game, and you damned well know it."

"And while we wait, tell me: What are you going to do?"

"While we wait?" Harrison asked and then shook his head. "No, my friend, there is no 'we' tonight. I told you, I do not need you here with me. You might have saved my life when I first returned to London and was accosted by the footpads, but right now I am in no need of assistance."

"I did save you from those ruffians, didn't I?"

"Don't go patting yourself on the back. You didn't arrive until after they'd cracked several ribs and cut the buttons off my coat."

Bray chuckled again. "There is that old adage—something about 'better late than never.'"

"And there is something about keeping the home fires burning as well, so go home. It feels like it's going to be a cold night. Your lovely bride is waiting. I intend to enjoy my drink and a few games of cards before I have my driver take me home."

"I have Louisa's blessing to enjoy a night of cards and drinks, and you are not going to keep me from it."

Harrison deliberately grinned and said, "So you have to get Louisa's permission to play a game of cards now?"

"I said blessing and you damned well know it. Just accept that I'm here and leave it at that, my friend."

Harrison clapped him on the back good-naturedly. "Why didn't you say so when you first came in? In that case, welcome. We don't have to wait for a table to come open. We'll find our own."

"Not so fast," Bray said. "First, tell me if you intend to back away and let the captain have Miss Rule without a fight."

Harrison's eyes narrowed. "What do you think?"

"I'd guess no but you've fooled me once or twice before."

Harrison drained his glass. "I'm going to make her forget there ever was a Captain Maxwell in her dreams."

Chapter 14

If music be the food of love, play on.
Twelfth Night, *Act I, sc. 1*

Ignoring the umbrella at his feet, Harrison left the comfort of his dry, warm landau and stepped down into a foggy mist. After several uninterrupted days of fairly nice weather, the usual spring gloom had moved in off the Thames to settle over London. He placed his hat on his head and then lifted the collar of his cloak against the chill of the midafternoon dampness and looked at the front of Angelina's house.

He'd managed to stay away from Angelina for several days. He needed to give Angelina some time before he started his pursuit of her. For most of his life he'd lived with no borders and without rules, pleasing only himself. But now he wanted something more than just pleasing himself. He wanted Angelina. And he wanted to please her, which meant he had to adhere to some of the rules of Society.

Maybe he should have stayed away a little longer,

given her more time, but he just couldn't make himself do it. He had to make sure she was all right and still handling Captain Maxwell's return with the same courage she'd showed the night he returned.

Harrison reached back into the carriage and grabbed the small pot of violets he'd bought for Angelina. He'd gone to the flower vendor to pick out a beautiful bouquet of spring's first flowers for her but then his eye had caught the discarded pot of neglected violets sitting near the man's trash heap. The shopkeeper said he was throwing it away because the flowers were too dead to sell to anyone.

That's what the owner thought, but not Harrison. There were only two or three of the short stems blooming, and those were wilted. What few leaves there were had turned either yellow or brown. The plant was definitely dying but it could be saved if someone knew how. So Harrison made the owner happy by buying it from him.

It would be the perfect gift for Angelina. She liked to take care of things. Taking in strays had proved that. She would enjoy finding the right place in her house to put the plant. He could see her adding a rich soil to it, watering it, talking to it, whatever the hell it was people did to bring plants back to life and make them flourish and bloom. What would she do with fresh flowers that needed no attention from her loving hands?

When he stopped under the overhang of the stoop, he reached for the door knocker but paused when he heard music. Someone was playing a fast melody on the pianoforte. He listened for a minute—and suddenly there came the most unbearable, high-pitched howling he'd ever heard. He squeezed his eyes shut and shuddered at the awful sound. Thank God it only lasted a few seconds. Then there was the beautiful peaceful music once more. He reached for the knocker again but jerked his hand down when the ear-piercing howling started anew.

"Damnation, what is that?" he whispered aloud to himself. Seconds later the yowling dog stopped and the melody continued.

Harrison looked from one side of the house to the other. Through the misting rain, a lone light shone from the front window on the left. If he was remembering correctly from his visit to the house last week, the music room was on the left. He glanced back at the street. His carriage was the only one he saw. His driver would never question him.

Throwing caution, reputation, and good sense to the wind, he stepped down off the stoop and walked over to the window. Harrison knew that spying on anyone, especially through a window, was against common decency's rules, but of course he wasn't known for following rules. Besides, curiosity was killing him.

He was tall enough to peek inside the room. The pane was foggy with condensation, but he saw Angelina sitting at the pianoforte, her back to him, with a small, white fluffy dog sitting beside her. That had to be Molly.

Harrison's breathing kicked up a notch and his loins thickened instantly at the sight of her. A lamp placed on the edge of the pianoforte bathed her in a shimmery golden light. She was on a red-velvet-cushioned bench, her rounded bottom clearly outlined by the way she sat on the skirt of her dress. Her spine was straight. There was a gentle slope to her feminine shoulders. Her golden-brown hair had been swept up into a chignon, showing her nape and slender neck. The lamplight made her tresses sparkle.

It stimulated him to watch the way her nimble fingers danced across the ivories while her hands and arms moved gracefully from side to side. Her shapely bottom moved and swayed with each note she played. He could tell she took great pleasure from the music. His desire for her grew fast and hot.

Everything about her was inviting.

The room she and the dog were in held only the pianoforte and two wingback chairs upholstered in a dark-green, wide-striped fabric with matching pillows. A small table stood between them. As best he could see, there was no one with Angelina but the dog, who watched her with rapt attention.

Ear-piercing howling rent the air again and Harrison shivered. There was a reason dogs were supposed to stay outside. Angelina looked down at the Maltese. The dog was doing its best to impress her. Angelina smiled and nodded her agreement, never hitting a wrong note in the melody.

Harrison smiled, too, and then he laughed when he saw her bend her head and touch her nose to the dog's nose; then she licked her chin. She laughed and patted her on the top of her head.

Now he knew what was going on. The dog would start howling at a certain place in the music. Angelina gave the Maltese her cue to chime in by nodding her head toward her. Watching Angelina play, he was beginning to wonder why he'd never liked music. As long as she was at the pianoforte, he felt he could listen to it for hours—or for a little while anyway.

He stood there watching her, listening, and thinking how he wanted to take those lovely hands of hers and place them on his bare chest and then slowly move them lower. He wanted to—

"What are you doing?"

Harrison swung around and saw an angry-looking Captain Maxwell standing on the stoop staring at him.

Bloody damn!

What were the odds of them both arriving at the same time? Fate was a nasty blackguard.

"Good afternoon, Captain," Harrison said and casually walked over to join him. The first thing he noticed was that the captain held a large bouquet of brightly colored, vibrant-looking spring flowers. Just as Harrison had started to buy for Angelina.

Maxwell had noticed Harrison's pot of half-dead violets, too.

The captain continued to stare at him with malice etched in every feature in his face. "Start explaining yourself."

The soldier was coming out in the man. Harrison didn't mind. He would have acted the same way if their roles were reversed.

Remaining calm, Harrison asked, "About what?"

Maxwell's scowl remained in place. "Looking in Miss Rule's window as if you were a Peeping Tom."

Now, that made Harrison angry, but he wasn't going to give the captain the satisfaction of knowing that. "She's playing the pianoforte," he said as the Maltese let loose with a shrieking howl that could have awakened the dead. "And the dog is singing for her," Harrison added. "What are you doing here?"

"I'm here to see Miss Rule."

Angelina didn't know Harrison was coming over. He wondered if she expected Maxwell or if he was showing up unannounced as well.

"What a coincidence. So am I," Harrison quipped. He reached over, lifted the door knocker, and rapped it three times. Barking sounded from behind the door.

"Quiet now!" Harrison heard the ill-tempered housekeeper yell.

The captain looked at Harrison with a curled-lip stance much the way Sam had looked at him that first day. Harrison had won over Sam; he had no desire to do the same with the captain, but he would like to keep things between them friendly. Maxwell was going to have to do more than this to intimidate him.

"Don't let me catch you looking in her window again."

"All right," Harrison said good-naturedly. "I won't let you catch me next time."

The door opened and Mrs. Bickmore looked startled for a moment to see two gentlemen standing on the stoop, both holding flowers. She recovered quickly. "My lord," she said and curtsied and then turned to Maxwell and said, "Sir, may I help you?"

"I'm here to see Miss Rule," the captain said.

Harrison smiled at the woman and said, "Me too."

Mrs. Bickmore stepped aside. They both walked in, taking off their damp hats. Angelina came walking out of the music room holding the small long-haired dog. She glanced from Harrison to Maxwell and back to Harrison again, and he knew. She *was* expecting the officer. Harrison was the interloper. He wasn't surprised, but he didn't like the way his stomach clenched for a moment.

Lady Railbridge came out of the drawing room, and her father was walking down the corridor toward them.

"Lord Thornwick, what a pleasant surprise," Mr. Rule said, smiling broadly and picking up his step.

"Good afternoon, Captain Maxwell, my lord," Lady Railbridge said, taking the dog from Angelina's arms.

"Lady Railbridge, Miss Rule, Mr. Rule," Harrison

and the captain said at the same time, neither of them willing to relinquish the right to speak first to the other.

"I'm sorry to interrupt your afternoon," Harrison said to Angelina when all the greetings had been acknowledged by everyone. "I only stopped by to give you this." He held the pot out to her. "I knew you would know what to do with it."

She took the wilted blooms from him and looked at them, seeming to study them. Then, as if the meaning of his gift became clear, she looked up at him, smiled, and said, "Thank you, my lord. I'll take care of the violets for you."

"Now that you're here, Lord Thornwick," Mr. Rule said, "I insist you stay and have tea with us. I've been wanting to talk with you about the possibility of you becoming a member of a small gentlemen's club I belong to. We don't have any peers. You would be the first. It would be an honor to have you join us. We've already voted on it so you don't need to do anything but accept."

"I'm honored, Mr. Rule, but I'm afraid it's not possible for me to stay today. Perhaps we can discuss it one day at the Heirs' Club."

Mr. Rule's eyes widened. "The Heirs' Club. Why, that would be splendid. I've never been there. I should like that invitation very much, my lord."

Harrison said his good-byes and left. He stopped on the stoop and replaced his hat on his head. There would be other times for him to see Angelina. The next time he wanted to see her, he'd come on a Thursday afternoon since that was the day her grandmother was always out of the house; with any luck her father would be, too. He'd prefer the captain not be around either.

Harrison would be gentle, cautious, and persistent in

his pursuit of Angelina. For now, it would be best if she didn't know he wanted to make her his. He would let her continue to think he had no interest in her other than what she'd asked of him.

Considering that huge nosegay Maxwell gave Angelina, the soldier might think that he'd won that round. But Harrison knew Angelina better than the captain did, and he hadn't.

Chapter 15

*Reputation is an idle and most false imposition; oft got
without merit, and lost without deserving.*
Othello, *Act II, sc. 3*

Lord Thornwick was gone almost before Angelina knew
why he'd been there. She looked down at the wilted violets and smiled again. That man was unbelievable. He
wanted her to take his plant and make it bloom again,
but why? Did he think that because she helped wounded
dogs, she could help a dying plant? She had no skills in
that area whatsoever, but she would see what she could
do to save it for him.

But on further thought, she knew it was not like Lord
Thornwick to care about a plant. It had to be that the
violets were an excuse for him to come over. But why
hadn't he simply asked her the proper way? Because he
seldom did anything the proper way.

What a devil he was.

"I brought you flowers," Captain Maxwell said and
extended the bouquet to her.

"Thank you, Captain, they're beautiful." She took
them in her free hand and smelled them. "And very fra-

grant, too." Handing both gifts to Mrs. Bickmore, she said, "Please put the flowers in water and bring them into the drawing room for us to enjoy. Put the violets in the kitchen for me to deal with later."

Though she had no notion how. She supposed she could try her hand at pruning and repotting them. Maybe she would put them in her painting room so they would have a lot of light. But whether they would revive she had no idea.

She turned back to Captain Maxwell and said, "It appears that the rain is steady."

"It is," he said. "I'm sorry the weather hasn't cooperated for a ride in the park this afternoon."

"It doesn't matter. We can do it another day. Let's go into the drawing room."

For the first fifteen minutes of Captain Maxwell's visit her father kept him busy with conversation. She and her grandmother would chime in from time to time. More often than she could count, Angelina found her thoughts drifting to Lord Thornwick and his sudden appearance at her house. Was it possible that he had known the captain would be visiting her today and for some reason he wanted to make an appearance, too? But for what purpose? To put Captain Maxwell on edge?— for surely the officer was when he'd first arrived, and Angelina didn't blame him. She had reserved this afternoon for him. The captain's body had been stiff and his expression definitely irritated, if not angry. She supposed it had to be happenstance that he and Captain Maxwell arrived at the same time.

When the chatting had died down and the tea had grown cold, Granna excused herself and her father picked up a book and moved to a chair by the window as was the custom of not leaving a young lady alone with a gentleman.

She sat on one end of the settee and Captain Maxwell on the other. She really didn't mind looking at his scarring or the patch. They didn't bother her now that she'd gotten used to them. What did bother her was that she didn't seem to have any eagerness to be with him or sit closer to him. She had been waiting for him to come home for over a year, so why wasn't she feeling desperate to talk to him and be alone with him?

It was all Lord Thornwick's fault. The timing of his arrival today had her and the captain feeling discombobulated.

"How well do you know Lord Thornwick, Miss Rule?" Captain Maxwell asked.

"Not very well," she answered and as soon as she'd said it, she wondered if it was the truth. Somehow she felt as if she was fibbing because, in a way, she knew the earl very well. He was commanding, arrogant, and self-assured. "Why do you ask?"

"I hesitate to mention this, and maybe I shouldn't."

"What?" she asked curiously. "Surely you must know that once you say maybe you shouldn't mention something, you have to. I will never sleep another wink now until you tell me what you are referencing."

He chuckled. "I didn't think about it like that," he said. His expression turned serious. "It's just that he troubles me."

Angelina feared that Captain Maxwell was seeing Lord Thornwick as a rival. That couldn't be further from the truth. The earl couldn't have made it any clearer to her that he had no interest in vying for her hand. He was only making a show of interest in her because she begged him to do it for the Season. And she was certain he kissed her only to unsettle her, and he had. He always seemed to be quite happy to do that. Though she would never mention any of these things to Captain Maxwell.

Instead, she asked, "How did he trouble you?"

"It was most disturbing, and I'm not sure I want you to be disturbed by it, too. Perhaps I should tell your father instead."

"Now you really have me curious and on the edge of my seat, Captain. You must tell me what you are talking about. If I feel my father should know we'll alert him at once."

"When I walked up to your house today Lord Thornwick was looking in your music room window."

She pursed her lips and studied on what he'd said. Doing something like that was a fanciful thing and it didn't sound like anything the earl would do. But then, the captain wasn't one to make up a story like that, either.

"That's odd." But not astonishing. Lord Thornwick was always full of surprises. Including bringing her a half-dead plant. It did give her an unexpected shiver of awareness to know he'd been peeping in at her.

"I thought so, too. I asked him what he was doing and he said he was watching you play the pianoforte. I heard you, too as I walked up the path, but I wouldn't go over to the window and spy on you."

Captain Maxwell seemed much more concerned about this infraction in manners than Angelina. "I'm afraid Lord Thornwick plays by his own rules, or maybe it's better to say that he plays by no rules. Not many acceptable ones anyway."

His expression questioned her. "Yet you don't seem upset by this realization."

"I'm not." She smiled at the officer, trying to reassure him. "There was no harm done." Now that she thought about it, it was actually quite amusing that

Captain Maxwell had caught Lord Thornwick looking in her window. As far as she was concerned, it served the earl right. Though she doubted the incident embarrassed him in the least.

"That's not acceptable behavior for anyone and especially an earl. I thought you'd be a bit more upset by his Peeping Tom antics."

"Perhaps I would have been if he had been looking into my bedchamber, but there is nothing to see in the music room. And it's not like he didn't have a reason. He heard the pianoforte playing."

"I think I should let your father know. I would hate for Lord Thornwick to make a habit of gawking at you through your windows."

Angelina laughed lightly. The image of the earl gawking at anyone was amusing and the very idea was preposterous. "That's not something I would ever concern myself with. Nor should you. And as far as my father goes it will not concern him, either, but by all means mention it to him if it will make you feel better. Now, Captain, I don't want to talk about Lord Thornwick. Tell me about India. I doubt I shall ever have the opportunity to go there and I want to hear all about it."

"It was hot where I was and very little rain." He stopped and sighed. "The Indian people are clever and hard workers from what I observed. As you can imagine, their customs are very different from ours."

Captain Maxwell continued to talk. She noticed that the longer she looked at him, the easier it was to ignore the wounded side of his face. She couldn't help but wonder what had happened, and she hoped he'd share it with her one day, though she'd never ask. Obviously there was a battle of some kind, or maybe a small skirmish. It must have been a pistol shot or perhaps a musket or maybe even the explosion from cannon fire. There

was nothing about the scarring that looked as if it could
have been done by the straight blade of a knife or the
firm contact of a fist.

"So I don't think I will ever be going back," he finished.

"And you're all right with that?" she asked. "Never
returning?"

He put his arm up on the top of the settee. "I have to
be. It's doubtful I'll stay in the army, now. I can no longer fight."

"I'm sure that troubles you."

He shrugged. "My commanding officer has discussed
with me the possibility of staying in the army and becoming a courier." He sighed heavily again. "I promised
to think about it, but it would probably be difficult for
me to become a messenger."

"But why? That is a very important duty, is it not?
To carry critical and classified documents back and forth
for the generals and other officials."

"I'm a soldier, Miss Rule. That's all I've ever wanted
to be."

"Oh." She didn't really know what to say to that im-
passioned statement. "Perhaps there is a role for you
somewhere in the army. I assume there is no hurry for
you to make a decision."

"Not so far," he said with an intense expression.
"Presently, I'm still considered to be recovering. Though,
I have no idea how much longer that will be the case."

"What would you do if you resigned your commission?"

"I have money saved. Enough to buy a small house
in a village somewhere or here in London. Not in Mayfair, of course, but if I continue to be frugal, I have ad-
equate means to support a wife and family. I will not
live as a pauper."

"No, I never thought you would."

He shifted in the small sofa and leaned toward her. "Miss Rule, I know I no longer look the way I did before I left for India, but I need to know that you would like me to continue to call on you."

Yes! Yes, of course.

He had been the man of her dreams for three years. But should she encourage him? The injury had left him vulnerable. She saw it in his face and heard it in his voice. Her heartbeat increased. Should she allow him to think they could be together if that might never be possible? There was no hope that the captain might be able to help her father pay his debts as she'd once hoped. She couldn't ask him to take what he had saved for a house and his future and give it to her father for his reckless behavior. Especially now that the captain was considering resigning his commission. No, she wouldn't ask that of him. She would get the money from the work of her own hands. Her father and his debts were her responsibility, and she would take care of them. Even if she had to paint day and night.

"Yes, Captain, of course," she finally said. "I would like for us to get to know each other. That is what the Season is for, is it not?"

He sat back again and looked at her curiously. "But there are others wanting to get to know you as well. Lord Thornwick?"

"My father certainly hopes he is," she said honestly, but avoiding the complete truth.

"How can I compete with an earl?" he said gruffly, throwing his body against the back of the settee in a frustrated manner.

Angelina forgave his slight show of temper. "Because you are a well-respected and honored gentleman just as he is. Captain," she said softly, "I just met the earl a few nights ago. I've waited for your return for over a year."

His stare at her face was intense. "So have I. You don't know. You can't know how I longed for yet dreaded coming home. Not knowing how you, or how anyone would receive me now."

She had a fairly good idea how conflicted he must have been.

He stirred restlessly and looked down at the floor before finding her gaze again and asking, "You're sure my appearance doesn't repulse you?"

His return to his appearance pricked a moment of annoyance inside her. How many times must she tell him? "Would I be sitting here having a normal conversation with you if it did? Do you think me that small-minded, sir? If so, I don't want you calling on me again."

"No," he said, his expression softening. "No. I don't think that. It's just that I've seen the way others stare at me. Believe me, I know this is not an easy face to look at."

"You have no reason to say that," she said earnestly.

"I've seen my face every day for the past five months." He closed his eye and shook his head briefly before looking back at her. "I pray each night that it will continue to heal but each morning I wake, look in the mirror to shave, and the scars are no better."

Her heart went out to him. She gazed at him with all the concern she was feeling for him about his insecurities. How could she help him? She wanted to reach out and touch his face, his hand, or something, but with her father in the room she couldn't.

"Give yourself time, Captain. I'm sure it's much better than after it first happened. The scars will continue to heal and lose their redness and fade with time."

"That's very good of you to say." He gave her a gentle smile. "Though I don't know that it's true."

"I do. It's the truth, and I don't want you to reference it again because it makes no difference to me."

His gaze stayed on her face. "I thought about you every day I was gone."

Her heart lifted and she smiled again. "I thought about you every day, too," she admitted frankly.

She heard his intake of breath. "I hoped you would wait for me but after my—after——I was afraid to hope since I, well, none of that matters now, does it. Thank you, Miss Rule. You've made me very happy."

Angelina smiled, too. She couldn't give up so easily on Captain Maxwell. This is what she'd dreamed of for over a year. To court him and to be his wife one day. She wouldn't forget that. She was certain that the captain would make her feel all the wonderful sensations Lord Thornwick had made her feel and more.

Her paintings would sell and she would pay her father's debts. Her whole future depended on it. Once she freed her father from the risk of prison, she would be free of the threat of an arranged marriage to a man who couldn't possibly be the right husband for her.

Chapter 16

And by the way let us recount our dreams.
A Midsummer Night's Dream *4.4.198*

A bell jangled as Bishop Worsley opened the door of Highgate's Furnishings and Antiquities Shop at Number Four-Fifty-Five South Lambert Street. It had taken several days, but he'd finally completed his search and decided which establishment they needed to approach about acquiring Angelina's paintings. He'd said he wanted a place that sold expensive items where only the crème de la crème of Society made their purchases.

Angelina was the first to step into the well-lighted room, followed by her grandmother and then the bishop who carried the large satchel filled with an assortment of her work. At once Angelina noticed the pleasant fragrance of spicy incense. The room was filled with well-placed furniture. Paintings, tapestries, and mirrors of every size, shape, and dimension hung on the walls. Different styles of urns, vases, lamps, and all manner of small household accessories were attractively placed around the room. A basket of fresh flowers was placed on one of the side tables and a silver tea service on another.

The shop owner evidently wanted to cater to the traditional buyer. There were none of the bizarre things that seemed to be so popular in homes the past few years. No stone gargoyles with big emerald eyes, no stuffed heads of boars, bears, or other animals, and no life-sized statues of Athena, Venus, Zeus, or any of the other Greek gods or goddesses. Almost anyone who entered his place of business would feel comfortable and find something conventional to take with them when they left. That the shop had such a large variety of things to choose from gave Angelina hope. According to Bishop Worsley, other than the duchess, this man was her best chance of obtaining money to help her father.

"Good afternoon, ladies, sir," a stout-built man of average height said, appearing from a room at the back of the store. "Welcome to Highgate's. I'm the owner and I'll be happy to assist you with any questions. Or you may feel free to browse on your own with no disturbance from me. Whatever you prefer."

"Thank you, Mr. Highgate," Bishop Worsley said, stepping forward. "I'm Mr. Hugh Walters. This is my wife, Mrs. Walters, and our niece Miss Paulette Savill. We'd like a moment of your time if we may."

Angelina breathed a sigh of relief at how easily Bishop Worsley handled the made-up names.

"Of course," he said with a closed-lip smile. "But my name isn't Highgate. That was the name of the shop when I bought it many years ago and I had no reason to change it. I'm Mr. Eyston. How can I help you?"

"We have some paintings we were hoping you'd buy from us to sell in your shop. We'd be pleased if you'd take a look at them and consider it."

The man glanced down at the satchel as if it were a

distasteful object, and then gave the bishop a dubious look. Angelina's heart sank.

"You have paintings in that?" the man asked.

"They are quite small," Bishop Worsley responded. "All miniatures."

"Hmm," he said, showing the first hint of interest. "I have been known to buy handcrafted items from individuals from time to time and I do sell some paintings. But I only buy the highest quality of merchandise."

"We knew that. That's why we came here. I wouldn't let my niece's paintings be sold just anywhere, you understand."

Mr. Eyston cut his eyes around to Angelina and then to her grandmother, who was pale as a ghost and looked as if she were about to faint. Angelina knew her grandmother was against doing this and wished she could have done it without her, but she'd insisted on coming along.

"I'm not promising anything, but come over to my desk and let's take a look at what you have."

They walked to the back of the shop, where there was a large dark wood desk. The elaborately carved trim work along the edges and down the legs was beautifully cut and tipped with gold leaf. Mr. Eyston quickly closed some account books and pushed them and other papers aside. Bishop Worsley set the satchel in the chair and opened it.

"I'll let Miss Savill take them out," the bishop said, looking at Angelina. "She knows best how to handle such delicate things. I'm afraid my big hands might drop one."

Angelina looked at the shop owner and knew at once he was already bored, completely uninterested but trying to be polite. If she was going to get his attention she had to make this visit personal. Even though her insides were quaking, she hoped her nervousness didn't show on the outside.

Swallowing her hesitation, she turned to him, held out her gloved hand, and said, "Mr. Eyston, I'm pleased to meet you."

His light-brown eyes widened with surprise as he took her hand and nodded. "Miss Savill, thank you for coming into my shop today. Now show me what you're offering."

Angelina took her time and laid out three snuffboxes, two mourning boxes, four miniatures, one whalebone, and two pieces of ivory on the desk. Bishop Worsley had already left all her fans with the duchess for her consideration so she had none to show.

Mr. Eyston looked at every piece as it came out but said nothing. He then picked up his spectacles, bent over the desk, and studied each piece. He remained quiet and so did everyone else. The minutes ticked by as he picked up first one, then another, for closer examination. Angelina thought her breathing would stop and her stomach would jump into her throat before he finally laid his spectacles down and turned to her.

"The painting is quite good."

"It's excellent, Mr. Eyston," Bishop Worsley said confidently. "Not many artists can paint so small and still have every detail in the face recognizable and you know it."

Mr. Eyston looked at Angelina again. "Is this all you have, or are there more pieces?"

"I have more of everything," she said cautiously. "I have been painting for a long time. I paint on fans as well but unfortunately I have no examples to show today."

Mr. Eyston folded his arms across his chest and looked down at her work again. "If I am interested," he said, looking back to Angelina, "would you be willing to prove to me you painted these and that you—how shall I say it—that you are not taking credit for anyone else's work?"

Angelina tried not to get her hopes up. "I would be happy to paint anything you might suggest."

"All right," he said. "I don't suppose you have paint and a brush in that satchel?"

She shook her head.

"Very well."

He went around to the other side of the desk and picked up the inkwell and quill. He set them down in front of her, then grabbed a clean sheet of vellum and placed it beside the ink. "I realize it's not oil and brush but if you can paint on ivory and whalebone, you can paint with ink. Show me something that will prove to me you are the artist."

Angelina moistened her lips and looked down at the ink jar. It had been a long time since she'd used ink but she could do it. But what would she paint that would best show her talent?

"Miss Savill? Is something wrong?"

She looked up at him. "No. May I borrow your spectacles, Mr. Eyston?"

He picked them up and handed them to her.

Her stomach jumped as she removed the satchel and sat down at the desk. "What kind of scene would you like?"

He looked down at one of the miniatures she'd painted of a gentleman and lady strolling in the park, pointed, and said, "This one."

Angelina relaxed. Inside she was smiling. He had selected one of the easiest things for her to paint: a lady and a gentleman in a garden. She picked up the quill and drew a two-inch circle in the center of the page about the size of a snuffbox lid. The gentleman would be the place she'd start.

Her confidence in her ability kept her hands steady. She wasn't nervous about what she was doing. She was anxious about whether Mr. Eyston would accept her work to sell in his shop. It was crucial to her plan.

Half an hour later her grandmother and Bishop Worsley were sitting on one of the settees in the shop but Mr. Eyston was still standing over her shoulder, breathing down her neck, watching every stroke of the quill. Her shoulders ached and her eyes were dry from the strain of looking through spectacles she wasn't used to.

"That's enough," he at long last said. "I'm confident you are the artist."

That cool, refreshing feeling of relief washed over her. Angelina laid the quill down and rose to face him. Her grandmother and the bishop walked over to join them at the desk once again.

"I'll need some time to evaluate each piece. I already have some clients in mind for some of these."

"That's wonderful to hear, Mr. Eyston," Angelina said, trying not to get her hopes up yet. This was only the beginning. He had not made any offers yet. "Thank you."

"I'd like to see everything else you have available by the end of the week if possible. After I evaluate all of them, I'll send over an estimate of what I'm willing to pay for each item."

Angelina felt tears of joy gather in her eyes at the possibility that her wild idea might actually work. "We'll have them to you by the end of the week."

Chapter 17

*Friendship is constant in all other things, save in
the office and affairs of love.*
Much Ado About Nothing 2.2.266–67

It was dark as midnight and freezing cold, too. The rising sun of dawn hadn't penetrated the gray skies on the horizon. A patchwork of early-morning fog hung low in the misty air and scattered as they slowly rode through it. Harrison's fingers and toes were tingling but his heavy cloak and the horse beneath his legs helped keep him warm.

"I'm beginning to think we should have waited until midday to ride in the park rather than at daybreak," Harrison said to Bray, who rode beside him.

"I was just trying to remember if this was your fool idea or mine so I'd know which one of us to call a bloody idiot."

"It was yours and you damned well know it," Harrison complained and then finished with a short laugh. "Can you believe we used to do this and actually enjoy it?"

"Ah, but years ago when we'd ride like this," Bray

answered, "we had spent the night gaming and were happy our pockets were full."

Harrison's horse nickered and blew puffs of warm air from his nostrils. "And we'd down numerous pints of ale and several glasses of brandy to keep us warm."

"Do you miss those days?" Bray asked.

Do I?

Harrison took in a deep cold breath and caught the odor of damp foliage. He remembered many rides in the park before, during, and after daybreak when he, Bray, and Adam were the scandalous scoundrels of London Society. Racing through the park on horseback or curricles was almost a nightly pastime, no matter the weather.

"No," Harrison admitted with a grin. "But I sure as hell enjoyed them at the time."

"So did I."

They rode in silence for a time. Through spindly, barren tree limbs, Harrison noticed that the first shards of pink split the sky in the distance. He heard the deep sound of a hound baying in the distance. It reminded him of Angelina's dogs. And that reminded him of Angelina's sweet smile, her fresh-as-rainwater scent, and the taste of her honeyed lips. He wanted to see her and he wanted to see her today. Hearing the dog's howl reminded him of an idea he'd had a couple of days ago but dismissed. A risky idea, but Harrison had never let that stop him.

"So tell me, why did you want me to meet you for an early-morning ride in the park?" Harrison asked.

"What makes you think I had a reason other than wanting someone to talk to while I exercised my horse?"

"Because I've known you since I was ten."

"Tell me it hasn't been that long?" Bray said dryly.

"It has. Do you have everything arranged for our journey up north on Sunday to see Adam?"

"I'm set. How about you?"

"I'll be ready. I want to see him but I also need to see Thornwick. I continue to get updates from my manager every couple of days, but he never tells me all I want to know."

Bray pulled the reins short and stopped his horse. Harrison did the same, thinking it was about time Bray decided to tell him what he had on his mind.

"I have some information for you, if you want it."

Puzzled, Harrison said, "Go on."

"First, I want you to know I didn't go looking for this. The subject came up while I was talking with some gentlemen about an issue that will be discussed in Parliament soon."

"All right," Harrison said, remaining cautious and curious as to what this was about. "But you need to know I haven't mastered being an earl, yet. I have no desire to wade in the political waters of Parliament."

Bray reached inside his coat pocket, pulled out a flask, and tossed it to Harrison.

"Good, you don't have to worry about that for the current session. This was about a military issue."

Harrison went still. It had to be about Maxwell.

"Am I going to need this?" Harrison asked, holding up the silver container.

"Only to stay warm."

"In that case." Harrison opened the flask and took a drink.

"The information I have for you is about Captain Maxwell."

For a moment Harrison wondered if he even wanted to hear what Bray had to say. Whatever it was, the information would not alter Harrison's plans in any way. He still intended to win Angelina's heart away from the soldier.

Harrison sipped the brandy again, replaced the top, and threw it back to Bray. "I had already assumed that."

"It concerns how his injury happened."

Now, that interested Harrison. His horse snorted, shuddered, and shifted beneath him, restless to get moving. "Go on," he said, reaching down to pat the warm neck of his mount.

"It didn't result from a battle, a skirmish, or any kind of brave act as I assume most of us suspected. It was an accident."

Harrison whistled under his breath. That was surprising news. "What happened?"

"His commanding officer said he was inspecting his loaded pistol and it backfired right into his eye."

"Damnation," Harrison whispered.

"It was a hell of a thing to have happened."

"I agree. I haven't heard any gossip. Is he claiming something different occurred?"

"Not that I know of. He's not telling anyone what actually transpired and his officers and the people who know are respecting his wishes and keeping quiet, too. That is, except for one officer who decided to divulge the information to the three gentlemen in our group."

Harrison's bay stirred restlessly again, causing Bray's horse to snort and stomp his feet, too. If that many men knew, it would eventually get out.

"I wonder why he wouldn't want anyone to know the details. It was an accident that could happen to any of us."

"But shouldn't happen to an officer. It's not that I think you should do anything with the information,"

Bray said. "I wanted you to know, too, since I had heard."

"I'm glad you told me. I admit I'd wondered. This is not my story to tell, and if I should hear otherwise, I'll keep my peace about what I know."

"I was sure you would."

Bray uncapped the flask and took a drink. "How are things going with you and Miss Rule?"

"Slow," Harrison responded, his stomach tightening just thinking about Angelina and how she made him feel. Taking his time wasn't what Harrison wanted to do, but it was the best approach for her. If he rushed her, she would get more confused about him than she already was. He knew something she didn't. She could swear to heaven and back that she was in love with Maxwell, but Harrison knew different. She wouldn't have responded to his kisses the way she had if that were the case. In time, as she got to know the officer she'd realize it. And Harrison had to give her that time.

"Have there been any more rumblings from Hopscotch?" Bray asked.

"Not since the incident at the Heirs' Club where he reminded me once again how serious the Prince is about his wishes for me to marry Miss Rule."

As if sensing he would get no more information from Harrison, Bray said, "What do you say we give these horses their heads like we used to? Fifteen pounds if I make it to the Serpentine before you do."

Harrison took a close look at his friend's mount. He wasn't familiar with the horse but he did know the stride, stamina, and speed of his bay.

He grinned at Bray. "Thirty and you're on."

Chapter 18

I have suffered with those that I saw suffer!
The Tempest *1.2.5–6*

She wasn't ready by the time Lord Thornwick arrived, but it wasn't her fault. Her father had rushed in the door minutes ago announcing that he'd just seen Lord Thornwick at the Heirs' Club and the earl had asked if he could take Angelina for a ride. And of course, her father had happily agreed he could come immediately since Angelina had no other plans.

No other plans!

It'd taken her three days to complete every painting she'd started but for one reason or another had never finished. Yesterday she'd carefully packed all her snuff- and mourning boxes, fans, and miniatures and had them delivered to Bishop Worsley, thinking her job was done and everything was in his hands. She should have known better. The man promptly sent her a note in return saying that she was to continue to paint every day, and as she finished each box or fan she was to send it to him. Already she was finding that while she immensely enjoyed painting for pleasure, she had little desire to paint because she needed to or someone demanded it.

While she dressed, Angelina was alternately frustrated and excited. Frustrated because she'd never get more painting done if she continued to have things happen during the day that kept her from it. And frustrated because she couldn't figure out what in heaven's name she was doing being excited about the prospect of seeing the earl.

Captain Maxwell, the man of her dreams, was back in London; he should be the only gentleman she was looking forward to seeing. He was kind, courageous, and wounded. He needed her support and love now most of all. Lord Thornwick was a strong, capable, and carefree man who had no worries and no problems. He certainly didn't need any compassion from her. That she was eager to see him made no sense to her. Her heart belonged to Captain Maxwell. She was sure of that.

Besides, what kind of man showed up unannounced to visit a young lady with a pot of wilted violets in his hands for her to nurse back to health? Though she had considered it a challenge to save them and make sure they bloomed again just to show Lord Thornwick she could.

She and the earl had seen each other in passing at one of the parties last night, and though there was no conversation between them, they had both done a lot of watching the other. Why she would bother, she had no idea. And now suddenly he wanted to take her for a ride in the park. She just couldn't figure him out. He followed no acceptable rules of polite behavior. What kind of gentleman would give a lady only a few minutes' notice?

There was no time to put much thought into what she would wear. She hurriedly donned an ivory carriage dress that was trimmed with dark blue ribbon around

the neckline and the cuffs of her sleeves. When
Mrs. Bickmore announced that Lord Thornwick had
already arrived, Angelina sent her down with matching
bonnet and cape and told her to find a parasol to take as
well.

Angelina stopped in the vestibule to calm her breathing from scurrying to change. She didn't have to worry
about pinching her cheeks. She was already flushed.
Much to her consternation, she always felt that way
when she looked at Lord Thornwick. He made her forget she was a calm, sensible young lady who wanted to
be in control of her future life.

She headed confidently down the corridor to the
drawing room, determined to ignore those unwanted
feelings the earl stirred up inside her. When she walked
through the doorway, her breath caught in her throat.
Lord Thornwick was on one knee on the floor, laughing
and playing with Molly and Mr. Pete.

He looked up at her and smiled and she felt as if her
heart flipped. A warm tenderness settled over her and
all her anxious feelings drained away. He could disarm
her faster than a hummingbird could flap its wings.

"Lord Thornwick, I apologize for being late."

Harrison rose tall and commanding. The now ever-
present butterflies in her stomach started swarming like
bees. Would she ever cease to have that sensual awareness when she saw him? He looked devilishly handsome
in a fawn-colored coat and dark-brown waistcoat with
brown trousers stuffed into shiny black knee boots.

"You're not late," he said as Mr. Pete barked and
jumped on his leg, trying to regain his attention. Molly
yapped, too, but couldn't be bothered to expend the en-
ergy to jump. "There was no time set. Besides, I was
enjoying getting better acquainted with your grandmother's dog and Mr. Pete."

She looked around. Except for the dogs, he was alone in the room. "Where's Papa?"

"After I arrived, he left to go tell the members of his club that I agreed to join and become a member. Apparently he didn't want to wait. He said he'd be back before we returned."

Another warm feeling washed over her. "It wasn't necessary for you to join his club, but thank you for doing that. I know it made him very happy."

"I did it because I may be asking a favor of him soon."

"My father? Really?"

He nodded. "After the library is rebuilt at Thornwick, I'll need someone to help me decide what books I need to replace all those that burned."

"That's right. I'd heard there was a fire at your home but no one seemed to know how bad it was. Was it very destructive?"

He shrugged and then rubbed the head of the jumping dog. "It will take time to repair all the damage, but it's begun now."

"Mr. Pete, stop that and leave Lord Thornwick alone. Sit. Sit."

The dog didn't acknowledge her and kept trying to get Harrison's attention. He rubbed the beagle's head again. It was her fault for not taking the time to properly train Mr. Pete, but the painting was more important at present.

She tamped down her feelings of appreciation and said, "I'll take the dogs out back and then we'll be ready to go."

"I'll help you," he said, scooping up Molly and handing her to Angelina. He then grabbed Mr. Pete and said, "Lead the way."

A few minutes later they picked up Harrison's coat, gloves, and hat, along with her things, on the way out the door. The grip of Harrison's hand was strong against her gloved hand as he helped her step into the curricle. He settled himself beside her and immediately released the brake, picked up the ribbons, and snapped them onto the horses' rumps. The carriage took off with a jolt and a rumble.

White wispy clouds scattered across a blue sky and the bright glare of the sun. Angelina opened her parasol and relaxed into the softly cushioned seat. It was a glorious day for a ride in the park, but she needed to be painting.

"Do I hear you laughing?" the earl asked.

Was I?

"Laughing? Me? I don't think so. You must be hearing things."

"Aren't you happy?"

"I guess so. I mean, yes, I'm happy. What an odd question. Are you happy?" she countered.

"Very," he said, turning off her street and maneuvering the horses to fall in line behind a curricle carrying another couple. "You seemed flustered when you walked into the drawing room."

I was.

"Flustered doesn't mean unhappy. Not that I'm admitting I was flustered, either, you understand," she added hastily.

"I suppose I could have given you more notice of my intention to take you for an afternoon ride."

"That would have been polite," she agreed. "And even better if you had asked whether I'd like to go rather than just telling my father you were coming to take me."

"Ah, I see. So as with the dancing—you want to be asked and given the chance to decline."

"Yes," she said with a smile. "That would be nice."

"I'll try to remember that." He glanced over at her

and offered a roguish grin. "I suppose being told takes some of the charm off the ride."

Very little, she wanted to say, but settled for giving him another smile instead.

"Tell me, how are your plans to save your father coming along?"

She had wondered if he would ever ask her about that. "My grandmother and I are working on something."

"That's good. What?"

"Nothing I want to talk about with you, Lord Thornwick."

A wrinkle formed between his eyebrows. "But I'm curious."

She smiled, feeling quite confident her paintings were going to produce enough money to help them pay down the debts. "I'm sure you are."

"There aren't many things two ladies can do."

"Not many, but some."

"You're not going to tell me anything."

"No."

"Fair enough. Did you enjoy your afternoon with Captain Maxwell?" he asked after a couple of minutes' silence.

She glanced at him, but he was keeping his eyes straight ahead on the horses. "Yes, we had a lovely visit," she said and watched him drive by the road that would have taken them to Hyde Park. "You missed the turn to the park."

He looked over at her. "I didn't miss it."

She twirled her parasol against her shoulder and said, "I'm sure we just passed it. If you look behind you, you'll see you indeed missed the turn."

"Did you think we were going to the park?"

Suspicion that all was not right seeped into her mind. "Didn't you?"

He laughed. "No."

"What do you mean? Didn't you invite me to take a ride in the park with you?"

"No, I only told your father I wanted to take you for a ride."

"You are very mischievous, my lord."

"Perhaps, but I never said we would be going to a park. I've wanted to do this since it first crossed my mind, but I always ended up talking myself out of it."

His words were like a needle prick. She knew he was only feigning interest in her to fool her father and the Prince, but that he felt the need to talk himself out of an afternoon ride with her stung.

Lord Thornwick will always be a scoundrel!

"But my father made a fair assumption, don't you think?"

He shrugged. "Yes."

"Well, no matter," she said, determined to enjoy the afternoon. "It's such a beautiful day, it will be nice to just ride and see the sights of London."

"I didn't say we didn't have a destination."

She looked over at him again, and once again he kept his eyes straight ahead. "So we are going somewhere?"

"Yes."

A feeling of excitement rose in her. Any normal young lady would be frightened to be in a carriage with a renowned scoundrel, and here she was feeling a delicious thrill of excitement.

"You aren't going to tell me where you're taking me, are you?"

"That would spoil the surprise."

Surprise?

What was the earl up to? She wasn't sure she could trust him to take her anywhere, but that didn't stop her nerve endings from tingling or keep her from wanting to go with him.

They had left the familiar part of town, past all the shopping. The houses were getting farther apart and the roads were less traveled and bumpier than the ones she was used to.

"I'm not sure this is a part of Town where I should be, my lord."

"It's not. But you are safe with me."

"I was speaking of my reputation, not my personal safety."

He laughed. "And you are right. Your reputation is always in danger when you are with me, Angelina."

"How well I know."

"And it's nice to know you still remember our kiss."

She would never forget it.

They took another turn and started down a long lane that was more two ruts in a path than a road. There were no houses on either side of the trail, but plenty of tall bushy shrubs and scrub trees showing new growth lining the way. A large dwelling came into view at the end of the lane. Unlike the drive up to the house, its spacious lawn was well tended with precision-cut yew and shrubs outlining it.

"Do the people who live here know we are coming?" she asked.

"No, but you don't have to make an appointment to visit."

It didn't surprise her for a moment that he would take her someplace where no prearrangements were necessary.

"I have to say I'm quite curious about why we are here."

He stopped in front of the house and set the brake.

He jumped down and reached back for her. "Take my hand. You're about to find out."

Leaving her parasol in the carriage, she walked with him up to the door. He rapped the door knocker. After a short time a well-dressed woman opened the door, looked at them curiously, and said, "May I help you?"

"We're here to see Mrs. Vaughan."

"Come in. I'll get her."

Entering an unknown house with Lord Thornwick was definitely against the rules of polite Society, but Angelina wasn't about to object without finding out why they were there.

The servant led them into a drawing room and said, "Wait here."

"Would you like to sit down?" Lord Thornwick asked.

"I'll stand for now," Angelina answered. She glanced around the room, noting a large, impressive portrait of a beautiful woman sitting in an upholstered chair, holding a Pomeranian. A stately-looking Pyrenees stood by her legs and a spaniel lay at her feet.

"Lord Thornwick."

Angelina turned to see the tall, beautiful lady in the portrait rising from a curtsy. She looked to be about the age of Angelina's grandmother. She wore a dark-lavender dress trimmed with black lace. The neckline of the bodice was cut low. A diamond-and-amethyst necklace that seemed more appropriate for evening wear than daytime hung around her neck.

Lord Thornwick introduced her as Mrs. Olivia Vaughan. Angelina thought the woman had one of the sweetest smiles she'd ever seen.

"Thank you for coming to see what I've done, Miss Rule."

"I didn't tell Miss Rule why we are here."

Mrs. Vaughan's eyes rounded. "Oh, well, then let's get right to our tour and show her. Follow me."

Angelina looked at Lord Thornwick and mouthed, *Tour what?*

You'll see, he mouthed back to her and motioned for her to fall in step behind Mrs. Vaughan.

They walked out the back door and down the steps. As soon as they were outside, Angelina heard dogs. Some barked and some yelped, but none of them sounded as if they were hurt or in pain. They started across a spacious lawn toward a huge building. Over the entrance was a large sign that read THE ANIMAL SHELTER FOR THE PREVENTION OF HYDROPHOBIA.

"You're not the only one who takes in wounded and starving dogs," Harrison said.

Angelina turned to Mrs. Vaughan and asked, "You help rescue injured dogs, too?"

"I do. Maybe on a little grander scale than you, but no matter how little one can do, it is all important. Lord Thornwick thought you might like to see what I do."

"Yes, thank you. I'd love to."

Harrison opened the door and they stepped inside a large barnlike structure. Around the perimeter were cages with dogs of varying sizes and breeds. Angelina guessed there were close to fifty cages. The dogs barked, yelped, scratched, and clawed, trying to get out and garner the attention of the friendly faces who entered their domain.

"I've never seen a place that has so many dogs," Angelina said walking farther into the building.

"We've been here less than a year," she said. "When my life became less complicated last year, I knew what I wanted to do. I opened a shelter to help those poor little creatures who have no home."

Angelina felt her chest swell. "That is so kind of you. That is something I would like to do one day."

"And perhaps you shall. I can't help them all but as you can see, I help all I can. I call it my dog sanctuary. By calling it a shelter for the prevention of the spread of rabies, I receive a lot of generous donations from friends and even strangers who have a fear of rabid dogs. Two gamekeepers look after the dogs for me. They feed them, exercise them, and tend their wounds if necessary."

"I don't know what to say. This is such a wonderful idea. I wish I could do something on a grand scale like this."

"If you've saved one, Miss Rule, you've helped."

"I wanted you to know this place was here," Harrison told her. "If you find a dog that needs help, send a note to Mrs. Vaughan and she will send someone to your house and bring him here."

"I only wish we could take all the street dogs," she added to Lord Thornwick's words. "Alas, we have to limit it to those who are starving or hurt and can no longer take care of themselves. I can't bear to see a wounded animal in pain and not do something."

"Neither can I," Angelina echoed.

Lord Thornwick remained quiet and let Angelina talk with Mrs. Vaughan about her shelter, about how she went about trying to find homes for some of the dogs. Angelina could have stayed the rest of the afternoon, but all too soon the earl said it was time to go.

Once good-byes were said, and they were settled back on the curricle, Angelina reached over and kissed Lord Thornwick on his clean-shaven cheek. She caught a whiff of shaving soap. His eyes brightened. His gaze swept up and down her face. Finally she'd done something to surprise him. That pleased her.

"That was quite unexpected, Angelina, but appreciated."

"Thank you for bringing me here."

He released the brake and gave the horses the command to move. "I'm glad I finally decided it was all right to bring you here."

"Why would you not want to? This is a wonderful place. And Mrs. Vaughan said I could bring dogs here anytime and she would see that they are taken care of."

"No," he said quickly. "She said for you to send her a message and she would send someone for the dog. And that is the way it must be handled."

Angelina wrinkled her nose at him as they started down the lane. "Why? This place is not a secret, is it?"

"No."

"Then I would like very much for you to tell me why you think I shouldn't come here to help or for a visit."

"All right," he said, continuing to glance at her. "I suppose I should tell you for your own good. Mrs. Vaughan has been a mistress to several wealthy and powerful gentlemen over the past thirty years. She's no longer in that line of business, but she is not someone who is acceptable for a young lady to associate with."

"A mistress? Oh, I see," she whispered. That was the last thing Angelina would have expected to hear.

"Does that shock you?"

Quite a bit.

"No, no," she fibbed, feeling heat rise up her neck and settle in her cheeks. "I mean of course I've heard of mistresses, but I don't think I've ever met one before."

"You'd have no reason to."

"It's just that she seemed like such a nice, lovely woman."

"Mistresses are nice, lovely women, Angelina. Why

would a man pay for the pleasure to share time with a shrew?"

"Of course you're right."

"Mrs. Vaughan is beautiful, intelligent, and discreet. She was sought after for many years. She could command any price she wanted and did. Once her beauty started to fade, she turned to other pursuits."

"That surprises me."

"What?" He looked at Angelina again and grinned. "That she went from taking care of two-legged animals to four-legged?"

"Of course not." Angelina huffed and then scoffed. "She is still a very beautiful woman. Her beauty hasn't faded."

"I agree with you," he said. Angelina was quiet while she opened her parasol. Finally she asked, "Was she your mistress?"

He glanced at her and chuckled. "So you are curious about that. I wondered if you would ask."

"How could I not after what you told me."

He remained quiet, looking at the horses trotting along the rutted lane.

"Was she?" she asked again.

Harrison's expression softened. "No, she was never my mistress."

Angelina believed him. "Then how do you know so much about her?"

"From other gentlemen."

"So men talk about their mistresses."

"Somewhat," he said as calmly as if they were talking about the beautiful weather. "Never in any great detail."

"Is it true that you once walked down a street in Mayfair with a mistress on each arm?"

He glanced at her. "So you've heard about that."

"It's true then?"

They left the deserted lane and turned back onto the main roadway. "It was a long time ago. I no longer try to shock people."

"Is it also true then that you have participated in orgies?"

That got his attention and he jerked his head around. "Where did you hear that?"

"From some ladies in my reading group who swear it's true."

"Angelina." He paused as if trying to decide what he wanted to say. When he'd made up his mind, he continued, "I am quite open with you about many things, most things, but there are some things I'm not willing to discuss with you and that is one of them."

So she had finally found a subject that rattled him. Thank goodness! She was beginning to think that he was unflappable. Good to know he wasn't. That tickled her, and she laughed.

His expression told her he didn't think that was amusing, but a few seconds later she saw the corners of his mouth twitch with laughter, too.

Chapter 19

You kiss by th' book.
Romeo and Juliet *1.5.110*

Harrison sat in his coach dressed in evening attire with his feet propped up on the opposite seat. A tin box of hot coals sat on the floor to keep him warm, and a flask of brandy helped him pass the time while he waited and watched Angelina's front door. It was the only thing he could do. He'd missed her the past two nights, having no idea which parties she would be attending or at what time she would be there. There was nothing to do but to follow her carriage to her first engagement of the evening.

He'd asked himself a thousand times why he hadn't kissed her the afternoon they went to see Mrs. Vaughan. It was a perfect opportunity. He'd wanted to. Started to. But he feared that if they'd started kissing on that lonely stretch of road, he might not have stopped until she was completely his. He wanted that, and one day she would want it, too, but she hadn't yet come to that realization. She needed more time. And as much as he disliked doing it, he had to give her that time to see that Captain Maxwell wasn't the man for her. Harrison was. He didn't know how, but he'd known it the moment he first saw her.

He was still thinking about Angelina and the officer. The afternoon she and Harrison had gone to Olivia Vaughan's house, Angelina said she had a lovely time with Maxwell. Had the officer seen her since then, had he danced with her again? Harrison had wanted to know more but at the time, he decided he wouldn't ask. He wanted Angelina thinking about him, not the captain. But Harrison couldn't let it go. He kept wondering if Maxwell had held her hand, if he'd kissed her.

His instinct told him no. He doubted the captain had spent any time alone with her during the afternoon. It was too wet for a ride in the park, and her father and grandmother had been home. Harrison was fairly certain one of them kept Angelina in sight at all times. Mr. Rule had already made it clear he intended Harrison would wed his daughter. But Harrison had to make sure.

The front door opened and Harrison sat up. He reached up and knocked his fist twice on the top of the coach, giving his driver the prearranged signal to follow.

Less than ten minutes later Harrison's carriage stopped in front of Viscount Thistlebury's house. Harrison stayed inside the coach until he saw they had entered.

He left his hat, gloves, and cloak with the servant at the front door. On both sides of the vestibule were rooms filled with people. At a glance Harrison didn't see Angelina in either of them. He walked down the corridor to see if there were other rooms where people might have gathered, but the dining room and book room were empty. The kitchen was filled with servants. It appeared the two front rooms were the only ones with guests.

He strode back to the vestibule and entered the drawing room. For a time he chatted with the Lord Mayor, but all the while he discreetly let his gaze search the packed room for Angelina. Not finding her, he soon left and entered the doorway on the other side. Lord Thistlebury immediately cornered him to let him know he'd heard about the rebuilding of Thornwick. Harrison remembered that the viscount was one of the gentlemen at the duel that morning who'd said that Harrison wouldn't take care of the place. Harrison smiled and told the man he'd invite him to a house party once the place was finished. In fact, he would invite all the men who'd doubted his ability to change from a carefree scoundrel to being a trustworthy earl for Thornwick.

Harrison soon spotted Angelina and set his gaze on her while he continued to keep Lord Thistlebury happy with news from the building project. Harrison had no doubt the man would be eager to spread the word. Just when he thought he was going to have to approach Angelina to get her attention, she caught sight of him. For a moment he would have sworn to anyone that she was glad to see him.

He remained a little while longer with the viscount and then excused himself from his host and moved to the doorway. As he'd hoped, Angelina's gaze followed him. He inclined his head toward the corridor. She wrinkled her brow and lifted her shoulders a little to indicate she didn't understand him. He took two steps backward, motioned with his head again toward the corridor, and walked out. There was no way she wouldn't understand that, he thought. He waited at the far end of the corridor and within a couple of minutes she walked out and looked straight at him.

Harrison felt that now familiar tightness in his chest and stomach. She looked stunning in a low-cut, high-waisted gown made from a flimsy, frothy-looking fabric that clung to her legs and outlined her shapely figure as she walked toward him. Three strands of pearls hung around her neck, a short single strand at her throat and a longer double strand on the enticing swell of her breasts. He was struck by an intense and immediate desire to possess her and make her his.

"Good evening, Angelina," he said as she came up to him.

"My lord, is something wrong?"

He had hoped for a sweet smile from her but he'd settle for less at the moment. "No. Should there be?"

"You were acting strange."

"Was I? I wanted to talk to you without being in the middle of the crush."

"Good. This gives me the opportunity to thank you again for taking me to see Mrs. Vaughan."

"And it gives me the opportunity to ask you more about your afternoon with Captain Maxwell."

Her eyes searched his cautiously. "Yes, but why would you want to?"

She was being evasive. She had to know that would irritate him. He thought he could live without knowing, but he was dying to find out if he had touched her, kissed her, and held her in his arms.

"I suppose you had many things to catch up on since he's been gone over a year."

"We are getting to know each other, it's true." She moistened her lips. "I told you, we never spent a lot of time with each other before he left. Remember, I hadn't had my debut so our time together was extremely limited."

"That's right," he agreed. "Captain Maxwell is more than a few years older than you, isn't he?"

She raised her eyebrows and seemed to ponder his question. "I don't know how old he is."

"I'd guess about twenty years older than you."

"Probably not quite that much, but age matters not to me," she assured him quietly.

"Tell me, did he talk about his injury and how it happened with you?"

She frowned and glanced behind her as if to assure herself no one was watching them talking alone in the dimly lit corridor. "No. I didn't expect him to. In fact, I'm sure it would be very difficult for him to talk about that horrifying time with anyone. Why do you ask? Why are you asking me these questions about the captain?"

Did she really not know that he was jealous and that it was eating at him day and night?

"I thought perhaps he might have told you how it happened. That you might have asked. Isn't it natural to be curious as to exactly what happened to him?"

"Yes, and I suppose I am," she admitted, then qualified by adding, "Somewhat. But that is being meddlesome, my lord. I would never ask him about it. How would you like it if I or someone else asked about your injuries?"

He gave her a puzzled grin. That was the hell of it. He had participated in all kinds of dangerous escapades for years and had never had a serious wound in his life. "What injuries would those be, Angelina?"

"Everyone knows you had a duel last winter," she said in a frosty tone. "That you killed a man, and you were shot, too. Obviously your wounds are not visible as are Captain Maxwell's, but surely you have them."

Oh, yes, he had wounds, but thankfully he had the kind of wounds that didn't show on the skin.

"It's true I dueled last winter, at the other man's insistence I might add. And I wounded him. But he is still very much alive. And I was not harmed. There were a dozen men who were witnesses and know the truth."

She gave him a doubtful look. "I heard you were shot, too, which is why you stayed away from London for half a year. You were healing."

Yes, he was healing. He had been wounded and was grieving the loss of Maddie, his brother, and their children. He was adjusting to a title he wasn't worthy to bear, and learning how to rebuild and manage the large estate he was never supposed to inherit. But Harrison didn't want her to know he'd ever been that vulnerable.

"Gossip is an amazing progression of facts that seem to have no truth behind them." He moved very close to her and softened his voice. "Just tonight I heard that Captain Maxwell kissed you on the afternoon of his visit."

She gasped and looked behind her again. "You did not hear that."

No, but I've been wondering.

"Does that mean his lips didn't touch yours?"

"Of course not," she said, seeming outraged by his fib. "Unlike the man standing before me now, he's a gentleman. A true gentleman. Besides, how could he have kissed me when my father never left us alone for even a moment?"

Good for Mr. Rule.

Harrison quickly surveyed the corridor and doorways for anyone who might be nearby. Seeing no one, he said, "The captain could have done something like this." He picked up her hand and hurried down the corridor with her following. It pleased him that she didn't try to stop him but willingly let him lead the way. He opened the back door and gently pulled her outside onto the stoop.

The lamp on the small porch wasn't lit but hazy moonlight shone down from the twinkling black sky. The cold breeze that drifted across his face did nothing to chill the heat in his loins.

"Ah—why are you bringing me out here?"

He dipped his head low and whispered, "So I can do this." He placed his lips on hers as his arms circled her and brought her up to his chest. She was stunned by his embrace and kiss. She squirmed and pushed against his chest for a second or two before lifting her arms around his neck, giving him access to hold her closer and tighter. With a contented sigh, she parted her lips, opened her mouth, and leaned against him.

Harrison loved the way she melted so easily into his arms. His lower body thickened and hardened instantly. He wanted her and he wanted her to know he did. He kissed her long and deeply. She sighed and matched his passion. Her response made him eager for more of her.

"Perhaps the captain has not been dying to kiss you, Angelina," he whispered against her lips. "But I have."

She tasted of fruit punch. He'd never liked the drink but on her lips it was heavenly sweet and satisfying. He loved the tempting depth of her mouth and searched it with his tongue, before letting his lips glide across her cheek to softly nuzzle the warm soft area behind her ear. She lowered her head to give him better access. He inhaled softly, slowly drinking in her womanly scent.

"You are sensual, Angelina," he whispered softly against her ear. "You cannot deny that. I know you feel desire deep in your soul. I long to bring it to life and release it for you to enjoy and savor."

"No, my lord, I'm sure that's not true," she answered,

but gave him no hint she wanted him to stop his kisses and caresses.

"One day, I will prove it to you."

His hands slid down to the small of her back, and then around her lean narrow waist. When she made no protest he continued his exploration. He moved his hands over the firm roundness of her buttocks and felt their firm shape beneath the thin fabric of her gown. She was slender, yet very womanly. His hands roved up and down the sensuous curves of her small waist, the gentle flare of her shapely hips and bottom. She allowed him the freedom to touch her supple body as he desired without protest.

He stopped kissing her and looked down into her blue eyes. "I've been waiting to kiss you and touch you like this, Angelina," he said in a voice husky with desire. "I've wanted to show you how much I want you."

Her eyes searched his. "But we shouldn't be doing this. We shouldn't kiss like this."

"You told me you had made no commitment to Captain Maxwell. Is that still the case?"

She moistened her lips. "Yes."

"Then we are hurting no one. And I don't know about you but this feels too wonderful to stop." He lifted her bottom and pressed her gently against his hardness. "I'll stop anytime you say."

He waited.

She remained silent, her eyes searching his.

"So should I continue?" he asked.

"Please," she whispered, closing her eyes and lifting her lips to his.

Harrison quickly covered her mouth with his before she had time to change her mind. Her lips were warm, sweet, and pliant beneath his. The slow exploration of her body caused a rampant hunger inside him. He deepened the kiss, letting his mouth cover hers more fully, more frantically.

He cupped her bottom again and pressed her against the hardness hidden by his trousers. She sighed into his mouth when he brought her tightly against him. Excitement surged inside him when she matched his eagerness, as if she had been hungry for his touch the way he had been for hers. His hand moved up her rib cage to settle over the deliciously soft, tempting fullness of her breast. His hand massaged, caressed, and teased. Beneath his hand, her chest heaved with determined breaths, and each skillful caress. A hot dizziness of sensation whirled in his head, making his body ache for more of her.

His lips left hers, and he kissed his way down the cool, taut skin of her neck. His tongue played in the hollow of her throat before he kissed his way down to the bare swell of her enticing breasts. A soft whimper passed her lips, and her arms tightened around him. Her fingers dug into the fabric of his coat.

Harrison had to taste her.

He pulled on the neckline of her dress and slid it off one shoulder while kissing the smooth skin of her chest.

"I want to look at you," he whispered. "But you have to say yes. You have to want it, too."

"Yes," she murmured.

He dipped his hand beneath her stays and gently lifted her breast from its hiding place. Shaded moonlight glistened off her lovely pale skin and dusky rose-colored nipple.

He swallowed against the torture of wanting her so desperately and knowing she couldn't be his at this moment. "You're beautiful," he said huskily, wondering if it were possible to be any more aroused than he was at that moment. "I knew you would be."

Bending his head, he covered her cool, firm nipple with his warm mouth. She gasped with delight. He tugged on it, nipped it with his lips, and sucked gently. It puckered invitingly. He loved the thought of making her feel deliciously good. All he could think was that this must be what heaven tasted like.

"We mustn't do this," she whispered but made no move to push him away.

"How can we not when it gives us such pleasure?" he whispered against her soft skin.

"It's not proper. You're not following the rules," she insisted as her head fell back, giving him greater access to her gorgeous body. She cupped his head to her breasts and moaned with sweet, satisfying pleasure. A tremor shook her body, making him want to risk more liberties. She was enjoying his touch as much as he hoped she would.

Somewhere, at the back of his mind, he heard talking and laughing, but the sounds were from inside the house. They were just outside the back door. He'd had no intention of taking things this far with her. A few kisses was what he'd had in mind, but he couldn't stop when she became so responsive and so willing to have him touch her, taste her, and mold his body to hers. Desire was raging inside him and he was having a hell of a time putting restraints on it.

Her skin was soft and warm despite the chill of the evening, her breasts were full and firm, and he was lost to the way she accepted his kisses and caresses and allowed him to bathe her skin with his tongue. His insides quivered. His body throbbed with a deep, painful ache. Right now he was tortured. He wanted to give her all the pleasure she wanted. He desperately wanted to press her against the door, lift her skirts, and make her his without further hesitation. That would settle once and for all who she belonged to, who had truly won her heart. He made a move to do just that when sanity rushed in and took control. It finally filtered into his brain that he couldn't treat her that way.

As much as it made his body ache with unspent desire, he reluctantly lifted his head, pulled her dress over her shoulder, and stepped away from her.

"It's not easy turning away from you, but I must," he said, sounding as breathless as he felt. "I hear voices. I don't want anyone to see us here."

"Neither do I," she said, arranging the neckline of her gown. "I don't know how or why I allowed things to go so far."

"Passion has a way of doing that."

She cleared her throat and admitted, "So I'm finding out."

He wanted her more than he could put into words, and whether or not she knew it yet, she was hungry for him, too. But not here. Not like this.

"I must go before I change my mind. I will leave by the back gate. That way no one will suspect we were out here together. If anyone sees you and asks why you were outside, tell them you felt faint and needed fresh air. No one will dispute that."

"How can they when it's true? I don't think I've ever felt so unsteady on my feet."

He kissed the side of her mouth and then turned to leave, but she said, "Wait."

He stopped and looked at her.

"When we were leaving Mrs. Vaughan's house and were on that overgrown stretch of road hidden from everyone, you didn't kiss me."

"That's right."

"Yet tonight you—you kiss me and touch me so intimately where there is great risk of being seen. Why?"

Harrison smiled. He liked that she was questioning his motives. That showed she was thinking about him and how he made her feel, even if she wasn't ready to admit it to him or herself.

"Though I'm seldom a gentleman, I do on a few occasions decide to be one. I wanted to let you know I can be a gentleman. I can, at times, follow the rules and do the right thing, but it is never as easy, enticing, or satisfying as doing what's forbidden."

He smiled before turning away and heading for the back gate.

Chapter 20

We cannot fight for love as men may do; we should
be wooed, and were not made to woo.
A Midsummer Night's Dream *2.1.241–42*

Angelina didn't know where he was. He was so confusing. Five nights had passed since she'd seen Lord Thornwick at any of the parties or balls.

Where was he?

Was she just missing him as she went from house to house each evening? Were they, as the poets wrote, two ships passing in the night? Or was he possibly deliberately avoiding her? But what was most confusing of all was why she should care. His kisses and caresses made her lose all rational thought. Whenever he kissed her, nothing else mattered. She didn't know how that could be, only that it was how she felt.

One afternoon he introduced her to a beautiful woman who had a heart for helping dogs; the next time she saw him he kissed her lips, her neck, and her breasts until she thought she would faint from all the glorious sensations. He'd made her feel things no proper young lady should ever feel. He'd asked her to admit to things she should have never thought. He'd caused her to let him kiss her and touch her in a way that should only be done by her husband—and now it was as if he'd disappeared from the face of the earth.

He was maddening.

Why should she care that he was missing? She should be happy if she never laid eyes on him again in her life, because he was ruining Captain Maxwell's home-coming. Angelina didn't want to think or care about the earl. She wanted Captain Maxwell to be the only gentleman on her mind.

Angelina had washed the paint from her hands in the kitchen before heading above stairs to change and put up her hair before Captain Maxwell arrived. She was eager to spend time with the captain. She wanted him to completely wipe all thoughts of Lord Thornwick from her mind.

By the time she made it to her room, Angelina realized she was weary. Late nights at balls and early mornings of painting were sapping her strength. Several times during the day she thought she might have to put her brushes away and rest, but she'd pressed on. Bishop Worsley had sent her a note saying that Mr. Eyston was most impressed with everything she'd sent. He'd also mentioned that he had an appointment with the Dowager Duchess of Drakestone. But he hadn't told her when that meeting would take place. His ending remark had been, "Keep painting!"

And so she had.

Her grandmother's maid had laid out a light-melon-colored carriage dress sprigged with a dark-orange thread and a matching ruffled pelisse. She started to un-lace her bodice and realized she heard a chewing noise coming from the other side of the room. Could it be what she was thinking? She walked around the foot of the bed and saw Mr. Pete chewing on one of her shoes.

"Mr. Pete!" she exclaimed, kneeling down to grab him. "What are you doing in here? And eating on my shoe as if it were a meaty bone. You naughty boy," she reprimanded, trying to pull the shoe from his mouth. He growled and held tighter to the soft leather, thinking she was playing with him.

"No. Stop. You must let go. Shoes are off limits. How did you get up here anyway?" He released the shoe and immediately scrambled to take it from her again. She threw it up on the bed, picked him up, and rubbed his head affectionately. Mr. Pete licked her chin and she laughed. "You are a sly little mischief maker. You are not supposed to be above the stairs. I must be more diligent about knowing where you are in the house. Perhaps Mrs. Bickmore can help me keep an eye on you."

At the sound of a knock she turned and saw her father leaning against the door jamb. His gaze had zeroed in on Mr. Pete, who barked a greeting to the master of the house.

"You aren't letting him sleep up here, are you?"

Her smile faded. Her throat tightened and so did her arms around Mr. Pete. He squirmed. "You know better, Papa. I found him just now when I came up to change."

Her father cut his eyes around to the wet and gnawed shoe lying on the bed and then back to her. His expression suggested he wasn't sure he believed her. "All right," he finally said. "Your grandmother is downstairs waiting for you. She said you were going for a ride in the park with Captain Maxwell."

"Yes, Papa."

He straightened his tall frame and asked, "Will you please tell me why you're going for a ride in the park with the officer and not Lord Thornwick when he is the one you are supposed to be secretly betrothed to?"

She bit down on her bottom lip as she rubbed Mr. Pete's back. "I don't know, other than Lord Thornwick has a mind of his own. I haven't seen him at any of the parties for several nights now. Have you?"

"Strange," he said and crossed his arms over his chest as his brow wrinkled. "Now that you say that, I realize I haven't seen him for a while, either. Odd for him to go missing in the middle of the Season. I think I'll ask around and see what I can find out about where he might be."

"There are so many parties, it could be that we are just missing him." She paused and then asked, "Will you let me know if you find out anything?"

"Of course. I think I'll do that this afternoon since you won't need me to chaperone you today. In the meantime," her father continued, "do I need to remind you that you shouldn't encourage Captain Maxwell or any other young man? I agreed to not having an engagement announced until the end of the Season but it's not fair for you to lead anyone into thinking you might be available for them to consider a match."

Her father had already reminded her. More than once. Angelina hugged Mr. Pete's warm body close to her chest, and he licked her chin again. "I know, Papa. I am careful not to encourage anyone about a possible future."

He gave her a pointed stare. "You do remember what will happen if we don't announce you'll be marrying the earl in a little more than three weeks, don't you?"

"Of course I do."

How could she forget? She was working hard to make enough money to give to her father so they would both be free of those debts or at the very least pay them down enough that the lenders would wait for the rest. She had already delivered two new paintings to Bishop Worsley this week. What she painted was small, but the work was so tedious it took a lot of time.

Half an hour later Angelina sat under a light-gray sky on the padded bench beside Captain Nicholas Maxwell. She folded her gloved hands in her lap and smiled contentedly. It was just the way she had imagined it would be. Well, except for the patch covering his eye. That was on his right, and he had intentionally made sure she was seated on his left. She settled into the seat, opened her ruffled parasol, and prepared to enjoy the afternoon ride to Hyde Park with the most dashing army officer in the world.

She couldn't count the times over the past year that she'd dreamed this day would happen. It seemed as if she'd always imagined herself alone with Captain Maxwell and free to explore feelings of happiness, excitement, and love. But now she knew there were other feelings to wish for as well. Divine feelings too joyous to put into words. Harrison had awakened her to such delicious delights she blushed at times just thinking about them, about the way he made her feel, the places she'd wanted him to touch her. And how she'd never even thought about him looking at her body, her breast, until he asked her if he could. Not only had she not felt any shame, she had wanted him to look at her. Look at her and find favor with her.

So now she had all those feelings, all that wanting, that eagerness to look forward to with the man of her dreams. The man she loved. Yes, it was going to be a good day even if there wasn't a warm ray of sunshine in the sky.

Captain Maxwell turned to her, smiled, and said, "You've made me a very happy man today, Miss Rule."

"Then that makes me glad, too, but tell me. What did I do to get such a glowing report?"

"Allowing me to take you for a ride in the park so everyone will see us together."

He reached under the seat, pulled out a plaid blanket, and laid it over her lap. He shyly placed his gloved hand over hers and squeezed for the briefest of moments before letting her go and releasing the brake. She'd expected a thrill, a tightening of her stomach or something, but she supposed the touch was too brief to give her the sensations.

Captain Maxwell picked up the ribbons and made three quick clicks against the horse's rump. The carriage took off with a jolt, a jangle of harness, and the clopping of hooves on hardpacked ground.

They rode in silence all the way to Hyde Park. At the entrance, he maneuvered the horses onto the narrow lane behind a shiny black barouche. The park was busy with carriage, horse, and pedestrian traffic as was expected for afternoons during the Season. Several small groups of people stood around talking, children and dogs played, and many couples strolled side by side. A few people had spread blankets and were enjoying refreshments as they chatted.

Numerous vendors had displayed their wares throughout the park. Some sold roasted nuts, sweet cakes, and meat pies. Others had various forms of entertainment for the parkgoers to enjoy, which were received with varying degrees of interest. A puppet show had a large crowd of more than twenty-five while a man playing a lyre had only one couple who'd stopped to listen.

"Would you like to park and walk or would you prefer a leisurely ride?" the captain asked.

"Why don't we ride for a little while longer and see if we can find an area that isn't so crowded."

"That sounds good to me," he agreed.

They talked about the parties in the evenings, the people they met and talked to, but there was more silence between them than conversation as they rode by the Serpentine and later down Rotten Row. When they passed other carriages, sometimes they would wave or nod. Angelina asked him more about India, Belgium, and other places he'd traveled, listening to every word. She had never traveled outside England and loved hearing what lay beyond the sea.

She had no idea what was going through Captain Maxwell's mind as they talked, but as for herself, she kept waiting to feel an exhilarating sense of awareness of him that hadn't yet happened. She couldn't understand why. He was a handsome man, so dashing in his red coat with its gold braid, buttons, and epaulets. She felt quite proud to be sitting beside a distinguished soldier with such an impressive career. It was easy to be comfortable, content, and even happy to be with him as they'd talked, but . . .

Where were the butterflies? The breathless, desirous, and expectant sensations she always experienced whenever Lord Thornwick was near? Perhaps it was that the captain wasn't focusing on her. He was busy with the horses, watching the traffic, making sure they didn't get too close to another carriage or the people walking in the park. Yes, that had to be the problem. He was distracted by his duty as the driver of the carriage.

"Why don't we stop over by those trees?" she said suddenly. "There don't seem to be many people in that area."

"That might be because it looks boggy," he said with

a smile. "It's low and there's been a lot of rain the past few days. We can try it."

"All right, let's go over and see if that's why everyone is avoiding the area."

Captain Maxwell guided the horses over to a stand of trees and set the brake. He helped her down and reached back for the blanket and basket he'd brought.

"You stay here. I don't want you getting your shoes muddy. I'll see if I can find a dry place to sit."

Angelina watched Captain Maxwell walk away. He was tall, his back straight and shoulders high. He wanted to find a good dry place for them to sit and not allow her to go traipsing around on soggy ground with him. He did the things she would expect a fine gentleman to do, but something was missing between them.

Within a minute or two, he returned. "I found a place. Stay right behind me and step in my footprints."

She obeyed and followed the captain's tracks as he instructed. She found herself wondering what Lord Thornwick would do in the same circumstance. A warm feeling settled over her and she smiled. She knew exactly what he would do. That man would defy the rules of convention, lifting her up in his strong arms and carrying her over to the blanket to set her down so the soles of her shoes would never touch the muddy ground.

Soon they were settled on the blanket. Captain Maxwell pulled from the basket two flasks and a linen cloth that held bread and cheese. From the first flask, he poured her a cup of punch; then he poured from the other into his.

"What are you drinking?" she asked after tasting the punch.

He looked down into his cup. "Brandy. It helps dull the pain." He took another drink.

Angelina's heart constricted. He was still in pain. How could she help him? "When you first returned, I asked if the pain was gone and you said it was."

"The real pain is gone, but believe me there is still a lot of imaginary pain."

She squeezed the cup in one hand and the handle of her parasol in the other. She'd heard that when a person lost a leg or an arm there was still pain even though that limb was gone from the body. Was that what he was referring to, or was there a deeper, darker, emotional pain that wouldn't ever heal?

"I'm not sure what you mean," she answered softly, hoping he would open up and share more with her.

He laughed with no merriment. "Nothing, forget I said that."

He'd meant something by his comment. She leaned toward him. "Perhaps it would help if you talked about what happened. I'm a good listener."

He gave her a look that chilled her. "No. It wouldn't help."

There was a whisper of bitterness in his voice. She supposed she could understand that. She'd never press him to talk about something so personal. She let it drop.

"Besides," he said, "I just want to sit here, enjoy my drink, and look at you."

"That would be boring for me, sir," she said trying to lighten the tone of the conversation. "Why don't you tell me about your family?"

"Three brothers. All married with children and all still in the army. No sisters."

"That certainly covered a lot of ground with a very few words. Do you get to see any of them when you're not on assignment?"

"Not often."

"Parents?"

"They've been gone a long time."

"I'm sorry," she said.

He shrugged. "My aunt seems to enjoy my visits. That's why I stay with her when I'm in London. Now that I've answered twenty questions for you, I have one for you."

"That was three questions, not twenty," she argued. "And very short answers from you, I might add."

"It felt like twenty." He added more brandy to his cup and stretched out his legs. "Other than Lord Thornwick, how many other serious competitors do I have vying for your hand, Miss Rule?"

That surprised her and for a moment she wondered if he knew about the arrangement between her father and the Prince, or the one between herself and Lord Thornwick. But no, there was no way he could possibly know any of that. Her father's debtors had agreed to keep his dire financial problems a secret, too. She was sure they wouldn't do anything to prevent the prospects of the Prince paying in full.

She hesitated, thinking to find a way to avoid answering, but in the end she simply said, "None that I know of."

"Good." He drank from his cup again and watched her over the rim. "I'm sure the reason there aren't more is because most gentlemen would not want to compete with an earl for a lady's hand."

"An earl and a captain," she reminded him.

His expression turned serious. "I want you to know that I will be able to take care of you, Miss Rule."

"I—no one would ever doubt your capabilities, Captain."

"I'm not an earl, but you will never go lacking for anything you might want."

"I'm sure," she hurried to say.

"I've been in the King's service for almost twenty years," he continued. "During that time I've lived with my aunt when I wasn't away with my regiment. I've saved quite a bit of money. Enough for us to live comfortably for the rest of my life if I'm frugal."

Angelina felt his desperation but she didn't know what to say. Even though she was sure she loved him, she suddenly realized she was not ready to commit to marrying Captain Maxwell. She hoped he wasn't about to ask her.

"That's admirable."

"I know it's not the right time yet. We still need to get to know each other better, but I want you to know that I have designs on no other lady but you."

Then kiss me, she thought. *Sweep me up in your arms, hold me tight, and show me how much you want me*. She wanted to feel his desire for her in his touch, his kiss, and his embrace. She wanted to feel his body tremble with need to hold her.

They were in a fairly secluded area of the park. She saw no one nearby. It was the perfect time for him to reach over and place his lips on hers. Less than three feet separated them. Didn't he know she wanted to experience his passion for her? Didn't he know she wanted to be kissed and kissed and kissed until she was dizzy with flaming-hot desire for him?

But instead of doing all the things she was dreaming of, wanting from him, he threw his empty cup into the basket and said, "We'd better go. I see rain in the distance."

Angelina felt bereft, and stunned that he wasn't going to take the opportunity to show her just what kind of designs he had on her. She emptied her cup into the dry grass and sighed. She was sure he desired her. Maybe he was too much of a gentleman. Maybe he just didn't know how to show it—unlike Lord Thornwick.

He had left her with no doubts about how desperately he wanted her.

Chapter 21

All is not well . . . Foul deeds will rise.
Hamlet *1.2.255–56 and 257.8*

The sun had come up and the lamps had been extinguished. The early-morning sky was a hazy gray. Harrison had sat at the card table and watched the sun rise above the horizon from the window on the far side of the room. He'd seen a few people pass by the tavern since dawn and knew there was a blustery wind outside that was promising rain. Perhaps it was just as well that he and Bray hadn't planned to start their journey home until tomorrow.

The evening had been like old times with Bray and Adam, staying up all night drinking, playing cards, and reliving in great and exaggerated details the escapades of their younger years. But none of them had drunk to the excesses they used to. Harrison was feeling quite mellow and ready for a few hours in bed. He suspected his friends were feeling the same way, too. Not that either of them would ever admit it to him.

When he and Bray had visited Adam a year ago, he

wouldn't go with them to the local pub for a tankard of ale. But at the time, it had only been three months since he'd lost his wife and child.

Harrison had been touring the world when it happened, but Bray had told him that Adam's wife had suffered for three days trying to bear his child. Harrison and Bray hadn't mentioned her or the baby last year, and not this trip, either. How could a man ever talk about what Adam had gone through? Harrison couldn't begin to imagine what it must have been like for Adam to stand by hour after agonizing hour and watch his wife die without giving birth. He must have been wild with desperation to help her. Harrison had never had a reason to feel that helpless, and he hoped to God he never did.

They assumed Adam knew they weren't there to intrude on his grief or his life. He would understand they just wanted to check on him once again to see how he was doing. Harrison was glad they'd made the three-day journey, glad to have found Adam in better spirits. Last year neither he nor Bray would have been surprised to hear that Adam had decided to end his life. He'd probably been closer to it more times than Harrison wanted to know, but now he was thinking that possibility had finally passed for his friend.

Harrison's thoughts turned to Angelina as was so often the case. He remembered how she looked the afternoon he kissed her in the garden: fresh and innocent. She was the very essence of goodness. Her long flowing hair had been tangled about her shoulders by the wind, and that big-brimmed hat made her all the more fetching. Her eyes were sparkling and her cheeks were flushed from the sun—and he hoped from his sudden appearance, too.

When he'd kissed her, touched her, and tasted her at

Lord Thistlebury's house, she'd looked more like the beautiful, captivating Greek goddess he'd seen the first night they met. She wore a flutteringly thin gown and a crown of pearls in her upswept hair. Angelina had a sensual way about her that had him thinking about her all hours of the day and night. And it didn't matter if she looked like a pure young lady ready for her first kiss or the invitingly sensuous young lady wanting a gentleman to show her pleasure, Harrison wanted her.

But winning her wasn't easy. She had a fierce sense of loyalty to Captain Maxwell, but he didn't think it was love.

He remembered the taste of her warm mouth, the feel of her satiny-smooth skin beneath his fingers, and the way her soft body responded to his when he pressed her against his hardness. At that moment she was as eager for him as he was for her. But he also knew she was holding on to the thought that she'd given her heart to Captain Maxwell. Harrison had no doubt he could make her want him, but could he make her love him?

Already he'd been gone five days and it would be at least three more before he made it back to London. He wondered if Maxwell had kissed her yet. Harrison didn't want him to kiss her, but he needed to. And the captain was a fool if he hadn't.

"You win, I'm out," Bray said to the fourth man at the table, an older gentleman, and the only one who'd played the entire night with them and had won as much as he had lost. Bray then looked at his friends and said, "And I'm ready to go find a bed anytime you two are."

Harrison and Adam looked at Bray and grinned. "We've been ready for half an hour. We were waiting for you to get enough."

"Well, let's get our coats and go get our horses," Bray said. "We have a fifteen-minute ride ahead of us."

"It's more like half an hour to my house," Adam corrected.

"Damnation," Harrison remarked. "Remind me why we rode so far to play a few hands of cards and drink a couple of tankards of ale?"

"Yes, why did we?" Bray added.

"Because it's the nearest tavern to my house and you two were insisting we had to have a night away from the cottage."

"You must move closer to the village," Bray said, and clapped Adam on the back as they walked outside the tavern.

"Better yet," Harrison said, "Why not come back to London with us?"

"That is a better idea, Adam," Bray insisted. "Do it."

"I have things here that need my attention," Adam said in a tone that let them know arguing would do no good.

A cold wind whipped against the side of Harrison's face as they stepped out of the tavern. They stood near the door pulling on their gloves and wrapping their scarves tighter about their necks. They were getting ready for the long walk to where they'd stabled their horses when they heard a man yell, the crack of a whip, and the pained yelp of a dog that sent blood curdling through Harrison's veins.

The three of them looked at one another and then in the direction of the sounds. On the opposite side of the wide street stood a beefy shopkeeper holding a whip in his hand. A thin blond dog had been tied to a hitching post. Anger rose fast and furious inside Harrison. He was choking himself with the rope that held him, trying to get away from the man. The crack of the whip sounded again. Another yelp rent the air. Harrison shivered as he, Adam, and Bray rushed toward the animal.

The dog's dirty white coat had two strips of blood about six inches long running across his back and shoulders and before they could get there, the man gave him another lash. Harrison thought of Angelina and how she tried to save dogs who'd been mistreated and neglected; he wanted to rip the whip from the man's hands.

The shopkeeper was a large man. He wore a white apron over his wide girth. His shirtsleeves were rolled up to his elbows even though it was near freezing outside. Harrison saw that the man's shop was a bakery, and there was no doubt the man enjoyed what he produced.

He wasn't the kind of fellow Harrison wanted to tangle with but for beating the dog, he'd make an exception and do it anyway.

Adam was the first to speak as they approached the shop. "What's the matter, mister?"

"This is the third day this whelp has been around stealing meat pies, trash, or anything else he can find around here," he said. "I aim to see he doesn't come back to my shop."

Harrison looked at the shelving the man had put out to hold his baked goods. The dog was tall and thin, but still a puppy, he'd guess. Harrison didn't know much about dogs but he looked to be at least part Pyrenees. He could easily jump up, put his front paws on the highest shelf, and help himself to a pie.

"Look at him," Harrison said. "The dog is starving. You can't blame him for taking the food. He doesn't know it's wrong."

"He will when I get through with him," the shopkeeper said, winding up the whip for another go at the dog.

"Why don't you just move your shelves up so he can't reach them?" Bray offered.

The man growled. "Get away from here, you trouble-makers. I don't need you three city knockers telling me what to do, and I'll not be going to extra trouble rebuilding my shelving just so a dog can't reach them."

"I can't let you strike the dog again," Harrison said.

"Nor can I," Adam said, kneeling down beside the dog to have a look at him.

"I won't, either," Bray added.

The baker threw his shoulders back defiantly, puffing out his large chest. "Who do you dandies think you are to come to my shop and tell me what I can and can't do?"

"Name's Adam Greyhawke."

"Bray Drakestone."

"I'm Harrison Thornwick and we're all telling you, if you try to strike that dog again you'll have be ready to pull all three of us off you."

"That I can do and be happy while doing it," the man said and Harrison saw his grip tighten on the handle of the whip. "But step aside. I'm going to finish with this mongrel first."

The man raised the whip and threw it toward the dog again. Harrison was the closest. He reached out, caught the end of the whip in his hand, and jerked. Even through his gloves he felt the sting of the leather strip. The shop-keeper was strong, but so was Harrison. He held tightly to the whip and managed to wind it around his arm a couple of times.

"Let go," the beefy man bellowed with a snarl. "You have no reason to meddle in my affairs." He took a couple of steps toward Harrison.

"That's right. Keep walking toward me," Harrison said in a deadly quiet voice as the man stopped danger-ously close to him. "You might be able to take one of us, and maybe even the second, but there is no way you will make it through the three of us. Now, if you are ready, I'll be the first."

Bray stepped up beside Harrison. "I never liked being second to anyone. I'll take him first. Besides, I can have him on the ground with a bloody nose before you get that whip off your arm."

"If anybody is going to be first, it will be me," Adam said, rising from where he'd been trying to untie the rope from the dog's neck.

Suddenly the shopkeeper was looking at a solid wall of men as tall as he was but younger and a whole lot more muscular. He seemed to consider trying to fight them all, then dropped the whip handle and started backing away.

"All right, take the dog if you want it and get out of here. Just don't let me catch it back around my store."

"Oh, we will take the dog," Harrison said as the three of them advanced on him. "But that's not all we're going to take." He took the whip off his arm and started curling up its length.

"Wh–what are you going to do?" the shopkeeper asked, his eyes darting quickly from Harrison to Adam to Bray.

"I was thinking maybe I'd let you see what this whip feels like across your back," Harrison answered. "What do you think, Adam?"

"You do that. I'd rather have a go at him with my fists." Adam swung his cloak off his shoulders and let it fall to the ground. "I haven't had a good fight in a long time, and I'm itching to have a go at this bugger. You can use the whip when I'm finished with him."

"What's this?" Bray complained. "After you two get through with him, what will be left for me other than a bloody carcass?"

"You're right, Bray." Harrison continued to advance on the man, backing him all the way up to the door of his shop. "I'd hate to see my friends get their clothes dirty. I'll tell you what. For now, we're going to forget this happened."

The shopkeeper gave a cautious smile.

"But while we take the dog over to that tavern and see to his cuts, we're going to watch you rebuild your shelving higher so it won't entice other dogs or animals to jump up for your bread and pies."

"I'll do no such thing. I said take the dog. That's enough."

"Suit yourself," Adam said walking toward him, too, and rolling up his sleeves as he went.

"Wait, wait!" the baker said, holding up his hands to ward off Adam's attack. "All right, I'll rework the shelving if that's what you want. Just stay away from me and keep that dog away from here, too."

Harrison picked up two meat pies from the man's stash of baked goods. "These are for the lashes you gave the dog. Now get inside and get a hammer and some nails and start working on that shelving before my good humor fades."

The man turned and stumbled into his shop.

Bray removed the knife from around his belt and cut the rope while Adam put the pies in front of the dog. He was wary but sniffed the food and finally started eating.

"I'll take the dog home with me," Harrison said, knowing Angelina would take one look and fall in love. She would tend his wounds and have him fattened in no time. "I know someone who will take good care of him."

"No," Adam said. "The dog stays with me."

Harrison started to object, but something in Adam's tone told him there would be no arguing about this. It was then that Harrison realized that Adam needed to rescue the dog as much as Harrison did. Adam hadn't been able to save his wife and child, but he could save a dog.

Adam needed the dog.

And Angelina?

Harrison smiled. The only thing she needed was him. She had enough dogs.

Chapter 22

Give me that man that is not passion's slave, and
I will wear him in my heart's core, ay, in my heart of heart,
as I do thee.
Hamlet 3.3.72–75

The music at the Great Hall seemed exceptionally loud to Angelina, and the crowd more boisterous than usual. She had danced with several gentlemen, including Captain Maxwell. She had talked with some of her friends from her reading and sewing groups, and had her fill of punch and champagne. But when all was said and done, she'd spent most of the evening watching the entrance to the ballroom, not wanting to miss Lord Thornwick should he come in and grace the ton's nightly gala with his presence.

"Well, I see you aren't sick after all," Helen Ramsey said, walking up to Angelina where she stood near one of the huge fluted columns.

"Did you think I'd been ill?"

"I thought you must be. You missed our reading society and sewing circle again this week. Actually, I think you've missed the last two or three weeks."

If anyone was going to be aware of Angelina's

absence from the group since the Season started, it would be Helen. She took pride in letting nothing pass her notice.

"It's really been busy since the Season started," she told the redhead staring at her with bright-green eyes.

"Busy doing what?" she argued. "I haven't even seen you at any of the afternoon card or tea parties. You can't be attending any more parties than the rest of us. And everyone but you made it to both events."

"Good," Angelina said, refusing to let Helen goad her into saying something she didn't want to say. "I'm glad everyone made it. There's always a lively discussion when the group is large."

"I don't know why anyone wants to be a member if you're not going to——oh, look. There's that poor Captain Maxwell dancing with Lady Eleanor. What a shame it is. He was so handsome and such a divine catch before he was disfigured like that."

"I think he's still handsome, Helen," Angelina said, instinctively coming to the captain's defense.

The young lady raised one eyebrow. "Are we talking about the same gentleman? You know he isn't. But perhaps if he wore a bigger patch to cover more of the scarring that would help."

Anger stiffened Angelina. "He needs to do no such thing. Time will fade the scarring so that's its hardly noticeable."

Helen rolled her eyes. "Look upon him however you wish, Angelina. But for his sake, I hope he doesn't think he can win Lady Eleanor's hand. The old duke will never let that happen."

"Why would you say that?" Angelina asked tightly, her anger rising at Helen's heartless words.

"Why wouldn't I? It's true. I know you have danced with him. Most of us have danced with him once or twice and we will continue to do so. We all feel sorry about what's happened to him."

"He is a courageous soldier, Helen. He doesn't need your pity or anyone else's."

"Well, he has it, so there," she said pointedly. "I wonder if the duke knows the captain is dancing with his daughter. Don't look so stricken, Angelina, I told you, we all feel sorry for him. Who wouldn't, but I mean, we certainly don't want to marry him."

Outraged by Helen's words, Angelina could only whisper, "You've talked about this with other ladies?"

"Of course. If you had bothered yourself to attend the meetings recently you would know what all the other ladies are saying. He's been the topic of conversation since he returned. I suppose if a lady had no other prospects of a good match she might consider marriage with him, but I mean can you imagine looking at him every day?"

"Yes, Helen, I can imagine doing exactly that," Angelina said, hoping she sounded as offended as she felt. "Captain Maxwell's face doesn't look horrible at all to me, and furthermore——"

"Wait." Helen held up her hand. "Before you reprimand me again, I know I should feel ashamed of myself for feeling the way I do about the captain. And I suppose I am ashamed. A little anyway. But I mean, wouldn't his children be frightened of him?"

Angelina gasped. "I'm going to stop this conversation with you right now before I do something I'll regret, like pull every hair from your head!"

Helen's green eyes rounded in fright. "What's wrong with you?"

"You! I don't want to listen to any more of your nonsense about Captain Maxwell and his appearance. What you are saying is madness. In fact, I'm going to go wait for the captain right now and as soon as he is off the dance floor with Lady Eleanor, I hope he will ask me for another dance. If he does, I shall dance with him. Excuse me." Angelina turned to walk off but swung back to Helen again. "And for your further information, Helen, I have already been for a ride in the park with him and I will enjoy another ride with him very soon. You can feel free to tell everyone you know. Though you probably would have anyway as you are the biggest gossip in our group."

"I am not. How dare you! I do not gossip!"

Angelina felt like stomping off but managed to walk away calmly, thinking she might never go back to the sewing circle or the reading society again. Foolish young girls, all of them. She didn't care what Helen said, Angelina refused to believe the only reason young ladies were dancing with Captain Maxwell was because they felt sorry for him. He was a kind gentleman of great integrity and courage; any lady should be honored to have him for a husband. Helen didn't know that because she was only interested in Helen.

Angelina would be happy to marry him should he ask her if—if only she could stop thinking about Lord Thornwick. That man was a distraction she didn't need. If she could stop thinking about his kisses and the way he made her feel when he looked at her, when he touched her. At times she wished the captain would be more forceful, more demanding, and in charge. More like Lord Thornwick. Then there were other times that she was glad he was such a gentleman and so respectful of her.

She knew what she needed. She just didn't know how to accomplish it. Captain Maxwell needed to kiss her. Yes, that would settle all her fears, she thought as she stopped near the dance floor. Surely if the captain kissed her she would feel the same way as when the earl kissed her. No, she would feel better, deeper, and even more glorious sensations than when the earl kissed her.

But the captain was a gentleman and Lord Thornwick couldn't be bothered with things like what was proper and what was not. If he wanted to do something he did, rules be damned. How could she let Captain Maxwell know she wanted him to kiss her? At the present, she didn't know. But she would invite him over and would find a way for him to kiss her even if she had to use some of Lord Thornwick's underhanded methods to do it.

"Miss Rule."

Angelina turned to see who had called her name and beheld the striking Dowager Duchess of Drakestone walking toward her.

"Your Grace," Angelina said and curtsied.

"I've been meaning to write you a note and thank you for having Bishop Worsley deliver some of your artist friend's work to me."

"No thank-you was necessary," Angelina said, her heart suddenly racing. "I'm glad to hear Bishop Worsley was able to help you?"

"So you didn't know he'd been to see me?" she questioned.

"I knew he had an appointment with you but I didn't know when or that he'd already seen you. I haven't heard from him in several days."

"Oh," the duchess said, seeming confused by her answer. She opened the fan she was holding and Angelina recognized the garden scene as one of her own.

"That's lovely."

"Yes, I'm especially fond of ones like this one that have the sparkle and shimmer on them. It looks like dew glistening on the flower petals, does it not?"

"Yes, it does," Angelina responded, flattered that the

duchess appreciated the care she took to make each flower look real.

"Tell me, do you know Miss Paulette Savill well?"

Angelina swallowed uncomfortably. She prayed the look in her eyes was not giving her away. She didn't know if it was a simple case of guilty conscience or if the duchess truly had a hunch that Angelina was the artist.

"Not too well," she fibbed with a huge attack of remorse for being untruthful, but she felt she had to do it. She had to stop the duchess from asking more questions she couldn't possibly answer. "I'm told she's very private about her life and her work and I respect that. I hope you found more than one fan that you liked."

Her Grace snapped the fan shut and said, "Oh, I found favor with them all, Miss Rule. I purchased everything the bishop brought with him and I asked him to bring more as soon as he could. They'll make wonderful little gifts when I attend house parties, don't you think?"

Angelina nodded and hoped she kept the shock from registering in her expression and her eyes, but she couldn't stop her sudden intake of breath. Why hadn't Bishop Worsley told her the duchess had bought all the fans and wanted more? And how much money did he get for the fans? Fearful excitement tore inside her.

"I told him I'd like Miss Savill to paint some fans for me with scenes I'd like to see. Perhaps a white peacock on a black fan. He was going to ask her. Do you think she'd do that for me?"

More painting?

Angelina didn't even want to think about that but knew she had to. The more she could paint, the more money she could make. She looked down at her hands. For a moment, she felt as if the duchess could look

straight through Angelina's gloves and see paint stains
on her fingers and know she was the artist.

"I—You—Bishop Worsley would be the best one to
answer that for you."

"Of course. You're right." The duchess looked at her
for a few moments longer than necessary before smiling and then walking away.

Angelina felt frozen to the floor. Could the duchess
somehow know she was Paulette Suvill? What would
Angelina do if she did? Her grandmother would be dev-
astated. Her father would go to prison. And Angelina
would be banned from Society for life. Heavens to
mercy! But she couldn't dwell on any of that right now.
She had to find her grandmother.

Forgetting about dancing with the captain, Angelina
whirled from the direction of the dance floor and went
in search of Lady Railbridge. They had to find out why
Bishop Worsley hadn't sent them word that the duchess
had purchased all her fans.

Another thought struck her as she searched the crowd
for her grandmother. Since the duchess had bought all
the fans—how much money would that be? Angelina
had no idea what price the Bishop had put on them. And
what was happening with the miniatures Mr. Eyston
had? She wondered if the bishop had finally made an
arrangement with Mr. Eyston. And if so, what was he
paying for the mourning and snuffboxes, and the other
paintings she'd had delivered?

After a frantic search of the ballroom, Angelina
found her grandmother sitting in the retiring room with
a small group of ladies. After speaking to everyone, Angelina managed to pull Lady Railbridge aside and tell
her what the duchess had said.

"Don't look so anguished, dear," Granna said and
patted her cheek affectionately.

Realizing her grandmother wasn't taking this as seriously as she was, Angelina said, "I simply don't understand why we haven't heard from him that he had sold every fan to the Duchess of Drakestone." Angelina didn't add that she also had a feeling the duchess suspected her of being the painter. That would only distress her grandmother, and Angelina was worried enough for the both of them.

"He is a busy gentleman, I'm sure. He can't come rushing over or sit down to write to us with every bit of news."

"Do you suppose Bishop Worsley has already completed the sale of the other things to Mr. Eyston as well?"

"I have no idea what he's been able to accomplish," her grandmother said, pulling her shawl tighter about her slim shoulders. "He told us it would take time."

"Her Grace didn't say when she purchased them, but it's been over a week since he told us he had an appointment to see her."

"And she may have just seen them today." Her grandmother's eyes narrowed. "What is this? It's not like you to borrow trouble this way. It's usually your motto to wait until you have something to worry about before you start wringing your hands."

Angelina was getting no help from her grandmother. She took in a deep breath. "Is that what I'm doing? Wringing my hands?"

"You are close to it. You must not fret about this. It could be that she just purchased them before coming to the party tonight. We have no idea. Replace that expression of worry with a smile, young lady. You must remember Bishop Worsley has things to take care of besides just your paintings. If we don't hear from him soon, I'll send a note to him and ask that he visit us. Now, does that make you feel better?"

Angelina smiled. "Thank you, Granna. I'm sure you're right. I will trust that he is working on my behalf and be done with it."

"That's my dear."

Her grandmother was right. She couldn't allow herself to worry about the bishop. Her grandmother trusted him completely. Angelina had to do that, too. For a little longer anyway.

The end of the Season was fast approaching.

Chapter 23

I'll smother thee with kisses.
Venus and Adonis *18*

Angelina sat up straight, took off her spectacles, and rolled her shoulders several times as she flexed her fingers. She sat in her painting room off the kitchen hunched over a fan. She'd received word from Bishop Worsley yesterday morning that the duchess wanted a black silk fan painted with nothing but a white peacock with his tail feathers open. That was no surprise to Angelina, but she had waited to start it until she'd heard from Worsley. The duchess probably had no idea how tedious it was to paint that tail. It had taken her most of the day.

He'd also written that he was still in negotiations with Mr. Eyston and would call on her and Lady Railbridge in the next few days. Angelina found that she was constantly either tamping down her excitement over actually selling her fans or worrying about whether she could make enough money to help her father before it was too late. If Bishop Worsley didn't come over soon, she would be very close to doing what her grandmother had accused her of—wringing her hands.

It had rained for three days so she hadn't been able to go out into the garden to paint, which made the laborious job a little more enjoyable. She loved feeling the fresh air on her face and hearing the sounds of nature when she was outside: birds chirping, bees buzzing by, and her dogs barking at passing carriages.

She'd chosen this room at the back of the house as her painting space for several reasons. It was well away from the drawing room where her father and grandmother often spent time. She loved them but their chatter could be a nuisance when she was concentrating on small details. There was a large window, which was a must. The hazy yellow glow of a lamp could never take the place of daylight when painting. It was where Rascal and Mr. Pete slept at night, and Sam when it was too cold for him to be outside where he preferred. Since the room was considered Angelina's and her pets' domain, not even Mrs. Bickmore ventured into it very often.

There was little furniture in the room: the desk and chair where she worked, an old settee that needed to be reupholstered, and a table to hold a teapot and cup. She looked over at the window. The floral-printed draperies were held back by dark-pink ribbons. In the sill sat the pot of violets Lord Thornwick had brought her. She smiled every time she looked at it. The brown leaves and wilted blooms had fallen off and now there were signs of new growth.

There was no clock in the room but Angelina assumed it was a little past midafternoon. She had worked since early morning. Her eyes were dry and her shoulders achy, but she had to keep painting. Every piece she could sell would bring her father that much closer to being free of his debt. And that would give her the freedom to choose her own husband.

Sam, Rascal, and Mr. Pete roused from their napping and started barking. "Stay," she said quickly before they could take off running toward the front of the house. Mr. Pete paid her no mind and raced out the door with his nails clicking on the hardwood floors as he went. "Quiet, Sam, Rascal, quiet."

The dogs looked at her, squirming and making dog noises as if to tell her there was something going on in another part of the house they needed to investigate along with Mr. Pete. "Sit," she said, and the dogs obeyed but continued to grumble. "It doesn't matter what you hear, the door, another dog, or the wind. You are staying put. If someone is at the door, Mrs. Bickmore will handle it, not you. And don't worry about Mr. Pete. He's still a puppy. It's my fault I haven't worked harder to train him, but I will as soon as I don't have to paint every day," she said, doing a little grumbling of her own.

The dogs eventually lay back down near the fireplace. Angelina replaced her spectacles on the bridge of her nose and picked up the lid and her brush. A garden scene was one of the easiest things for her to paint, but she would love to know if she needed to paint more or if scenes of the park were more popular—or her favorite, which was a handsome gentleman kissing the hand of a beautiful young lady.

"Good afternoon, Angelina."

Angelina was so deep in thought that when she heard Lord Thornwick's voice, it startled her. Rascal and Sam jumped up and barked. She rose and settled the dogs again before turning her attention to the handsome earl. He looked so dashing dressed in his dark trousers, buff-colored waistcoat, and camel-colored coat, but what melted her heart was seeing him holding Mr. Pete in his arms. She felt a sudden urge to rush into Lord Thornwick's arms and welcome him with a kiss.

Instead, she drew her eyebrows together in irritation at the thought of being so happy to see him.

She said to the rogue, "I'm sure I told Mrs. Bickmore that she must always announce you."

The corner of one side of his mouth lifted with a smile. "It didn't do any good."

"Obviously."

"Apparently this puppy is not free to roam in the house unattended," he said, rubbing his open palm down Mr. Pete's spine.

"None of the dogs are."

"Mrs. Bickmore was trying to chase him. She was only too happy for me to catch him for her and bring him to you." He put Mr. Pete down and then patted Sam and Rascal, who'd both come over to sniff him and say hello.

"I'm sure," Angelina mumbled and looked down at her paint-stained apron and the old, simple gray day dress she wore beneath. Part of her hair was tied back with a black scarf and the rest of it she quickly brushed away from her face, knowing there was nothing else she could do to make herself more presentable.

Suddenly frustrated, she said, "Didn't you stop to think that it might not be convenient for you to drop by my house unannounced?"

"I can't say it crossed my mind."

"Do you ever plan to let me know in advance when you are going to come for a visit?" she said, feeling more than a little annoyed that he seemed to enjoy catching her with paint all over her hands and her apron while he looked absolutely splendid.

"I just returned to London and you were the first

person I wanted to see." He moved in closer to her. "I missed you."

"I find it difficult to believe that's true."

His gaze stayed on her face. "It is. And it matters not to me if you have paint on your hands or your apron." He smiled. "I like looking at you. Like now. It's the first time I've seen you with spectacles on."

"Oh," she whispered and quickly removed them and laid them on her worktable.

"You don't have to take them off for me. I rather like them. I think they make you look scholarly."

"Nonsense," she huffed, trying to wipe a smear of white paint off her hand. It wouldn't budge so she gave up.

He looked down at the fan. "Painting again. A white peacock. It's lovely."

"Thank you," she said, looking around for her dome to cover it. Finding it on the floor by her chair, she placed it over the fan and then said, "It's all finished but the drying." She looked up at him and had to admit to herself that she was glad to see him—but he didn't need to know that. "Now, tell me why you are here."

"I told you." His gaze fluttered up and down her face. "I wanted to see you."

That's all? He wanted to see her. Why did comments like that from him always make her stomach feel like it was a sanctuary for butterflies?

Her heart started pounding in her chest and she started remembering how intimate their kisses were the last time she'd seen him. Forcing those thoughts away, she said, "Where have you been?"

"The Duke of Drakestone and I went to visit a friend up north, and on the way back I stopped by Thornwick to check on the rebuilding of the house."

"I didn't know if you were gone or if I was just missing you at the parties."

A curious sparkle lit his eyes. "Would you have liked for me to tell you my plans?"

"What? No. No, I certainly would not," she said, feeling a little flustered. "It matters not to me where you go or when."

"Are you sure about that?"

"Positive."

"You do a lot of painting," he said.

"I enjoy it." *Or I used to before it became work*, she thought.

"You know most of the portraits in Thornwick were destroyed in the fire, but some of them were only damaged. Perhaps you can help me find someone who would be willing to take them and copy them to a new canvas. I mean, I know nothing about painting and you could look at an artist's work and let me know if you think the person would be capable of doing a good job for me."

"I—I suppose I would be willing to help you find someone who could repaint or repair the portraits for you."

"Thank you," he said softly. "I appreciate that."

Lord Thornwick reached down and picked up one of her hands and looked at it as he said, "The Maltese is missing from the pack."

His hand was warm, strong, and clean. Hers was small and streaked with paint. "She's with Granna."

"It's Thursday. Is your grandmother visiting her friend this afternoon?"

He remembered that I mentioned that.

Her breaths quickened. "Yes," she said and looked down at her hand in his.

He lifted her hand to his mouth, placed his lips on the heel of her palm, and licked across a small swath of green paint. With hooded eyes he looked at her and asked, "And where is your father?"

Angelina's heart started pounding so loudly she was sure he could hear it. "I don't know."

He gently rubbed the wet paint with his thumb until it disappeared from her hand. "But he's not at home?"

"No."

She tried to stop her body from reacting to what he was doing. She tried to stop her mind from racing to thoughts that shouldn't be there. Both her body and her mind betrayed her.

He licked a spot of blue paint on the knuckle of her middle finger and rubbed it, too. His hands were gentle and careful not to press too hard on her skin.

"Good."

"Why do you ask?" she said, but she felt sure she knew.

"It's useful information." He looked down at Rascal, who didn't bother to acknowledge him, and then to Sam whose short ears perked up. "If you hear anyone coming down the corridor, bark."

Her heartbeat sped up. "Why did you say that to them?"

"Because I've missed you and I'm dying to kiss you again."

The determination on his face could only be called predatory, heated. Primal. A shiver of anticipation and excitement raced through her. Her breaths became short gasps.

She backed up a little. "You are not supposed to kiss me the way you do."

"I know." He kept advancing on her. "But you do enjoy it, don't you?"

She wanted to say no but couldn't.

"You can stop me anytime you want to. Just tell me no and I'll back away."

And then she knew she couldn't say no. Because the truth was, she wanted him to kiss her again. He drew her into his arms and up to his chest and claimed her lips for his own. As if it were the most natural thing for her to do, Angelina leaned into him and parted her lips. Harrison accepted her invitation and invaded her mouth with his tongue, alternating between short darting thrusts and long exploring strokes. His lips pressed hers long and hard, with deep feeling that stole her breath and left her senses reeling and wanting more.

She slipped her arms beneath the warmth of his coat and around his firm waist, pulling herself closer to him. She slid her hands up his ribs, past his broad back, wanting to feel the power in his shoulders.

Harrison ran his hands skillfully up and down the front of her apron, pressing them over her breasts, quickly awakening searing desire inside her. He gently squeezed and massaged her through her clothing. With his thumb and forefinger he searched for and found her nipples. He kneaded them seductively. His caresses were meant to entice her, stir her senses. and make her want more . . . and they did.

Angelina loved the way he was making her feel. A whispered sound of pleasure floated past her lips. Her body was responding eagerly to his touch.

"Now do you believe I missed you? That I had to see you and kiss you?"

"Yes," she whispered. At the back of her mind she heard an odd sound from the dogs, but Lord Thornwick's touch had her beyond thinking about anything except for how he was making her feel. Her mouth clung eagerly to his rough and demanding kisses. She slid her hands down to the firm muscle of his buttocks. She filled her hands with him.

The earl trembled and she smiled beneath his lips as he moaned and caught her bottom in his hands, too, lifting her up to his hardness.

"Feel how much I want you," he said between kisses.

"I do," she whispered.

Angelina melted against him, yielding to his strength as he pressed against her again and again. She heard the dogs continue to growl but pushed away the sounds in favor of the pleasure of the earl's touch.

"Now tell me you missed me, Angelina. Tell me you were waiting for me to return and kiss you like this."

She was about to say yes when she heard a warning growl from Sam. The dogs were no longer playing with one another. Something was going on between them. Sam could hurt Rascal or Mr. Pete within seconds. She pulled away from Lord Thornwick and twisted her head around to look behind her. All three dogs were holding a single piece of white cloth in their teeth, trying to pull it away from the others.

Breathlessly she pushed completely out of Harrison's arms and turned toward the dogs. "Sam, Rascal, Mr. Pete, what do you three troublemakers have there?"

They paid her no mind, but continued growling.

As if sensing that they were about to lose what they held, Sam snapped at Mr. Pete. The puppy yelped.

"Sam! Sit. Bad dog! Rascal, sit." Rascal and Sam obeyed immediately. Mr. Pete, thinking he had the item all to himself, was about to run away with it when Harrison caught him up in his arms and tore the cloth from his mouth.

"What were you three fighting over?" he asked and held up the item: a lady's stays.

"Ah!" Angelina gasped and jerked them from Harrison's hands, then hid the garment behind her back. Flames of heated embarrassment burned her neck and cheeks. All she wanted was for the floor to open and swallow her.

"It's too late to hide it now, Angelina. I've already seen it. And I might add I've seen stays before. Though maybe not ones with so much lace on them."

To Lord Thornwick's credit, after his remark he pressed his lips together tightly to keep from laughing out loud. It did little to soothe her. She saw a wicked glint of humor in his eyes and his shoulders shaking with mirth. It had to be Mr. Pete who had wandered away and pilfered the stays from the laundry basket.

"Come on, all three of you are going outside," Angelina said. "Now!"

She fled from the room and sent the dogs out the back door and into the misting rain. She didn't want to go back and face Lord Thornwick, but she had to deny her mortification and just do it. On her way back to Lord Thornwick she stopped and stuffed the corset into a cabinet. Later she would put it in its proper place.

She put on a brave face and walked back into the room, hoping to appear as if nothing had happened. The earl was standing in front of the window looking at the violets he'd given her.

"All they needed was some morning light and the right amount of watering," she said, hoping he wouldn't make any further reference to her unmentionables.

He turned and gave her a tender smile. "I knew you would know what to do."

"You can take them back home now. I've nursed them back to health for you. The new growth should produce blooms in a few days."

He frowned. "These aren't mine," he said. "I bought them for you."

She looked puzzled. "You bought half-dead violets for me?"

He nodded. "What would you do with flowers that needed no loving attention?"

"So you thought because I like to take care of wounded dogs, I would like wounded flowers, too."

He gave her a rueful smile. "Was I wrong?"

She smiled, too. "No, Lord Thornwick, thank you."

"It's Harrison." He leaned back against the window frame and crossed one foot over the other. "You must call me Harrison when we are alone. Especially now that I've seen—"

"Don't," she said firmly and held up her hand.

He laughed and it was so genuine and so wonderful that she started laughing, too. She might end up ruing the day her father said she could keep Mr. Pete.

"So after all we have been through together now, what is my name?"

She supposed it was a bit ridiculous for her to continue to call him Lord Thornwick after their passionate kisses. "Harrison," she said. "But only when we are alone."

"Accepted," he said and walked closer to her. "Tell me, has Captain Maxwell kissed you yet?"

Does he know I wanted the captain to kiss me?

"What? No," she said, feeling heat rise in her face again. "I've told you. Unlike you, he is a gentleman, an officer, a man of honor who follows the rules of Society."

His eyes seemed to pierce hers as if he were trying to see into her soul and test her honesty. "But he is still a man."

"He is a man and a very fine man," she defended, feeling her hackles rise.

"If he desired you as much as I do, he would not let manners, rules, or anything else stop him from kissing you."

"That is not true. He respects me."

"I respect you greatly, Angelina. I wouldn't do anything to hurt you. I desire you more."

She backed away from him. "I don't want to talk about Captain Maxwell with you."

"Fair enough. I don't want to talk about him, either. But I do have a suggestion for you. If he won't kiss you, you need to kiss him."

Had he read her thoughts? Perhaps he had. Still, she said, "That's an outrageous suggestion."

"Maybe, but think about it anyway." He walked past her but at the door stopped, looked back, and said, "If Captain Maxwell really wants you, I think it's time that he starts fighting for you."

Harrison turned and walked out.

Chapter 24

*The lunatic, the lover, and the poet are of imagination
all compact.*
A Midsummer Night's Dream *5.1.4–6*

Angelina's plan was working like a well-wound clock. She and Captain Maxwell were sitting in the park on a blanket at the very same spot they had been little more than a week ago. The weather was cooperating, too. The stormy-looking skies had kept many people away from the park. Even Captain Maxwell had suggested they not go for fear they would get caught in a downpour. It had taken some talking but she had convinced her grandmother to allow them to go, insisting that many times gray skies didn't lead to heavy rain.

A worried excitement churned inside her. One way or another, she was going to see to it that Captain Maxwell kissed her before he took her home. Things had been unsettled and sometimes tense between them since he'd come home, but today she was going to put an end to those feelings. She was going to rediscover the wonderful feelings that had given her so many happy memories the year he was gone. She would not let Lord

Thornwick and his scoundrel ways of seducing her come between her and Captain Maxwell any longer.

She couldn't.

After they were comfortable and the refreshment basket had been opened, Angelina asked, "Are you drinking brandy again, Captain?"

"Yes," he answered. "But not for the pain today. I am drinking simply because I enjoy it."

"Does that mean every day you are getting better?"

He looked down into his cup. "I like to think so. How is your punch?"

Angelina cleared her throat. "In need of a bit of brandy," she said.

He blew out a half laugh, half grunt. "I don't think your father would approve if I laced your punch with this."

"We don't always have to follow the rules, do we? Besides, he doesn't have to know. I mean, I won't tell him, will you?" She held her cup out to him.

"No, of course not. Still, I don't think we should do that, Miss Rule."

"I do," she insisted. "Some rules were made to be broken, and this is one of them."

He turned his head, looking from one side of the park to the other. "All right," he said. "I don't suppose a little will hurt." He set his cup on the blanket and opened his flask. He poured a mere drop or two into her cup.

Angelina was having none of that. She took the flask from his hand and added a generous amount to her cup. If she was going to find the courage to force the captain to kiss her, she had to mask some of her inhibitions. With Harrison she didn't have to worry about such things. He simply took charge and did exactly as he wanted, leaving her no choice but to be swept away by his pursuit of her. That was what she was going to have to do to the captain this afternoon.

She handed Captain Maxwell the flask and took a big drink of the punch. "Whew!" she whistled and then coughed a little from the burn in her throat.

Captain Maxwell laughed again. "I tried to tell you brandy is too strong a drink for a lady. Maybe next time you will listen to me?"

"I do believe this is something that should be sipped rather than gulped. It tastes nothing like champagne."

"Now, there is a lady's drink. I think you should pour that out and have only punch." He reached for her cup but she moved it away from him. His expression changed from humor to annoyance. He didn't like her not listening to his suggestion. Good; that was a start. He needed to be stronger and more in command.

"I said it was different. That doesn't mean I don't like it. I will sip it," she said, and she did. It still burned but went down much easier the second time. "I've noticed that you dance with many ladies each evening."

"Have you now?" he asked, sounding pleased.

She nodded and sipped again.

He picked up his cup and stretched his legs out before him, crossing one foot over the other. "Do I detect a hint of jealousy from the lovely Miss Rule?"

Did he? She really didn't think she was jealous. She wanted other young ladies to appreciate who he was and what he'd done as an officer in the army. She wanted them all to want to dance with him and want to spend time with him. What she felt was happiness that the ladies were not letting his disfigurement keep them from enjoying his company. He was relaxing, and she took that as a good sign that the afternoon was going well.

"It tells me that many young ladies are delighted you are seeking their attention."

"But what about you? Are you happy that I am seeking your attention?"

"Of course. You know you don't have to ask that question of me."

His eye narrowed. "I think I do."

It was now or never. She looked around them. There was another carriage in the distance, and someone rode on horseback even farther away. No one was close enough to know if they were there kissing or whispering.

Her stomach jumped. She put the cup down, rose up on her knees, and moved closer to him. "I want you to kiss me, Captain."

His Adam's apple moved as he swallowed slowly. "Do you now?"

"Yes," she said, her courage growing now that she'd actually said the words. "It's time. I've been wondering what it would be like to receive a kiss from you since I was sixteen years old."

He placed his cup on the blanket, rose up on his knees, and looked around them just as she had. "I won't keep you waiting any longer," he said. "I think we've both waited long enough for this."

"Too long," she whispered.

The captain lowered his head toward hers.

Angelina remembered that Harrison had told her the first kiss should always be with eyes open so she did as she had when Harrison kissed her and watched the captain's face while his lips touched hers in a tender kiss. It puzzled her that Captain Maxwell's eye was closed. But something else puzzled her more. The lack of response inside her. His lips were warm but there were no tingles on her skin, no butterflies in her stomach, and no desirous sensations racing to invade her most intimately womanly parts. There were no fireworks shooting through her senses.

Suddenly he jerked away from her so roughly she almost fell back. "Why did you do that? Don't do that!"

"What?" she asked, astonished by his tempestuousness, by the angry expression on his face and the fury in his voice. "What did I do?"

"You kept your eyes open. Why did you do that?"

He almost spat the words at her. Heaven help her. She thought she was supposed to. Lord Thornwick had told her to watch the first kiss, but she couldn't tell Captain Maxwell that. Frustration turned her hands into tight fists. "I'm sorry, I thought I was supposed to keep my eyes open."

"You were looking at my scars."

"No!" she defended, unable to understand why he was so angry at such a simple mistake. How could he have misunderstood so badly what she had done?

"You wanted see my face close up so you could decide if you could live with looking at me day after day. Morning and night."

"Stop that," she demanded. "You know that isn't true." That feeling she'd had since he'd arrived that everything was going to be good between them today fled from her. "I thought it was the right thing to do."

There was no way she could explain the reasoning behind her action. She should have known that anything Harrison had asked of her would not be normal and shouldn't be done at all. Why had she ever listened to the one man who never followed any acceptable rules of behavior?

"Know this, no matter how many times you look closely at me the scars will not change. This is the way I will look for the rest of my life."

Her heart was beating so fast she felt light-headed. "I've told you that your scars don't bother me. I don't even see them anymore when I look at you."

He shook his head and looked down at the ground. "Don't lie to me, Miss Rule. How can they not when they bother me at times to the point I feel I will go mad from the wishing, the wanting to look as I once did?"

Her heart broke for him at his honest admission. Of course they vexed him. This debacle, this pain he was going through now was her fault for keeping her eyes open.

No, it was Lord Thornwick's fault that the captain was affronted by her and she was shaking like a leaf in a thunderstorm. If she could get her hands on Harrison right now she would cheerfully strangle him with his perfectly tied neckcloth.

Captain Maxwell lifted his head and stared directly at her. "I don't want you ever looking at me that closely. Ever again."

"I won't," she said softly, hoping to placate him. "I didn't know. I'm sorry. You must believe me I'd never do anything to deliberately hurt you."

He ran both hands through his hair as he exhaled loudly and groaned. Her heart broke a second time. She wanted to hug him. Make up for the terrible mistake she made. She wanted him to lay his head on her breast so she could comfort him. She wanted to somehow ease the pain inside him, but she was afraid to touch him.

He coughed and sat back on his heels once more. He was calm again. The vehemence had faded from his expression, but she was still shaking. He picked up his cup and took a long drink.

"Yes, of course, I know," he finally said. "I'm sorry, Miss Rule. I lost control for a moment and stepped over the line. It's just that—I didn't expect you to——I know you weren't doing the things I accused——"

"You don't have to explain," she said, cutting him off.

"But I do," he said earnestly. "Sometimes such strong

anger overcomes me and gets the best of me. There are times I can't stop myself. And at other times, the anger comes rushing out before I realize it."

His contrite expression, his sadness filled her with sorrow. "It's all right," she whispered with the compassion she was feeling. "I understand. And I'm sure that will get better with time, too."

"I've tried to tell myself I've dealt with my lot in life. Many times I've told myself this. Then suddenly something will occur as happened just now between us and it proves to me I haven't accepted it. I've only hidden my feelings once again, for a time."

"That sounds perfectly normal to me, Captain," she said and gently placed her hand over his. "It's only been a few months. There hasn't been enough time for you to heal every wound."

And she believed that. This was the man she loved. She had always loved him. She didn't know why Harrison was now the man she dreamed about, the man she longed to see, and the man she wanted to hold her, kiss her, and caress her. Those feelings should be for the man who was with her right now. She felt desperate to recapture what she'd once felt for Captain Maxwell, but she didn't know how to do it.

"You are being very gracious. I should have known with your first kiss you wouldn't know how it's done."

She averted her eyes, not wanting to admit it wasn't her first kiss. "I didn't mean to distress you. Can we try it again?" She rose up on her knees. "Will you kiss me again? This time the right way, with my eyes closed?"

Angelina's stomach quivered but not in the same wonderful way Harrison created. It was in a nervous twitter for fear of doing something else wrong. She closed her eyes and lifted her face to his. When his lips made contact with hers she sighed, wanting desperately for it to be different this time. She waited for him to escalate the kiss. She wanted him to slant his lips and move them passionately over hers and allow her to feel his desire for her.

All of a sudden, Harrison's words were ringing in her ears. *If he won't kiss you, you should kiss him.*

Without further thought she reached up and wound her arms around his neck and moved in closer to him, pressing her chest against his. She tried to ask him with her movements to circle her with his arms, catch her up in his strong arms the way Lord Thornwick had. She wanted to feel him hold her as if she were the most precious thing he had ever held.

They kept kissing. Her feelings of desire would come for the captain. They would. She needed more time. He needed more time. But they would come. They had to.

But they didn't. They kissed longer and longer. Finally his arms slid around her and he pulled her close, but she felt no stirrings of passion from him or herself. All she felt was sadness.

"Oh, my love," he whispered against her lips. "My love. I've waited so long to hold you like this. After the pistol exploded in my face I never thought I'd hold you in my arms like this. I never thought you'd be mine. Tell me you'll marry me."

Marry him?

Angelina stiffened and broke away from the kiss.

"Did I rush you?" he asked.

She moistened her lips. "No, no, it's just that I didn't expect you to say that right now, today."

She sat back down and picked up her cup and took a sip, feeling like she wanted to cry. Captain Maxwell was a courageous and kind man. A handsome and capable man, the man she thought she loved, but now she wasn't sure she wanted to marry him.

Maybe it was just that they didn't have a good start with the first kiss. She should never have kept her eyes open. It hadn't felt natural. It was the wrong thing to do. That must have been the reason the stirrings of wanton desire and earth-shattering passion had eluded her and, understandably, the captain.

When she looked up at the captain he had a satisfied smile on his face, but she didn't feel satisfied at all. And it was all that blasted Lord Thornwick's fault. It was as if he'd reached into her heart and stolen her love from Captain Maxwell right out of her chest.

"You've known I was going to ask you to marry me."

Yes, and she used to want that, too, but now, now she couldn't say for sure that was what she wanted. "I'm not ready to—to answer you."

His eye searched her face. "I understand."

Angelina felt like crying. It wasn't supposed to be this way, she thought, and felt the first drop of cold rain.

"We've got to hurry," he said.

Angelina opened the umbrella while Captain Maxwell threw their cups in the basket. They ran for the carriage. He helped her step up just as a deluge started. She knocked him with the umbrella as he jumped in beside her on the seat. He laughed, and she laughed, too, but felt no real joy. She was sad.

"Hold on," he said. "We'll have to go fast."

He gave the ribbons a strong snap and the horses took off. The carriage bumped and jangled through the park. They hadn't gone far when Angelina saw a small, drenched dog limping, trying to stay off his right front paw, and headed right in front of their speeding carriage.

She grabbed hold of the handle of the bench and yelled, "Stop! There!"

Captain Maxwell yanked the ribbons so hard the horses reared and screamed. The curricle bucked and shuddered, almost throwing her from the bench. In an instant the captain dropped the reins, jumped to his feet, and slid his sword from its scabbard. The shrill sound of metal scraping against metal chilled her to the bone.

"Where?" he shouted, holding his sword in the air. "Where are they? I'll fight them!"

Angelina sat frozen in fear at the long sharp blade held so closely to her face. Her heart was pounding so hard she thought she might lose her breath. The captain's expression held a faraway, disturbing glaze. The rain pelted him as he searched the horizon in every direction.

"It's a dog, Captain," she whispered softly. She pointed in the foggy distance. "See. Put your sword away. There's no enemy, it's just a crippled dog."

He looked down at her. Confusion flashed across his face. "A dog?" He blinked slowly. "A dog," he said again. "I thought there was——never mind. I understand." He slid the sword back into its sheath.

The shearing sound of the blade entering its casing sent shivers up Angelina's spine all over again and she trembled.

"Do you mind helping me down, Captain?" she said, quietly. She pointed in the direction of the animal, who continued to limp along in the downpour. "I must help him."

"You can't save every stray, Miss Rule," he said flatly. "You must know that by now."

"I think I finally do, Captain. I can't save them all. I can't even save most of them, but I can save that one, and I'm going to with or without your help."

She then looked up at him with clear eyes. It was as if she were seeing him for the first time. Not a handsome soldier, not a wounded soldier, not even a wounded man. Just a man. A man she respected. A man she was honored to know, but did she love him as she once had?

"Very well, Miss Rule," he said stiffly. "Stay here under your umbrella. I'll get him for you."

"Thank you, Captain," she whispered, as a tear rolled down her face.

Chapter 25

I never did repent for doing good, nor shall not now.
The Merchant of Venice *3.4.10–11*

Angelina said good-bye to Captain Maxwell at the door, refusing his offer to let him help her with the shivering dog. She'd wrapped the puppy in her cape and held the umbrella over them on the short ride home.

"I've been watching for you since the rain started," Mrs. Bickmore said, opening the door for her. "Give me that soggy cape."

She tried to take the cape and saw it move. She jumped back. "What's that?"

"It's just another dog, Mrs. Bickmore." She stuffed him in the woman's arms. "He's really quite calm and will be no problem. Where are the others?"

"In their room where they're supposed to be," she replied, being very careful how she took hold of the dog.

Angelina knew she couldn't put a strange dog in with three pals. That would be asking for trouble. "Put him in the china and cutlery closet and give him something to eat and a blanket. I'll take care of him later."

"Look at you," Mrs. Bickmore said. "Your dress is sopping and probably your feet, too. Lady Railbridge asked that you join her and the Bishop Worsley in the drawing room as soon as you arrived, but I think you should get out of your wet clothing first."

Hope shot through Angelina. "No. I'm fine," she said, nervously untying the ribbon on her bonnet. "A little damp but not wet. Just go take care of the dog for me please."

At last, she thought, walking into the drawing room, peeling off her damp gloves. Bishop Worsley sat in one of the wingback chairs and her grandmother on the settee. Angelina looked at their faces, hoping to glean if the man had favorable or unfavorable news for them.

"Angelina, the skirt of your dress is soaked."

"And I'm thankful you have a fire going, Granna. It will dry in no time," she said, walking over to the fireplace and standing in front of it.

After proper greetings her grandmother said, "I didn't think you would ever return, dearest."

"I'm here now," she answered, rubbing her cold hands together.

"Good. Bishop Worsley wouldn't say one word about what he's accomplished until you arrived."

Angelina felt an uneasy gnawing in her stomach. After her afternoon with Captain Maxwell, she didn't know if she could take any more disappointments.

"I've been a bit worried," she said, looking at the man, "since it's been so long and we haven't heard about your progress. Just demands to paint more."

"I know I told you a project like this would take time. A lot needed to be done."

"You did," she agreed anxiously. "I had hoped it wouldn't take as long as you expected."

He reached down into a satchel at his feet and pulled

out a dark-green velvet pouch tied with a gold braided cord. He handed it to Angelina. It was heavy.

"There is enough money in there to pay every one of your father's debts."

"What?" Her heartbeat raced and her knees went weak. She looked from the bishop to her grandmother, who appeared just as shocked. "How do you know? How did you know how much he owed?"

Bishop Worsley shrugged. "It was the first thing I had to check on. I needed to know how much money you needed. It's easy to find out what gambling debts a gentleman has if you know the right people to ask."

The pouch got heavier as Angelina held it. Enough to pay all his debts!

She wanted to believe what he said was true, but she couldn't. She had hoped they'd get enough to help them buy more time, but to completely pay everything—it was too much for her to accept.

"This will pay off all his debts?" she asked again.

"All the ones I found about anyway. I suppose there could be more."

"I'm stunned," she breathed softly as she hefted the bag and settled on the settee by her grandmother. "You were paid this much money for my paintings. I had no idea. I just assumed my father's debts would be so much more than I would be paid for my work. This is truly unbelievable."

Bishop Worsley chuckled and crossed one leg over the other, making himself comfortable in the chair. "No, no, Miss Rule. I see no reason not to tell you the truth. I mean, yes, the duchess bought all your fans and paid well for them. She asked for more, which you delivered, and she has also paid for them. Mr. Eyston gave you a handsome price for your miniatures and boxes as well, but it would be wrong of me to allow you to think you made enough to pay your father's debts. You didn't." He shook his head. "They were enormous. In fact, if this house didn't belong to someone else, you wouldn't be living here right now."

Lady Railbridge gasped.

"What are you talking about?"

"Suffice it to say, what you received from all your pieces would have hardly paid the interest on the money he owed."

Angelina swallowed the lump in her throat and looked at her grandmother.

"I have no idea what he's talking about, dear," she said, shaking her head. "Your father never made me privy to any of his affairs."

Angelina looked at the bishop. "Then what did you do to garner this?" She held up the heavy bag.

Her grandmother suddenly jumped up and said, "You didn't, Bishop Worsley!"

He smiled and slowly rose, too. "I did, Lady Railbridge. I did exactly that and I enjoyed every moment of it."

Angelina joined them standing up. "What? Tell me what you did."

"He gambled with your money. That's what he did," Granna said as if she were spitting something distasteful from her mouth.

Her accusation didn't wipe the smile off the bishop's face. It only enhanced it. "Yes, that is exactly what I did, Miss Rule. I took the money that came from your paintings and I gambled with it and I had the time of my life. I doubled it over and over again." He closed his eyes and breathed in as if he were smelling the most heavenly perfumed rose. "It was as if I couldn't lose. I've never had a winning streak like it. I doubt I shall ever have another."

"How could you?" Angelina asked in horror. "That's what happened to my father. Gambling over and over again got him into this trouble."

The bishop smiled. "Ah, but he lost, and I won."

"You could have lost it all, too," she said, her voice rising as the bag in her hand felt heavier and heavier until suddenly she threw it onto the sofa. "I would have had nothing, no hope of ever helping my father if you had lost."

"You never had any hope of helping him with what you could sell, either, Miss Rule. The moneylenders would have laughed at you had you arrived with the money you made. That is why I took the chance. Now, you can hate me for it. But that is the truth."

Angelina didn't know what to say. She wanted to force him to admit he was wrong about that, but she couldn't. In her heart, she knew he was right.

"I've always loved to gamble," the bishop continued. "Haven't been able to do it for a while. In fact, Lady Railbridge, I promised your husband I'd never do it again. And God rest his soul, I hadn't until you came to see me. It was too tempting to pass up. Two ladies trusting me with a couple hundred pounds." He smiled the sweetest smile Angelina had ever seen. "What were the odds that would ever happen to me? It was a dream come true. I haven't had my hands on that kind of money in years. How could I not test my mettle and see if I'd lost my touch with the cards. I made enough to pay your father's debts and more."

"How much more?" Lady Railbridge demanded.

"Doesn't matter," he said, then looked at Angelina. "I kept that as my payment. You don't mind, do you?"

Do I?

"No, of course not. I'm just astounded you would take the risk knowing what was at stake."

"That's what makes gambling appealing. I took chances because I had nothing to lose. As for you, Miss Rule, life is full of risk. But you already knew that or you wouldn't have come to see me."

He was right.

"I don't think there is anything left to say except thank you and good-bye, Bishop Worsley," her grandmother said stiffly.

He nodded. "If you have more paintings, Miss Rule, I'll be happy to continue to represent Miss Paulette Savill."

"No," Angelina and her grandmother said at the same time.

"It may not change your feelings for me right now, Lady Railbridge, but I've always wanted to do something for you. Your husband was kind to me when I didn't have a friend in sight. I feel like I have repaid him now and I appreciate you giving me that opportunity."

"I don't approve of the way you repaid him, Bishop Worsley," her grandmother said, her chin high in the air. "You could have lost everything."

The bishop made no comment but looked at Angelina and said, "I'm glad it worked out for you. You know where to find me if I can ever be of help again."

Angelina didn't approve of his methods any more than her grandmother, but she wouldn't worry about that. It was done and she was thankful. She'd gotten exactly what she wanted. She kissed Bishop Worsley on the cheek before he left.

"Granna, you know what this means," Angelina said as she looked at the dark-green bag lying on the settee where she'd thrown it.

She nodded. "Your father no longer has to fear prison."

"And I will be free to choose who I will marry."

"That's true. Your father has no reason to force you to marry Lord Thornwick, but before you make your decision think long and hard. And then choose wisely, my dear."

Angelina looked down at her hands. There was a spot of paint on her wrist. She remembered how Harrison had wet the paint with his tongue and then gently rubbed it off with his fingers. Flames heated her skin just thinking about that moment. He'd made her feel like she was the only lady he'd ever wanted.

Why had fate sent Lord Thornwick to come between her and the man of her dreams? She wanted to love Captain Maxwell. She wanted to help him recover, give him her devotion, and revel in their passion for each other. He deserved to be truly loved.

But Angelina feared that wasn't her dream anymore. There was a time she knew for certain that Captain Maxwell was the man for her. And now she wasn't. It had nothing to do with his scars. She was convinced of that. It all had to do with what she felt when the Earl of Thornwick walked into the room.

Chapter 26

I understand a fury in your words but not the words.
Othello *4.2.32–33*

After Angelina had seen to the injured dog and sent a note to Mrs. Vaughan, she changed out of her damp dress and went back into the drawing room to wait for her father.

She anxiously paced in front of the window, in front of the fireplace, and around the settee. She'd walked to the back of the house to check on Molly, Mr. Pete, and the new dog, too. She looked out the window at Rascal and Sam who were sniffing around the wet bushes, and then retraced her steps into the drawing room to start all over again.

The afternoon grew late. Mrs. Vaughan's worker arrived to pick up the injured dog, Mrs. Bickmore lit the lamps and stoked the fire, and her grandmother said she couldn't bear to watch Angelina pace another step and retired to her bedchamber to rest.

Angelina first thought she would rush her father as soon as he walked in the door and shove the money into his hands. Thankfully, her common sense took over and she discarded that idea from her mind. And several others equally ridiculous. The best thing to do would be simple and straightforward. Now she waited, albeit with bated breath, for him to come home so she could surprise him with this good news.

When the front door finally opened Angelina's legs went weak and she quickly sat down. She heard him talking to Mrs. Bickmore in the vestibule, knowing he was removing his cloak, hat, and gloves. Counting to ten didn't calm her. Inhaling deeply three times didn't calm her, neither did wringing her hands.

She looked at the velvet bag. She hadn't touched it since she'd thrown it onto the settee. But staring at it now calmed her. Why specifically she wasn't sure, unless it represented the fact that she could now decide for herself who she would marry. And, while she hadn't made the money that was in the bag, it was because of her plan, and her determination that the bag was full. Harrison crossed her mind and she smiled. She wondered what he would say if he knew she had broken the rule that said ladies and gentlemen of Society did not go into trade. However risky it was, with her grandmother and Bishop Worsley's help she'd accomplished exactly what she'd set out to do. That gave her enormous satisfaction.

"Good afternoon, Angelina. How are you this wet afternoon?"

She rose on confident, steady legs. "I'm very good, Papa, and you?"

He laid the newsprint on his favorite chair and then walked over to the side table and poured himself a drink from the crystal decanter. "Splendid. And shouldn't you be in your chamber getting ready for tonight's parties?"

"I will soon. I've been waiting for you to get home."

"That's nice to hear, my dear." He picked up the

newsprint and sat down, ready to enjoy his drink and the afternoon edition. "Will we be dining at home tonight or will there be supper for us at one of the parties?"

Angelina remained standing. Watching him. "I believe we'll dine here before we go."

"Good. I always like that better."

He took a sip of his drink and Angelina knew she could wait no longer. She picked up the velvet bag and said, "I have something for you."

He laid his newsprint aside and looked curiously at her as he took it from her. "What's this? It's heavy."

"Open it," she said, her stomach starting to jump again.

He pulled on the drawstrings and looked inside. "Good Lord!" He looked up at her with wild blue eyes. "Where did this come from? How did you get this?"

She understood his shock. She'd felt the same way when Bishop Worsley showed it to her. "I sold my paintings. My fans, miniatures, and boxes. Everything I've painted the past few years. There's enough money in there to pay off all your debts. There's no longer any need for you to be at the Prince's mercy."

His mouth hung open in disbelief. His wide eyes narrowed, and his face turned red as he jumped up out of the chair. "What the devil have you done, girl? What do you mean you sold your paintings? How could you and to who? You don't have anything worth this amount of money. Out with the truth of this right now."

Angelina took a step away from him, and her legs hit the back of the settee. Surely he would calm down once she explained everything about Bishop Worsley to him. "A friend of Granna's——"

"Lady Railbridge!" he interrupted. "I should have known she had something to do with this. Where is she?" His voice rose angrily. "I knew I would rue the day I brought her into this house to help me care for you."

Angelina had expected her father to be shocked, maybe even angry about what she had done, but not hostile.

"Papa, none of that is important now."

"You give me a sack of money like this and you say it's not important how you obtained it? You say you sold your paintings like a backstreet tradesman and you think that's not important to me?"

Angelina's happiness was evaporating fast and her courage was fading even faster. She didn't know what to say except, "I don't understand, Papa. I thought you'd be happy to be able to pay your debts yourself so you wouldn't be obligated to the Prince or anyone else."

"But I'm not paying them off myself, am I? You are!" he yelled. "By subjecting yourself to ruin, ridicule, and probably no small amount of danger, too. And with the things that you treasured most."

Angelina had never seen her father so enraged. This wasn't what she'd expected. "They were not treasures, Papa. And even if they were, you are more important than anything I have. I would have sold everything I have to keep you from going to prison."

His hand clutched the neck of the bag so tight his knuckles were white. "I can't imagine what madness came over you to do this. And that your grandmother aided you! I'm glad your mother didn't live to see this day."

"Papa, no," she said, his words slicing like a knife through her heart. "Don't say that. I only wanted to help."

"Help who? I didn't need any help!" he said, so vehemently his face shook. "The Prince agreed to pay all my debts and my daughter was going to marry an earl. An earl, by the way, who would have taken very good care of us both. What in God's name could have possibly made you think I needed help? You are the one who wasn't happy, Angelina. You did this for you and that captain and not for me at all."

Angelina was astounded. Was that true? Had she done it all for herself all along? Yes, she wanted a choice in who she married, but she also wanted her father to be free of the threat of prison, free of the Prince paying his debts.

That was not wrong.

From somewhere deep inside herself she found the courage to shore up her confidence. Calmness settled over her again. Her shoulders and her chin rose a notch. "It is true that I wanted to be free to choose my own husband, but that is not the main reason I did this, Papa, and you saying it won't make it so. I know I did this for you."

He looked as if he was going to say something else but didn't. He picked up his glass of port and drained it before he brought it down from his mouth. He then threw the glass into the fireplace. The shattering noise made Angelina flinch.

Her father walked out the door clutching the heavy bag without saying another word.

For the second time that day Angelina felt close to tears.

Chapter 27

What win I, if I gain the thing I seek? A dream,
a breath, a froth of fleeting joy.
Lucrece–*211–12*

Harrison watched Angelina dance with yet another gentleman. He knew she didn't like to dance, but there was something else wrong with her tonight. Her face was tight, her movements stiff. Maxwell had to be the reason. What had the officer said to her? Or done to her?

Harrison was close to winning Angelina's heart. He was sure of that. Perhaps he had already. But he hadn't won her. She had an irrational sense of duty to Maxwell that was driving Harrison insane. Yes, the captain needed her, but Harrison did, too.

"You were always so much like my son. You and Adam Greyhawke, too."

"Your Grace," Harrison said, and kissed the Dowager Duchess of Drakestone's offered hand. He was studying Angelina so deeply he hadn't heard Bray's mother walk up beside him. "I think that's the first time you've ever given me a compliment."

She gave him a doubtful expression. "Perhaps, and if so, don't ever expect another."

"After that one, another will not be needed."

She smiled. "You know, he never would have gotten into any trouble, and would never have been as wild as he was a few years ago if it hadn't been for you two."

"I take full responsibility for all your son's bad behavior, Your Grace."

"Mr. Greyhawke must share in that, my lord. I know you and Bray recently went to see him. Tell me, how is he doing now that it's more than a year past his tragedy?"

"It's difficult to speak for anyone else, but we thought he seemed better."

"Good. Have you seen Bray tonight?"

"No, but I haven't been here long."

"Hmm," she said, and for some reason she pretended to be distracted for a moment. "How about Miss Rule? Have you seen her?"

"She's on the dance floor."

The duchess raised her eyebrows. "Yes, I thought you would know exactly where she was."

Harrison realized too late that he had just been fooled by the duchess. "It's hard for a gentleman to miss such a lovely lady."

"I'm sure," she replied. "When you speak to her will you tell her I want to see her? I want to ask her about a fan."

"You are assuming I will speak to her?"

Her Grace smiled again. "Oh, you will."

The duchess opened her fan and Harrison saw a beautiful white peacock with its tail spread wide. His body went still. He'd seen that fan at Angelina's house the day she painted it. How did the duchess get it?

"This is lovely, isn't it?" she said, looking down at the fan.

"Very," Harrison agreed, keeping his voice level and feigning disinterest.

"It's by the same artist who paints Miss Rule's fans."

Harrison had no doubt of that. "I'm afraid I don't know much about fans."

"No reason you should. I have a question for Miss Rule about the artist."

So do I.

"I hear the artist also paints miniatures and mourning boxes," the duchess continued.

Yes she does.

"If I see Miss Rule, would you like for me to tell her you're looking for her?

"Yes, do that for me, my lord. And give my regards to my son when you see him as well." She closed the fan and walked away.

Harrison's body tightened. Oh, yes, he knew Angelina had painted that fan, and the duchess knew it, too. The duchess didn't miss anything.

So Miss Angelina Rule knew how to break Society's rules when she wanted to. But if she was doing what he thought she was, he had a few things to say to her. He knew she and her grandmother were looking for a way to pay her father's debts, and now he knew why she was always painting.

He wanted answers from Angelina, and he couldn't get them fast enough to suit him.

Harrison had been coming to the Great Hall for over ten years. He knew every dark corridor, every servants' door, every nook and cranny. He intended to find a place he could talk to Angelina where they wouldn't be disturbed.

As soon as the gentleman escorted Angelina back to

her grandmother, Harrison spoke hastily to Lady Railbridge. To Angelina he said, "Come with me for a glass
of champagne, Miss Rule."

Then not giving her time to accept or reject him, Harrison touched her elbow and guided her away from her
grandmother.

She stopped and lifted her arm away from his. "Excuse me, my lord, but didn't you promise to give me
time to accept or reject an offer from you before just
rushing me away?"

Harrison was in no mood for this but he said, "I didn't
forget, but I have something very important to discuss
with you. Would you please join me?"

She nodded.

Instead of taking her to the champagne table, he
whisked her out a servants' door hidden behind one of
the large fluted columns. The corridor was dimly lit. He
knew they would see a servant or two pass by them, but
in all his years of sneaking young ladies out for a few
kisses, he'd never had a servant say a word to them or
tattle.

"Why are we going in here? Where does this lead?"

"The servants use it. Don't worry, we're going no farther than a few feet from the door."

She stood under the yellow glow of a lamp. Her hair
sparkled. The low neckline of her dress showed the
beautiful swell of her lovely breasts, and a row of gar-
nets hung around her neck. Her face was still tight.
Something was wrong with her. But he'd find out about
that later. First things first.

"I saw something tonight."

She blinked. "Something that would be of interest to
me?"

"Yes. A fan."

Her eyes twitched at the corners, just enough to give her away. He didn't really have to say anything more.

"There are many fans in a ballroom, my lord. Which one are you referring to?"

"Have you noticed how you call me my lord when you feel you are telling me something I won't like?"

"I'm sure that's not true."

Her eyes searched his. There was something unreadable in hers and he was trying to figure out what it was that was bothering him. "It's true. Why don't you have a fan with you tonight?"

She looked down at her gloved hands and for a moment he thought she was looking at something that wasn't there. "I don't know. I guess I forgot to bring one."

"You forgot, or is it that you don't have one?"

Her lids flew up. She looked at him with her black-fringed, blue eyes. She moistened her lips and backed against the wall. "Of course, I——I have plenty of fans. Why are you questioning me about this? Surely you don't care whether or not I have a fan with me. Nor did you need to drag me into this darkened corridor to ask me about it."

"I remember the night the duchess stopped us and was interested in your fans, and I told you she would buy them."

Angelina kept silent. A sadness filled her eyes, and he knew for sure what she had done.

"You sold her your fans?"

"No—no." Her chest heaved.

He placed his hands on the wall on either side of her shoulders. "Why?"

"No," she said again, and then quickly added, "Yes, if you must know. I sold my fans to the duchess. I sold my snuffboxes, my mourning boxes. Everything else I've ever painted. I sold it all!"

His stomach tightened. She was too bold and daring for her own good.

"To who?"

"To who, Angelina?" he asked again.

Tears filled her eyes. She looked away and shook her head. "Most of it to a shopkeeper. The rest to the duchess."

The thought of her going into a shop and selling her paintings hit Harrison hard. Damn, she was filled with more courage and determination than he'd given her credit for. He'd known she wanted, planned to do something to pay her father's debts so she would be free to marry Captain Maxwell, but Harrison had always assumed that help would come from Lady Railbridge finding a private source to loan her father more money. Harrison never dreamed Angelina would sell her artwork.

"Tell me which shop and I'll buy it back for you."

She frowned. "I don't want it back. Besides, it didn't do any good," she whispered. "It was—I thought I was helping."

Please don't cry, Harrison thought. He never wanted to be responsible for making her cry.

He spoke quietly, soothingly. "Angelina, do you have any idea how much your father owes? You could never sell enough fans and paintings to buy him out of prison."

"You're wrong!" she said earnestly. "I did get enough. I didn't do it by myself, I had help, but I gave Papa enough money to pay his debts."

Harrison stiffened. How? He leaned in close to her. "What kind of help did you get?"

"A man named Bishop Worsley took the money and multiplied it by gambling."

"Damnation, Angelina," he said, taking hold of her shoulders. "Did your grandmother agree to this?"

"She knew about it, yes."

"Why would you do something that risky? Why would you involve yourself with a professional gambler?"

"You know why," she whispered softly. I wanted to be free to make my own choice. To marry who I pleased because it was my decision and not because I was being forced."

She pushed hard on his chest, shoving him away from her. Her hands did little to hurt him but her words cut like a blade.

"This is what you have been doing. You have been painting every day so you wouldn't have to marry me."

"You nor anyone else I didn't want to marry," she said on a choked-back sob. "I gave the money to my father. He has it now."

Harrison sucked in a deep breath. She was free now to marry anyone she wished. He shouldn't have been surprised by what she'd done, but he was. He knew she liked to take care of things, people, and dogs. It stood to reason she would do everything possible to take care of her father's debts, too. She'd told him she would, but he had underestimated her.

He wouldn't be guilty of that again.

"I would have paid your father's debts," Harrison said.

"My father is not your responsibility. He's mine and I took care of him."

"And now you are free to marry the captain."

She wouldn't look at him. Harrison's first thought was

that he'd lost again. He'd vowed he would never fight for another lady, but he had. Angelina was worth it. And he had fought fairly. But he knew what Angelina didn't seem to know yet. She didn't love Maxwell.

Without further thought he took hold of her arms again and said, "I love you, Angelina. I want to marry you."

Her head jerked up and her eyes watered again. Her chest heaved. "You lie."

"No. You know I have many vices, little patience, no boundaries, and I ignore rules, but I do not lie. I love you. Say you'll marry me."

Her eyes searched his face. For a moment he thought she would agree but then she said, "I can't."

He winced inside. "It's time for you to make up your mind who you love, Angelina. Captain Maxwell or me."

It was the most difficult thing he'd ever done, but Harrison turned her loose and walked back through the servants' door and into the ballroom.

He headed toward the exit. He loved her. He wasn't sure he knew it until after he'd said it. There was never any doubt he wanted her. From the moment he saw her, he wanted her to be his. Now he knew he loved her and he wanted her to know it, too.

Walking slowly, he headed for the exit. He hoped she'd come after him. He wanted her to come after him and tell him she loved him, too.

But she didn't.

Chapter 28

I did love you once.
Hamlet *3.1.115*

It had been raining since Angelina awoke.

Saying good-bye to a long-held dream wasn't easy. she'd worried all night and all morning that she might not be strong enough to do it when the time came. She was sad, and anxious, but before she could tell Harrison she loved him, she had to tell Captain Maxwell she didn't love him and couldn't marry him. It was the right thing to do. She owed it to him to be honest with him about her feelings before she committed to Harrison.

She sat on the settee with Captain Maxwell, her grandmother dutifully in a chair sipping tea. Angelina had asked the captain to come over. She would always smile when she saw him, feel such pride at knowing him, but without the passion or desire for him, she couldn't marry him. She had to let him know that she loved Lord Thornwick.

"Granna," Angelina said, "would you mind giving me a few minutes alone with Captain Maxwell?"

"Oh, that wouldn't be proper, dear. You know that."

"You needn't go too far, Granna, and it won't be for long. Please give us a short time together."

Her grandmother searched her eyes. "Well, I——are you sure you want to do this, Angelina?"

"Yes, please." She knew her grandmother thought she wanted time alone so the captain could propose to her. The captain probably thought that, too.

There was no need to sit back down after her grandmother left the room. Captain Maxwell wouldn't be staying long.

He surprised her by taking hold of her hands and saying, "Thank you for arranging for us to be alone." He smiled and looked down into her eyes. "I had hoped we could have a few minutes so I could properly ask you to marry me before I speak to your father. I was too hasty when we were in the park."

Rain had fogged the windows. The low-burning fire hadn't taken the chill off the room. Captain Maxwell's grip was strong and warm, yet still Angelina pulled her hands out of his and stepped away. She wondered if this would have been easier had it been a beautiful, sunny day.

When she looked at him, so handsome in his red coat with its shiny gold buttons, braids, and epaulets, a sword by his side, she wavered. But then Harrison with his teasing smile and passionate embrace came to mind, and she found all the courage she needed.

"Captain," she said. "I asked you to come over today so I could tell you I can't marry you."

He blinked fast and continued to stare at her. "It's the patch," he said with no emotion.

She'd feared he would think that. "No," she said firmly. She would not let him accuse her of that again.

"You say that, yet you won't marry me." He stepped closer to her. "You are the one who gave me a reason to live when all I wanted to do was die. I'd remember your sweet smile, and I'd tell myself I had to come back for you. I never thought I'd be good enough for you because of my scarring, but I knew you were waiting for me. I had to take the chance you would accept me as I am."

"Your appearance has nothing to do with my feelings."

"When I came home you encouraged me to call on you. I thought you had decided you could live with the way I look."

Her gaze searched his face intently. She needed him to understand. "I encouraged you because I had hopes I'd still have the same feelings for you that I did when you left."

Captain Maxwell hit his chest over his heart with his fist. "I still have the same feelings for you."

It broke her heart to say, "But I don't have them for you."

"The patch and my scarring offend you," he said roughly. "Just say it."

"No," she insisted adamantly. "That isn't true so stop saying it. It has nothing to do with your patch or the scarring. Your manner and treatment of me are perfect. You are a true gentleman. It has nothing to do with you. It's me."

"Stop trying to spare my feelings, Miss Rule. Please give me the dignity of the truth. You're beautiful and I am a monster with one eye. I have horrid scars. You will have to look at them every day of your life. Our children would have to look at me. Their friends will make fun of me."

"You don't know what you are saying," she declared,

feeling her own temper flaring because he refused to believe her. "I wanted to love you, Captain. I did love you at one time, but not anymore and not because of your appearance. I haven't wanted to tell you I can't marry you for fear you'd assume exactly what you are thinking. My decision has nothing to do with you and everything to do with me." Her voice softened. "I was sixteen when I first saw you. I loved you the way a sixteen-year-old loves the first handsome gentleman she sees. You were older, a soldier, and so dashing in your uniform. I don't know any way to say it other than my love for you didn't grow up with me. I love someone else."

"The earl."

"Yes," she answered quietly. "I'm in love with him. I wanted it to be you. You were the first man to set my heart to fluttering. I dreamed about you while you were away, and when you returned I tried to force myself to love you because I wanted to so badly. But no matter how hard I tried, I couldn't make it happen. I have great respect for you, but I don't love you."

He shook his head and said, "I can make you happy. I know I can."

"No. I don't know if Lord Thornwick wants me after, after some things I have said to him, but I must try to make him see that I love him, and I want to be his wife."

"Oh, he wants you, Miss Rule," the captain said bitterly. "You can be sure of that. But he will never love you, or be true to you, or be good to you."

In her heart, Angelina knew Captain Maxwell was wrong. Harrison had already been good to her in so many ways. He agreed to saying he would marry her at the end of the Season when, at the time, it was the last thing he wanted to do. He took her to the shelter where she could send wounded animals. He allowed her to take her time and realize that the captain was not the man she loved after all.

"I don't think you are right in that, Captain. I believe Lord Thornwick loves me and that he will be true to me. But in any case, it's a chance I'm willing to take."

"My injury doesn't keep me from being a man." He spoke harshly. "I want, I feel, I get angry."

"I know," she agreed.

"The earl doesn't deserve you. I do!"

"That is enough, Captain," she said, feeling annoyance rising again. "There's nothing more I can say. I think it's time you left."

"You can say it is love for the scoundrel that pleases you, but I know why you have told me no. I know that it's because you are afraid when I make you mine, you will be repulsed by me."

She flinched at his words. "How dare you say that? How dare you suggest I am that weak and shallow? You may be thinking that, but I would not be." Anger fierce and hot rose up in her. Without thinking, she reached up and yanked the patch off his head.

He yelled and covered that side of his face with his hand. "Give it back!" He lunged for the patch with his other hand. She quickly snatched it behind her back. He grabbed her again and tried to reach around her.

"Why did you do that? Give it to me."

"No!" Angelina struggled with him. She tried to pull his hand away from his face while he tried to reach behind her back. "I will look at you!" She struggled, wadding the patch tightly in her fist.

"Give it to me!"

"No! Look at me. I will prove you are the one who is afraid of what you look like. It is not me. It's you!"

Captain Maxwell yelled something about her being

a wicked woman who led him on a merry chase. Suddenly he brought his hands down and grabbed both her upper arms and held her like a vise. He was so irate he forgot that the injured side of his face wasn't covered. There wasn't a gaping black hole as she'd imagined. The lid was closed as if he were asleep. It wasn't even anything that would make her take a second look if she passed him on the street.

She stopped struggling.

He looked down and saw both his hands gripping her arms. He jerked his hand back up to cover the scarred side of his face. "What have you done?" he whispered in an agonized voice that saddened her to her core.

"I've proven to you that you are the one who has a problem with your appearance. It is not me. I have no problem looking at your face." She held his patch out to him.

He took it and slipped it on his head, settling it over his eye. "There is no eye there," he mumbled.

"No, but you are not a monster, either. I am not screaming or running away. I'm not horrified. I'm in awe of your courage and your determination to keep living your life as the strong confident gentleman you are."

"That does little to soothe me, Miss Rule."

He turned and stomped out.

Chapter 29

Courage mounteth with occasion.
King John 2.1.82

Slashing rain beat against the window of the carriage. It had started storming just as Harrison's coach had stopped in front of Angelina's house. There had been a steady drizzle all day, but suddenly the bottom seemed to fall out of the dark-gray sky. It looked as if no end was in sight. But Harrison wasn't going to let a little rain stop him.

Captain Maxwell needed Miss Rule. She would care for him. In time she would heal him. But Harrison needed her, too. He'd never told her. Never even hinted at it and never would let her know he was lost, he had been wounded, too. And he wasn't ready to stop fighting for her.

Telling her he loved her last night was a risk. Now that she'd had time to think about what he'd said, he needed to see her.

The umbrella would be of little use in the wind so he settled his hat low on his head, picked up the small basket of apricot tarts and hid them under his cloak, and stepped out of the carriage. Stinging rain pelted the side of his face, and he splashed in puddles as he hurried toward the stoop. He knocked once on the door and the dogs took over and did their part to let everyone in the house know someone had arrived.

A few moments later Mrs. Bickmore arrived. "My lord," she said, eyeing the basket in his hand. "Come in. Come in."

Harrison stepped inside, took off his dripping hat, and handed it to the housekeeper. "Thank you, Mrs. Bickmore."

"It's a shame you came out on such a bad day. There's no one here to see you. It wasn't storming when Lady Railbridge left so she decided to go ahead to her weekly outing. Mr. Rule is out, too. I don't expect either of them back before the storm lets up."

"Did Miss Rule go with one of them?"

"No, but she's resting and asked not to be disturbed."

Resting?

"Is Miss Rule ill?" he asked.

"I don't think so, my lord," Mrs. Bickmore said, looking at the basket again. "Lady Railbridge said something about her being very tired because she didn't sleep well. She wanted to lie down."

"And you say Mr. Rule is out as well?"

"Quiet, you beasts!" she turned and yelled to the dogs, who hadn't managed to settle down, before giving her attention back to Harrison. "I don't know when to expect him. Truth be told he'd been gone a couple of days now, and Lady Railbridge doesn't usually return until late."

Harrison looked at the tarts. He heard wind whipping around the house, and rain beating against the door and the windowpanes. Angelina was in her bed and unchaperoned. Harrison wasn't leaving without seeing her.

Could he do it?

Harrison knew when he'd decided to come to Angelina's house that he was going to fight for her with all he had. At the time, he didn't know what that was going to be, but now he did. It was a hell of a thing for him to do, and maybe it wasn't fair to the captain, but Harrison was going to do it anyway.

"In that case, Mrs. Bickmore, why don't you make yourself a cup of tea, sit down, and enjoy these apricot tarts?" He extended the basket to her.

"Oh." Her eyes rounded in delighted surprise at the thought of savoring one of the sweet cakes as she took the basket and caught the scent of the fruit. "Oh, but no, I couldn't do that, my lord." She shook her head. "I'll save them for Miss Rule." She reached for the basket. "She'll have them when she gets up."

"I insist these are yours to eat, Mrs. Bickmore. They're best when eaten warm, and my cook just took them out of the oven and wrapped them. I'll bring Miss Rule some more at another time. These are yours."

A smile spread across her face. "Well, if you insist," she said, peeking inside the cloth. "You're right, they are still warm. And they smell delicious, too."

"They are. Make yourself a cup of tea to go with them." He took his hat from her. "Go on now. I'll see myself out."

"If you're sure."

Very sure.

He smiled. "I am."

Harrison held tightly to his hat and watched Mrs. Bickmore walk down the corridor and disappear into the kitchen. As quietly as possible, he turned and took the stairs two at a time. None of the lamps had been lit at the top, and the thunderous skies had that part of the house almost dark. Two doors were on one side of the corridor and three on the other. He had no idea which room was Angelina's, but with no one else in the house but her, he didn't have to worry about knocking on the wrong door.

The dogs had finally settled down. He didn't want to make any noise that might disturb them again. He walked quietly up to the first door and knocked softly. He heard nothing. No sound came from the second, either. He then moved to the center door on the other side of the corridor and knocked.

"Come in," he heard Angelina say.

A surge of anticipation thudded in his chest. She could scream. She could throw him out, or she could welcome him. His hand closed around the cold knob. He turned it and pushed slowly on the door. It creaked slightly. He opened it only far enough to quickly slip inside, and then he softly closed it behind him.

Their eyes met across the room and held.

"Harrison," Angelina whispered, and she rose up in the bed. The covers fell away and she quickly grabbed her pillow and clutched it up to chest. "What's wrong?"

"Nothing," he answered.

The sight of her in her bed aroused him instantly. She was bathed in a soft yellow light from a low-burning lamp on the bedside table and the crackling flames in the fireplace. She was invitingly beautiful in a white long-sleeved night rail. Her glorious golden-brown hair tumbled across her shoulders. He remembered the rainwater smell of it, the silky feel of it.

"I'm not dressed. How did you get up here?"

"I walked."

She looked exasperated by his answer, but he expected that, and shock, too. He had invaded her private chamber without an invitation. It was downright brazen of him, and proved him to be the scoundrel he'd been accused of being. But, looking at her, he was glad he had come up to her bedchamber. Passion had always flared hot and quick between them whenever they were alone together. Looking at her now, he knew today would be no different.

"What are you doing here if nothing is wrong?"

From behind him, he felt underneath the knob until he found the key and turned it, locking out anyone who might try to enter. Expectation of what might happen filled him. He knew he was where he was supposed to be, but did she?

"I wanted to see you," he said, but it was so much more than that. He'd been consumed with yearning for Angelina almost since the first time he'd seen her. He took off his hat and laid it on the stool in front of her dressing table.

"You're not supposed to be in my bedchamber."

Her voice was raspy, giving him hope she'd let him stay.

"I know. When I heard that you were resting and your grandmother and father were out of the house, I couldn't resist the temptation to come up and see you."

He swung his damp cloak off his shoulders and laid it on the stool beside his hat.

"Mrs. Bickmore is here."

"She let me in," he said, giving her reassurance he didn't break into the house.

"I can't believe she allowed you to come up here."

He smiled. "She doesn't know I'm up here with you. She thinks I left." He shrugged out of his coat. "She's in the kitchen having a cup of tea and eating the tarts I brought you. If my luck holds, and the dogs stay quiet, she'll put her feet up and take a nap when she's finished."

She kept her gaze locked on his. "What are you doing?"

Taking a chance. A big chance that she wanted him as much as he wanted her.

"Removing my neckcloth," he replied, unwinding it and dropping it on top of his coat. "And my collar, too." He unfastened it and added it to the pile.

"You're, you're undressing?"

He nodded while her beautiful blue eyes questioned him intently.

She swallowed hard. "You can't do that."

"Then tell me to stop, Angelina," he said, tugging his shirt from the waistband of his trousers and pulling it over his head. He sent it the way of his other things.

She remained silent staring at his bare chest. He was having the effect on her that he'd hoped for. But she was having the desired effect on him as well. Just looking at her sitting on the bed caused the hardness between his legs to throb. He didn't mind that she was taking her time. He had no doubts this was right for both of them, but she needed to be sure, too. In the meantime, his desire for her, his eagerness to make her his, grew stronger with each passing second.

"It's time for you to make a decision."

Harrison sat down on his clothing and tugged and yanked one calf-high, damp boot off while keeping his gaze locked on her face. If she bolted or asked him to leave, he'd have to dig deep to find the strength to do it now that he'd gotten this far.

"There's still time to tell me to stop, Angelina." He pulled off the other boot, set it down beside its mate, and rose to stand before her dressed only in his trousers.

The burning heat of long-denied craving for her tingled in every nerve of his body. He had imagined himself lying with Angelina in her bed many times during the past few weeks. Now that he was so close to that happening, he was desperate for her answer. He was impatient and determined to know right now if she would choose him or the captain.

"So tell me, Miss Rule, are you going to break the rules and let me stay or should I re-dress and leave?"

Chapter 30

I crave no other, nor no better man.
Measure for Measure *5.1.423*

Angelina's breath stalled in her throat. She was captivated by Harrison's wide bare chest and lean, narrow hips gleaming in the glow of the lamplight. Beautifully defined muscles along his rib cage rippled and flexed with movement while he took off his boots. She'd had no idea he would be so stunning beneath his clothing.

He didn't know, but she'd already made her choice. Harrison was the man she loved. The man she wanted to spend the rest of her life with. It hadn't been easy to give up on her dream of marrying the handsome soldier dressed in his pristine uniform, but what she'd felt for him was only a young girl's fancy of what true love was. There was no reality to what she'd felt for the captain. Because they had never touched, or kissed, everything she'd felt for him was only in her imagination. Harrison showed her the difference between what was real and what was imaginary. She had no doubt that what she felt for him was true, lasting love.

The storm continued to rage outside. The wind howled, rain beat against her windows, and thunder rumbled ominously in the distance. Inside her heart, Angelina was at peace. And she knew exactly what she wanted.

Staring at Harrison's questioning expression, her breaths grew choppy with anticipation for what was to come. The few lingering doubts she'd had earlier vanished the moment he started undressing. Her body and her mind relaxed. She was ready, eager, and happy. She was going to keep her eyes open and witness her coming of age with Harrison. The pillow fell from her hands and dropped to the floor. She scooted away from the edge of the bed and without a word held up the covers and invited him to join her.

Harrison's gaze swept hungrily over hers and he walked toward her. When he made it to the bed he didn't hesitate. He simply crawled in, stretched his legs down beside hers, and gathered her in his strong embrace. Warmth curled enticingly around her. She gloried in the feel of his firm, bare back as her arms circled him. With his hand he brushed her hair away from her face, and smiled at her.

Angelina beckoned without saying a word.

Their lips met; their tongues touched with a sweet, satisfying mingling of their breaths. He kissed her longingly, and lovingly. Their lips moved together sensuously, languorously as they kissed and kissed. Angelina didn't think they had ever kissed in such an unhurried manner or for so long.

His hand slid slowly down her unbound breast. Through the thin cotton of her garment he fondled her with tenderness that sent heat flaring between her legs. Her nipple stiffened beneath his gentle touch and her abdomen tightened in response. Letting his hand drift down to her waist, he gently squeezed the indention before moving over the flare of her hip and back up to her breast again. With an open palm, he followed the same leisurely pattern down past the slope of her waist, to the rise of her hip, and back up to tease her erect nipple again and again.

Harrison took his time and so did she, allowing herself the freedom to explore without restraint the strong contours of his shoulders, back, and slim waist. They were eager but not hasty in their pursuit of touching and seducing each other. He had always been a commanding man; their kisses and embraces were usually so intense and fierce they took her breath away. It thrilled her now that he wasn't in a desperate rush but was giving them time to enjoy lying together, side by side for the first time.

When she felt his fingertips working the ribbon at the neckline of her shift, she helped him by parting the bodice and sliding the garment off one shoulder, revealing the swell of her breasts in the lamplight. Her shallow breaths and keen awareness of what was about to happen made her chest rise and fall rapidly.

With tenderness that touched her deeply, his warm breath and lips skimmed across her skin as he kissed the crook of her neck and shoulder, leaving a faint trail of moisture on her skin and a tightening in her most womanly part.

Harrison continued to kiss along her collarbone to the hollow of her throat, up the side of her neck, and under her chin. She kissed his cheeks, the side of his mouth, and under his eye all while a burning need for more of him was slowly building inside her. Their long-denied desire to possess each other couldn't stay banked much longer.

Harrison looked at her and whispered, "Angelina, I have yearned for the day you would be mine."

"So have I."

"No doubts or fears?"

"Plenty of fears about what we are doing, but no doubts. Now, can we continue?"

He chuckled softly and rolled her onto her back. He pushed her garment lower, exposing one breast, and greedily covered her nipple with his mouth as he settled the hard, heavy weight of his loins against hers. She sighed with heavenly pleasure and lifted her chest to him. He continued to cup, caress, and knead her breast with his strong yet gentle hand, sending wave after wave of pleasure to that intimate part between her legs.

Angelina ran her hands up and down his back, over his strong neck and into his thick, lush hair. She nuzzled the warmth of his shoulder with her nose and lips, letting her tongue taste his heated skin time and time again.

She went dizzy with pleasure as he pulled her nipple deeply into his mouth, sucking gently and forcing her to whisper what her body craved, "Give me more, Harrison. Give me more."

In answer to her plea, he shifted his lower body off her and let his hand slip down the plane of her leg as he gathered up her chemise to her waist. His hand rested on her bare hip for a moment before exploring her waist and then sliding over her abdomen to the warmth between her legs. Her thighs tightened instinctively, but he gently nudged them apart and found her soft, moist center with his thumb and forefinger. He rubbed, circled, and lightly pressed her center, teasing her, filling her with an exquisite joyous pain. She savored the spreading warmth of being awakened to hot, indescribable pleasure.

Somewhere at the back of her thoughts, she wanted to do something for him, to make him feel what she was experiencing, but his fluid, gentle touch left her incapable of doing anything but writhing with smoldering rapture. Spiral after spiral of new and glorious sensations twirled, whirled, and built inside her with every second that passed. She could do nothing but what she'd said she wouldn't do by closing her eyes, throwing her head back, and moaning softly.

Harrison's lips left her breast and found hers. "Not yet," he whispered. "It's best you feel this way when I enter you."

"No," she answered breathlessly. "Don't stop."

But he already had by the time her words were out of her mouth. She felt him push his trousers down his legs and kick them away. As his hand came up their bodies he grabbed the tail of her shift and pulled it over her head. Angelina helped him fling it away as they kissed madly.

He rose up over her and settled his hard thickness between her legs. He slid one hand beneath her head and tangled his fingers in her hair. With his other hand he returned to her womanly center and continued his gentle assault on her senses.

"Do you know what to expect?" he asked huskily, looking into her eyes.

"Yes," she answered and then shook her head. "No. I'm not sure."

"Just trust me."

"I do."

His lips met hers with intense urgency. He plundered her mouth, his tongue swirling and skimming into the depths and along the lining of her lips. Angelina matched his fierceness as their lips and tongues clung together in desperation to finish what they'd started.

She felt his shaft bearing down on her with gentle, persistent probing. A moment of pain made her jerk in surprise.

"Angelina," he whispered against her lips, "it had to happen."

"I know."

Tightening his hold on the back of her head, rubbing her center with his thumb, he asked, "Is the pain gone now?"

"Yes," she answered with a smile and hugged him to her as he slowly moved deeper and deeper inside her.

Harrison rocked his lower body against hers, and Angelina felt him slowly filling her with each movement. His kissed her lips, her cheeks, and her eyes. His movements were confident, commanding, and always gentle. Their breaths, their sighs, and their moans of passion joined as beautifully as their bodies as he pressed deeply into her. She matched his slow rhythm with movements of her own. His hand continued making dizzying sensations build inside her until an explosion of rapture splintered through her that was so heavenly, she thought she might stop breathing.

While she was still feeling the remnants of her glorious culmination, Harrison stopped moving, moaned softly, and eased his body down on hers, shuddering and quietly gasping.

A feeling of immeasurable satisfaction flowed over Angelina and she relaxed upon the bed. Harrison rested his weight upon her, burying his face in the crook of her neck.

They lay there for several moments with neither of them moving, their arms and legs entwined, basking in the afterglow of their lovemaking.

"Will it always be so powerful?" she asked.

"Always," Harrison answered, and rolled over on his side, pulling her with him. She rested her head on his shoulder, and he cuddled her close.

"Do you also know that taking your maidenhood makes you mine? I will not give you up, Angelina."

His bold declaration made her chest swell with love.

"You are the man I love, Harrison. I want no other."

He smiled and kissed her softly. "It's about time you told me that. I love you, Angelina, and I want no other. Do you want me to tell Maxwell about us?"

She rose on her elbow and looked at him. "You want him to know about what just happened between us?"

He chuckled. "No, my love. This afternoon will always be our secret. I meant tell him that you are mine now and he will have to stand down."

"I've already told him."

His embrace tightened and eyes searched her face, looking for truth. "When?"

"Before you arrived today. I told him I couldn't marry him because I love you."

Relief washed down his face, and his body relaxed again. "How did he take the news?"

She sighed heavily and thought about telling him about the argument and that she tore the patch off Captain Maxwell's face. Maybe in time she could tell him that but not now, not while the episode with the captain was still so raw.

"Not well."

"Understandable."

"It was very sad for me."

"It had to be done."

"I'm only sorry I couldn't make him believe that my rejection of his proposal of marriage had nothing to do with his scars. I don't think he'll ever believe that."

"You know the truth and so do I. That's all that is important."

"I tried to explain that I had loved him when I was younger but while he was away, I grew up and realized that dream wasn't reality. It wasn't a lasting love. The love I have for you is very different from the love I had for him."

Harrison laid his forehead on hers for a moment and then kissed her sweetly. "I'm glad you realized that before it was too late. I was so afraid you'd let your deep compassion for him be mistaken for love."

"I almost did, but when he kissed me, I never felt the desire for him that I feel for you."

His brows rose with teasing amusement. "So he finally got the courage to kiss you, did he?"

"He had the courage all along," she said, knowing there would still be times she'd have to defend Captain Maxwell; Harrison might as well get used to it. "You obviously forgot that he is a gentleman."

"And you obviously prefer a man who is not."

She kissed the side of his neck and breathed in deeply. "I prefer you."

He rolled her on her back and kissed her lovingly for a moment before he rose from the bed and picked up his trousers. "I would very much like to show you once again how much I love you, Angelina, but I'd rather your father not come home and find that we have anticipated our wedding vows this stormy afternoon."

"I don't think he'll be home anytime soon." She sat up and leaned against the headboard. "I think he's gambling again."

He pulled his shirt over his head. "What makes you say that?"

"You know I gave him the money yesterday to pay his debts. When he left, I assumed he'd gone to take care of them. But he never joined us at the parties and he didn't come home last night. He left with the money. I fear he took it and is gambling with it."

By the look on his face, she knew Harrison thought the same. "I will go and see if I can find your father." He reached down and kissed her lips again. "I must find him so I can properly ask for your hand in marriage."

She felt as if her heart would swell out of her chest. "You're aren't teasing me, are you, Harrison?"

His brows drew together. "It was settled we would marry before I crawled into your bed. I assume you will say yes to my proposal."

She smiled and laughed, throwing her arms around his neck. "Yes, you know I love you and want to be your wife."

"Then as much as I hate the thought, I must leave. Usually every gambler ends up at White's. I'll go there and wait, talk to others who come in and see if anyone has seen him."

"What will we do if he's gambled all the money away again? Will the Prince still pay his debts if he finds out Papa had the means and didn't do it?"

"It matters not to us what the Prince thinks or does. We will marry. You and your father will be my responsibility. I will pay his debts."

Her breath caught in her throat. "Do you mean that?"

He sat on the edge of the bed and said, "Come here." He placed his hands on the sides of her head and said, "I will take care of you and your father. Your grandmother, too. You just worry about taking care of me."

"I will take care of you forever," she said with all the love she was feeling.

"That won't be long enough," he whispered and laid her back on the bed.

The storm was waning but the passion between Angelina and Harrison wasn't. He made love to her again before Angelina dressed and went below stairs to keep Mrs. Bickmore busy while Harrison stole out of the house.

Chapter 31

Lay on, Macduff: And damned be him that first cries,
"Hold, enough!"
Macbeth 5.8.33–34

Anger wasn't something Harrison had to deal with often. He didn't let many things bother him and even fewer rile him. Perhaps it was that he'd seldom cared enough about anything to be bothered with the emotion. But Captain Maxwell was about to get the best of Harrison's easygoing nature.

It was clear the man had consumed numerous pints of ale, and though he hadn't gotten to the point he was slurring his words, Harrison knew he was only a tankard away. Harrison hadn't wanted to play cards with the captain when he'd approached the table but there was an empty chair and an unwritten rule of conduct that if a man asked to join a game, you welcomed him. That's one rule Harrison would have happily broken if the other gentlemen at the table would have complied.

The crowd at White's was thin. It was that time of early evening when most gentlemen were at home hav-

ing their dinner or preparing for the night's round of parties and balls. Harrison had questioned a few of the
men but none of them had seen Angelina's father. There
was only one other club Mr. Rule belonged to, and Harrison was thinking he'd quit White's and see if the man
was at the smaller club.

Captain Maxwell had lost the first two hands. Harrison had no idea how someone could get through almost twenty years in the army and not know how to play
a hand of whist. Harrison and the other two gentlemen
at the table were very good at cards and knew how to
play the game to their best advantage. Harrison had actually thought about finding a way to let the officer win
after his first loss, but quelled that idea. Win or lose, it
was best to play fair.

By the third game Harrison had had enough of the
officer's remarks and decided the hand they were playing would be his last. He didn't like the way Captain
Maxwell completely ignored the other two gentlemen at
the table and kept commenting about what an excellent
player Harrison was and how Harrison was going to
have to give him some lessons so he could get better –
as if Harrison would– and all the while downing a good
bit more ale.

Without warning Maxwell stood up, knocking over
his chair. He placed his hand on the hilt of his sword,
looked menacingly at Harrison, and said, "You cheated,
Thornwick."

Harrison frowned but kept his seat, and surprisingly
remained calm. The other two men at the table carefully
laid down their cards. There wasn't anything Harrison
disliked more than being called a card cheat unless it
was being called a coward. And he hated defending
himself over either one. He never minded being accused
of anything he'd done wrong. The Lord and everybody

else knew there had been plenty. If necessary, Harrison didn't even mind owning up to whatever it was he was being accused of. He just didn't like being condemned for something he didn't do.

"I don't have to cheat, Captain. I'm that good."

The man huffed out a laugh. "Because you cheat. I know this isn't the first time you've been caught. I say you have a problem with playing fair."

Harrison looked at the two other men at the table. Thankfully they were remaining still and quiet. Harrison knew Captain Maxwell's claim had nothing to do with cards. It was all about Angelina, and because of her, Harrison had to try to smooth this over.

"The only gentlemen who ever accuse me are the ones who've had too much to drink and are unhappy with their own play."

"Is that your style? You don't drink much knowing the others will. Do you wait until they are deep in their cups before you switch out your winning card?"

"You need to go home and sleep it off, soldier."

"Don't call me that," he snarled. "I'm not a soldier anymore and you damn well know it."

It was getting harder to do, but Harrison knew sometimes the wisest course of action was to keep his peace no matter the enemy. "It doesn't matter, it's an admirable title and you deserve it," he said, not liking the fact he was trying to placate the sore loser.

"I don't need you feeling sorry for me."

"Believe me, I don't," Harrison said honestly. "Now either sit down and play or leave."

"Why would I or anyone want to play with a cheater? You're not getting out of this one, my lord. Admit you cheated and I'll let it pass if the other gentlemen are willing, but keep in mind, once you do, you'll never play cards with anyone in London again."

Harrison didn't want to do this. If the captain wouldn't leave, Harrison would. He rose and when he did the other two men stood up and backed away from the table, too. That action caused all the other gentlemen in the room to stop playing and focus on the disturbance.

"I am not admitting to anything I'm not guilty of. I don't cheat." He turned to leave but the captain stepped in front of him.

"You can't just walk away, coward."

Harrison wished he hadn't called him that. It was mighty tempting to just coldcock the blackguard and lay him out flat. Instead, Harrison tried again. "Don't do this, Maxwell. I don't want to fight you."

The officer jerked his gloves from his belt and threw them to the card room floor. "Now you don't have a choice."

Harrison looked down at the gloves. Damn, he hated duels. If he fought Maxwell and wounded him, or worse killed him, Angelina would never forgive him. But if he didn't fight the man, Harrison didn't know if he could forgive himself.

It was best he try again to get out of this the easy way.

He looked at the other two men who had played with them. "Did either of you see any unacceptable moves by me."

"No, my lord," they said in unison.

"Have you ever in all the years we have played?"

"No, my lord," they repeated.

"Good." He nodded to them. "These men have no reason not to be truthful, Captain. That should be good enough for you."

Harrison turned to leave. In a flash Maxwell slid his rapier from its scabbard and had the tip pressing under Harrison's chin. Harrison froze. Damnation, that man was fast with a sword.

Gasps and low murmurings sounded around the room. Chairs scraped against the wooden floor as more men stood up. Maxwell continued to press the blade into the skin under Harrison's chin. His head was tilted back as far as it would go, but still the sharp tip pierced Harrison's flesh. He felt the puncture and a trickle of warm blood run down his neck.

There was nothing like the sharp point of a blade to let someone know you meant business. Damn, Harrison didn't want to fight the man.

"What's going on here?"

Harrison heard Bray's voice before he saw him come up beside him. "Put that sword away, Captain or I will put it away for you."

"Stay out of this, Bray," Harrison said.

"Like hell I will."

"This is my fight."

"You are unarmed and in no position to fight right now. I am. Remove your blade, Captain," Bray said again.

Although Harrison couldn't see it, he knew that Bray had drawn the dagger he always wore belted around his waist.

"I caught this man cheating at cards, Your Grace," the officer said.

"I've known Lord Thornwick since we were lads," Bray replied. "He doesn't cheat."

"Everyone changes, Your Grace. I guess he did. He's a coward, too. He tried to walk away from my challenge."

"I'd say that makes him an intelligent man, not a coward."

"I don't know many soldiers who would agree with you on that."

"This is the last time I'm saying, put down that sword." Bray's tone said the arguing was over.

Captain Maxwell whipped his sword through the air and sheathed it. Harrison's head fell forward. He moved to grab Maxwell, but Bray's arm landed across his chest, stopping him.

"It's the earl's choice," Maxwell said smugly. "He can fight me at dawn or he can walk away now and be branded a coward and a cheat for the rest of his life."

"I'll meet you at Martin's Ditch off Blackburn Road," Harrison said in a deadly quiet voice.

"Choose your weapon?" Maxwell said just as quietly.

"You want this challenge. You decide."

"Swords at daybreak," the captain said with a sneer, then added, "No mercy," and strode out of the room.

Rumblings of voices scattered about the room. Harrison thought he'd fought his last duel a few months ago. Damn, he'd wanted it to be the last. Maybe the man knew the Prince was already threatening him with prison.

"You don't have to do this, Harrison," Bray said, handing him his handkerchief.

"I didn't know you were here." Harrison pressed the white cloth under his chin and winced from the sting. Maxwell's blade hadn't gone deep but it was damned sharp.

Bray slid his dagger back into its holder. "One of Louisa's sisters is having a music lesson on the pianoforte."

"You don't need to say more," Harrison said, remembering that the only pianoforte music he'd ever enjoyed was Angelina's.

"No one believes you are a cheat or a coward."

"I know, but it doesn't matter."

"Do you really want to fight a man with one eye?"

"Of course not," Harrison said in an exasperated voice, pressing the handkerchief tighter against the cut. "He left me no choice. I will meet him at dawn."

"How long has it been since you held a blade?"

"Longer than I will admit," Harrison said, feeling none too confident that he could take the captain. The man was a soldier. He'd lived by the sword.

"This is madness," Bray argued. "I can have him picked up and sent to Newgate."

"That will settle nothing. It will only prolong it."

"It will give Maxwell time to sober and rethink this affront to your character."

Harrison looked at the bright-red blood on the white handkerchief. "This isn't about cards. This man wants to kill me and if I stood in his shoes, I'd feel the same way."

Understanding lighted in Bray's eyes. "So he knows he's lost Angelina."

Harrison nodded once. He didn't have to guess at what the army captain was feeling. Harrison knew. The man had lost his eye, his ability to be a soldier, the lady he loved. Captain Maxwell probably no longer cared if he lost his life as well.

"He won't change his mind and I'm not in a mood to forgive him should he." Harrison looked up at his friend. "I am at peace about this, Bray."

"In that case, I'm your second?"

"I don't want to involve you in this."

"You're not. I am."

Harrison nodded.

"Change your shirt and get your sword. I'll get us a room at the fencing club so you can practice."

Harrison started to walk away but Bray stayed him with a touch to his shoulder.

"This is a no-win duel for you, Harrison. If you wound him, she'll never forgive you, and if the unthinkable happens . . ."

"I understand. My honor demands I answer his challenge."

Chapter 32

They durst not do't; they could not, would not do't.
King Lear 2.2.215–16

She woke with a start. A door had slammed below stairs. Booted feet were climbing the steps fast.

"Angelina!" her father called.

Her heartbeat raced as she looked out her window. It was still dark. What was going on? She pushed the covers back.

"Angelina!" he called again.

She scrambled out of bed and was donning her robe when he rushed inside, slamming the door against the wall.

"You must dress and come with me at once!"

"What's wrong?" she asked. "Did your lenders not accept the money?"

"No, no, of course they did and were quite happy. It's Lord Thornwick. He's in danger and you must help him."

Harrison!

Her heart jumped into her throat. "What kind of danger?" she asked, running to her wardrobe to find a dress.

"That foul Captain Maxwell has challenged him to a duel at dawn. We must stop him. The carriage is waiting."

Frantic, Angelina looked back to her father. "A duel? Captain Maxwell and Harrison? But why?"

"The captain accused him of cheating at cards."

"That's preposterous," she exclaimed, pulling out a simple carriage dress that would be easy to put on. "Lord Thornwick would never cheat."

"It was just a ruse, my dear. I'm sure the true reason is you. To his credit, I'm told Lord Thornwick did his best to talk Maxwell out of the challenge. The fool just wouldn't listen."

"Where are they?" she asked, frantically pulling out a pair of shoes.

"What's going on?" her grandmother asked from the doorway.

"Help me dress, Granna. I must hurry. Lord Thornwick is in danger."

"I've heard they are meeting at Martin's Ditch," her father said. "I think we can catch the earl before he leaves his house. I'll wait below stairs. Hurry!"

A few minutes later their landau arrived in front of Lord Thornwick's town house. The carriage was barely stopped before Angelina had the door open and was waiting for their driver to help her down. Harrison's carriage was still there. Thank God he hadn't left yet.

Not waiting for her father, Angelina raced to the door and hit the knocker several times. The door jerked open and she saw the Duke of Drakestone. Harrison was behind him with his cloak and gloves in his hand.

"Harrison, don't do this," she whispered, rushing past the duke and stopping in front of Harrison.

His eyes swept lovingly up and down her face. "Angelina, what are you doing here?"

"Papa heard about what you have planned and told me. I had to come," she said.

Her father rushed in the door behind her. Harrison gave him a murderous look. "You shouldn't have told her."

"I had to. She's the only one who can talk you out of this foolish stunt. Besides, she would have never forgiven me if I hadn't."

"Wait outside," Harrison said. "Both of you."

The duke and her father went out and closed the door. Angelina flung herself into his arms and he caught her up tightly to him. He was warm and strong and he was hers. She couldn't lose him in a duel.

"Don't do this, my love," she pleaded, her arms circling his waist. "Please, don't do this."

He held her tightly for a moment and kissed the top of her head then set her away from him. "I want you to go back home with your father. I will come to you there when this is over."

How could he tell her that? "Don't ask that of me." Her throat ached from holding in the fear churning inside her.

"You must. A duel is no place for a lady."

"It's no place for anyone. I will talk to Captain Maxwell and I'll get him to——"

He grabbed her upper arms with his hands. "It's too late for that, Angelina. Everything is set and it cannot be undone."

"Of course it can," she insisted. "This is madness! I don't care what he thinks about you. I'm asking you not to go."

"If I could do this for you I would, but I can't."

"Does the captain think I will love him if he forces

you to wound him further? I will tell him again, I will never love him. I love you."

"It's not about love for him anymore, Angelina. It's about revenge and it can't be stopped. Go home and I will come to you there when this is over."

"You are good with a pistol, right?"

He nodded.

"So you'll only wound him. Like that other man. The one you dueled with last year, right?"

He smiled. "Thank you for your faith in my abilities, my love, but this will be with a blade."

She remembered the sound of Captain Maxwell sliding his sword back into his scabbard and she shivered. "But he's a soldier. He must be very good."

Harrison shrugged.

Angelina shook her head. "I don't understand why you have to do this, my love. How can I let you do this?"

"You can't stop me. Angelina, my honor is the only thing that makes me deserving of you."

At that moment she knew she couldn't change what was to happen so she had to be the one to change. She couldn't be a weak, whimpering lady, though she desperately wanted to be. Those feelings had to be denied. Angelina had to be strong and confident for Harrison. He had to know she had faith in him to know what had to be done and his ability to do it.

She squared her shoulders and lifted her chin. "In that case, I can't leave you to face this alone. I know you will handle this like the gentleman you claim you aren't. I understand that, but I must be there for you."

His eyes searched her face. She remained courageous and steadfast though inside she felt as if she were falling apart.

"Very well, you and your father can ride with me, but once we are there you must stay in the carriage, stay quiet, and not try to stop this. I must have your promise, Angelina."

Could she do that? If she gave her word she would have to. It broke her heart anew to say it but she relented and whispered, "I love you, Harrison. I promise I will stay inside the carriage until the duel is over."

He hugged her to his chest and whispered, "I love you, Angelina."

Chapter 33

Take honor from me, and my life is done.
Richard II *1.1.183*

Harrison sat in his coach with his eyes closed and the back of his head pressed against the velvet cushion, resting his eyes, remembering how alluring Angelina was with her gorgeous hair spilling over her shoulders to caress her breasts. He didn't ever want to forget that memory. Or her soft sighs, her gentle touch, or her eagerness to enjoy, to give, to fulfill both their cravings for each other.

She was sitting on the opposite seat from him, with her father. He couldn't touch her so he thought of her, deeply and longingly. He didn't want her with him, but he couldn't deny her. He had no doubt of her courage or strength no matter what might happen.

He wore his favorite over-the-knee boots, breeches that didn't bind, and a white shirt with full sleeves, forgoing the coat, waistcoat, and neckcloth, knowing the less clothing to worry with, the better. For hours, he'd swung the sword until his arm ached and then fenced some more. After a couple of hours' sleep he and Bray had readied to come out to the dueling site.

There could be little doubt that Captain Maxwell was good with a sword. How could he not be, having been a soldier for the better part of twenty years? Still, the man was handicapped by his blind side. Harrison had to use that to his advantage.

The carriage door swung open. "It's time," Bray said, holding Harrison's sword in his hand.

"Everything has been attended to?" he asked.

"Exactly what you wanted. No time limit, no interference by anyone, and no halting the fight once it begins."

"But—" Angelina leaned forward. "What does that mean?"

"Angelina." Harrison spoke her name softly and shook his head. "Remember your promises to me."

She hesitated and started to argue then leaned back in the cushion again and folded her hands in her lap. It would not help him if she troubled him now. "I do and I will remain quiet, but remember I love you."

Harrison smiled at her. "I will not forget that." He then glanced at her father. "See she stays inside."

"I will sit on her if I have to, my lord. Be careful."

Harrison picked up his coat from the seat, stepped outside the coach, and shut the door. He didn't want to do this. He wanted to be through with dueling. Turning away from the carriage, he surveyed his surroundings: more than two dozen men standing around a small clearing, several carriages lined in a row opposite his. Trees budding with spring, dew shimmering in patches on the ground. Air chilly but not cold. The low murmurings hushed and for a split second it was so quiet, Harrison could hear his own labored breathing.

Until now, he had fought fairly for Angelina. He dug

into his pocket, pulled out a crudely made eye patch, and started fitting the black fabric over his right eye.

"What the devil are you doing?" Bray said. "Give me that." He reached for the eye patch and Harrison swerved away from him.

"I'm making this an equal fight," he said, tying the thin leather strips at the back of his head.

"It's fair without that," Bray muttered. "You aren't as proficient with a sword as he is. I've let you do some dangerous and fool-hearted things in my life."

"As I have you," Harrison countered,

"But at the time, we were young, and had no respect for life or anything else. You have Angelina now. It's downright foolish to handicap yourself this way."

"Maybe."

Bray let out a heavy sigh and flattened his hand against Harrison's chest. He looked him directly in his eye and said, "You know what you're doing, don't you?"

Harrison remained quiet. You're hoping the patch will make him angry, make him reckless."

"Like I said, I'm hoping to make this an equal fight. I never said it was fair."

Bray held the sword out to him. He started to reach for it but heard Captain Maxwell yell from the other side of the clearing, "Take it off!"

Harrison looked at the soldier. He'd removed his regimentals and like Harrison wore only trousers, boots, and shirt.

"You are mocking me by wearing that! Get it off!"

Harrison saw rage light in the captain's face as he stomped toward him without his sword in hand. "I am giving you an equal chance, which you wouldn't have otherwise. It's the only way I can honorably fight you."

Maxwell gave him a murderous look as he quickly closed the distance between them. "Take it off now, you coward." He pointed his finger at Harrison. "Or I will rip it off after I have torn your head from your shoulders!"

Harrison was getting damned tired of the man calling him a coward. "You can try," he said calmly and continued his leisurely stroll to meet him.

The captain let out a yell and charged Harrison, catching him in the chest with his shoulder. The wind swooshed out of Harrison's lungs. He stumbled backward and fell onto the ground. The captain leaped on top of him and clawed for the patch. Harrison held him off with a tightfisted blow to his chin that stunned him.

Harrison threw the man off him and sprang to his feet. Maxwell was on his feet just as fast and came up swinging at Harrison. He sidestepped him, backed away, and motioned with both hands for the captain to come at him again.

"I'll gouge both your eyes out and see how you like that!" Maxwell shouted on a ragged breath and took another swing at Harrison.

Harrison ducked but a quick right caught him under his eye, sending splintering pain through his face as his head snapped back. Regaining his balance, Harrison plowed his fists one right after the other into Maxwell's stomach. The man grunted and came back at Harrison with a powerful glancing hook to his abdomen.

Shouts from the crowd drew closer but Harrison kept his focus on the raging soldier in front of him. Sucking in a short, shallow breath Harrison connected to the man's jaw with a hard jab. Bloody spittle flew from the captain's mouth as he grabbed for Harrison's patch again. Another hard right caught Harrison on the side of his mouth, smashing the tender flesh against his teeth, ripping his lip and sending a shower of blood that sprayed his chin.

Evading Maxwell's long reach, Harrison gave him a powerful uppercut to his chin and then two quick jabs to his midsection. Sweating, Captain Maxwell staggered backward then suddenly lunged forward again, knocking Harrison to the ground. The captain pounced on top of him, and once more clawed for the patch. With a surge of strength, Harrison rolled the man over and grabbed him around the neck by the crook of his arm, forcing him to gasp for every breath.

"I'm assuming you changed your mind as to the choice of weapons and took fists," Harrison said between labored breathing. "Wise choice."

"Hell no, I didn't," Maxwell sputtered, trying to leverage his body with his feet and pull himself away from Harrison's grip.

Harrison grabbed his wrist with his other hand and tightened the pressure against the officer's throat. "I could snap your neck right now, and no one would fault me, Captain."

"Fault you? They expect you to do it and so do I. We agreed to the rule 'No mercy.' "

"I never did like to follow the rules."

"Go ahead. You say you are not a coward. Prove it. You say you're not a cheat. Then prove it and don't let me cheat death again. Kill me. Kill me!"

For a split second Harrison was tempted to do just that. Maxwell wasn't yelling empty words. The soldier wanted to die, and he wanted Harrison to see that it happened. The distaste of that rose like bile in Harrison's throat. He reached up and ripped the patch off his eye and slung it away.

"There are at least a dozen men here who will swear

you came at me with your fists in this duel," Harrison said quietly. "I accepted your challenge, defended myself, and won." Harrison let go of the man and roughly shoved him away.

"Coward," Maxwell said with a swollen lip. "The rules of the duel said to the death."

Harrison staggered to his feet and stared down at the sweaty, bloody man. "We've already established what I think of rules. If you want to die, find someone else to do your dirty work for you. I don't have the stomach for it. This duel is finished."

He started toward his carriage. The door pushed open and Angelina sprang from the cab and ran toward him. He caught her up in his arms and held her gently against his dirty, damp shirt.

"Your lip is cut and you're bleeding," she said, placing her open palm against his cheek.

He could have told her his hands, jaw, and ribs were hurting like hell, too, but all he said was, "I'm fine."

"I'm so thankful you weren't seriously hurt." She glanced over at Maxwell, who still lay on the ground. "That neither of you was. That there were no swords used."

Harrison looked into her eyes. Her compassion for the soldier was still there. He knew it always would be and Harrison didn't mind. That was who she was. He loved her for it and had no doubt of her love for him. "Do you want to go to him?" Harrison asked.

Without hesitating or bothering to look at the captain, she said, "No. He must find peace with what happened to him, but I can't help him do that."

All Harrison's pain ebbed away. He circled her with his arm and started to walk toward their coach when he heard the sound of a carriage racing and bumping over the rough ground. He turned to see the coach barreling toward them at breakneck speed. Four guards on horses flanked each side of it. The carriage stopped near them and Mr. Hopscotch stumbled out the door, almost falling in his haste.

"Stop the duel! Stop the duel!" He ran to the center of the clearing and looked around. The onlookers stared at him as if he were demented. He saw Maxwell still lying on the ground, and then spotted Harrison by his carriage.

"You're late," Harrison said. "It's over."

Hopscotch ran his open palms down the front of his coat as if he were wiping something off them. "Yes, I see that now. But all seems well."

"It is. You can tell the Prince that he can stop sending you with guards. My dueling days are over, Mr. Hopscotch. Miss Rule and I are getting married as soon as the banns are posted."

Harrison looked down at Angelina. "You do accept, don't you?"

She smiled. "It is with great pleasure that I accept, my lord. But what is this about the guards?"

"It's a long story, my love and if fate continues to smile on me, I should have about fifty years to tell you about it. Let's go prepare for our wedding"

Epilogue

I know no ways to mince it in love but directly to say
"I love you."
Henry V 5.2.125–26

Something disrupted Harrison's sleep. His eyes fluttered open to bright sunlight splintering into his bedchamber from a slit between the two drapery panels. He felt warmth beside him. He smiled. It was Angelina's rounded bottom snuggled against his hip. It must have been her movement that roused him.

What a nice way to wake up.

It was their first morning at Thornwick since becoming husband and wife. The house was a long way from being finished but Angelina was just as eager as he was to return and oversee the rebuilding.

He turned his head and saw her long tangled hair spread across her pillow. Moving slowly so he wouldn't wake her, he eased away from her just enough so he could look at her. The color of her skin was beautiful. Her back was straight and her shoulders softly rounded. His gaze drifted to the indention of her small waist, on to the flare of her womanly hip, down the smooth plane of her thigh, and all the way to her shapely legs entwined with the sheet. She was as lovely from the back as she was from the front.

Harrison knew how lucky he was to have such a passionate wife. She was also honorable and loyal to a fault. Those weren't the only things he admired about her. She was a nurturer, too. In the years to come, she would know how to manage their unruly sons and how to counsel their innocent daughters.

He could have easily lost Angelina to the captain And almost had. Harrison meant it when he told her he didn't harbor any ill feelings concerning the captain and his challenge to the duel. Hell, Harrison might have tried the same if he'd lost Angelina. But he wouldn't be so generous if Maxwell made any further attempts to continue his grudge. Harrison had meant it when he said their fight was finished.

An odd sound caught his attention. He couldn't place what it was but it sounded like it was in the room with him. He listened intently for a moment, but all was quiet again. He reached over and tenderly kissed the back of Angelina's shoulder. He breathed in the warmth of her scent. It was heavenly woman. They had been up late and he didn't want to disturb her, but his body was telling him to stop the nonsense of letting her sleep and pull her into his arms and awaken her with kisses.

The sound came again. Was that the *grrr* of a dog? And was that a gnawing sound? He slowly rose in the bed and sat up. He glanced around the room. Clothing, shoes, and stockings were strewn about the floor, but he saw nothing amiss. He was about to lie back down when he heard a dog growling. This time he was sure. There was a dog in the room, but which one and how the hell had it gotten into his bedchamber?

Harrison spotted his trousers on the floor beside the

bed. He reached down, picked them up, and slid his legs into them, pulling them up his hips as he eased off the bed. Angelina stirred but didn't wake.

With quiet steps he walked around the foot of the bed to the other side and saw Mr. Pete with his front paws forward, his hind end up in the air, chewing the devil out of the toe of one of Harrison's boots.

With no thought for his slumbering wife and in a voice loud enough to unsettle the dead, he exclaimed, "You little cur!"

Harrison dove to grab the boot out of the beagle's mouth but the little dog was quicker and dragged it just out of his reach as Harrison hit the floor on his knees and skidded. He stretched to grab it but Mr. Pete snarled and pulled it back just far enough that Harrison missed it again.

"Harrison, what's wrong?" Angelina said. "What's going on?"

"Your little mongrel is using my boot for a bone," he said, reaching for the third time and grabbing hold of the heel. Mr. Pete growled, shook his head, and sank his teeth farther into the leather. Harrison pulled and the beagle gave a valiant effort to hold on but his small jaws were no match for Harrison's strength. Finally he had to let go of his new boot bone.

Harrison rose to his feet. Mr. Pete barked up at him several times, as if to say, *Give it back and let's play again*.

Harrison examined the boot. The once shiny toe was scratched, skinned, and chewed. The little devil's teeth had made holes and frayed the softer leather at the top. The boot was beyond repair.

"I'm so sorry, Harrison. Is it ruined?"

He glanced over at his startled wife. She was wiping

her sleepy eyes with one hand and pulling the sheet under her chin with the other.

"No," he lied. "It's fine."

"I don't know how Mr. Pete got above stairs and into our bedchamber. Maybe one of the servants accidentally let him out of the storage room while we were having dinner last night. I'll take him back down immediately."

Harrison dropped the boot to the floor. He heard Mr. Pete grab it and drag it away. "You'll do no such thing." He walked over, put his hands on each side of her face, and smiled down at her. "It's just a pair of old boots. And good morning, Lady Thornwick. You are looking especially gorgeous this morning. Maybe that's because we are finally home."

She looked up at him with a questioning expression. "You're not angry at Mr. Pete?"

Well?

"Why should I be?" he said with a smile. "I have others."

"I know men can become very fond of their boots. I hope it wasn't your favorite pair."

Harrison searched her beautiful blue eyes and remembered something Bray had said to him months ago: *I like Louisa's sisters, but even if I didn't, I'd put up with them because Louisa is worth it.*

That's the way he felt about Angelina's dogs. He liked her dogs, but even if he didn't, he'd tolerate them for her.

"I'm certain. From this day forward there will be a new tradition at Thornwick. Dogs will be allowed to run free in the house."

She smiled and laughed and wound her arms around his waist as she hugged him to her, placing her cheek against his bare abdomen. "Even I have limitations about how much freedom the dogs have in the house, and the first rule of order is that they don't belong above stairs. We must have our space and they must have theirs."

Harrison liked that idea. He cupped her head to him. "In that case, I'll leave all the rules to you."

"Now that is very generous of you, my lord," she said with a laugh. "No reason for you to start making or following rules this late in life, is there?"

He reached down and kissed the top of her head. "You are the only rule I want."

She looked up at him with her beautiful blue eyes. "Thank you for understanding. Mr. Pete is still young and has not been properly trained yet. I love you even more than I thought possible for being understanding about my pets and my father. Thank you for paying off the rest of his debts."

He grinned and crawled into the bed with her, pulling her into his arms as he joined her.

"I should have paid them all, but for your craftiness. You will keep your promise to never sell another fan or painting, right?"

"I will, my lord. Besides, I'll be too busy helping you restore the Thornwick paintings that were damaged in the fire. And hopefully, my father will be too busy helping you replenish the library to even think about gambling for a long time to come."

"A very long time." Harrison kissed her lips and looked lovingly into her eyes. "You are the perfect mistress for Thornwick, Angelina. My father and my brothers would be pleased."

Her eyes watered. "I don't think you could have said anything that would have pleased me more."

"It's true. You will help me restore my family's legacy with strong sons and beautiful daughters."

"Should we start working on trying to get those sons right now, my love?" she asked as she rolled him onto his back and straddled his hips.

"Please do, my love," Harrison said and thrilled to his wife's touch.

Author's Notes

Dear Readers,

I hope you have enjoyed the second book of my *Heirs' Club of Scoundrels* trilogy. With Harrison and Angelina's story, it was fun to explore the feelings and emotions a young lady might experience as she grows up and discovers that the heartthrob of her youth is not the man she loves enough to want to spend the rest of her life with.

During the Regency, the possibility of being thrown in debtors' prison for not paying what you owed was very real. There were several debtors' prisons located throughout England. Though no prison was pleasant, some debtors' prisons allowed the inmates the freedom to receive visitors and to continue conducting their businesses.

Dueling has been around almost since the beginning of time. Queen Elizabeth I officially made it a crime in 1577 but that didn't stop the practice and hardly even slowed the countless duels fought each year, which numbered in the thousands throughout Europe. There are many recorded cases where gentlemen were prosecuted for attempted murder or for the murder of an opponent while dueling. Generally, though, authorities and the courts were sympathetic to the principles and code of honor.

By 1840 there was a dramatic decline in dueling. Some historians think this was in large part because of a growing middle class, anti-dueling campaigns, and intellectual trends against violence.

The addition of the Prince Regent weighing in on Lord Thornwick's dueling and the threat of prison was written entirely for entertainment and has no historical basis in fact.

If you missed the first book in the Heirs' Club trilogy, *The Duke in My Bed*, you can get a copy at your favorite bookstore or online e-retailer. Watch for *Wedding Night with the Earl* in March 2016.

I love to hear from readers. Please visit my website at ameliagrey.com, like me at facebook.com/AmeliaGrey Books, or email me at ameliagrey@comcast.net.

Happy reading!
Amelia

Read on for an excerpt from Amelia Grey's next book

WEDDING NIGHT WITH THE EARL

—coming soon from St. Martin's Paperbacks!

"Would you like to try?" the earl asked.

To dance?

Katherine hedged. "That's two questions."

"You asked two," he reminded her.

She had. It wasn't his fault he didn't know that London's ton had nicknamed him "the beast." Swallowing her concern, she said, "All right, no. Wait. I mean yes, of course, yes, I'd like to try, but isn't it very obvious why I can't?"

There was a glow of something in his eyes that she hadn't seen in them before. She wasn't sure, but it looked like anticipation or perhaps hope.

The earl stepped closer and bent his head toward hers. "I believe I can teach you?"

"What?"

Was he teasing her? Mocking her? Maybe he was a beast. Didn't he know how vulnerable she was when it came to her injury? But how could he? He didn't know that since she'd fallen down the stairs when she was nine years old and reinjured her leg, that she hadn't taken a step without her cane. She couldn't.

A cold hard chill shook Katherine's body. She gathered her shawl about her neck once more. "No." She leaned heavily on her cane and backed away from him. "You have no right to even suggest you could do that."

"Maybe not a quadrille, but I could teach you to waltz. A slow one. I would hold you firmly, but properly, and gently guide you."

"I said no. Now, excuse me. It's late, I should go inside."

Lord Greyhawke took hold of her upper arm when she started past him and stopped her from leaving. His hand was firm, warm, possessive. "I know I can teach you. Right here, right now on your front lawn, if you will let me."

She moved as if to pull her arm out of his grasp, but he held her tighter, letting her know he was in control and she would go nowhere until he was ready to release her.

The very thought of his proposal caused her stomach to twist into a knot. "No," she whispered above the roaring in her ears.

The earl held out his other hand to her. "Trust me," he said in a persuasive tone.

Trust him?

"Give me the cane," he said.

His confidence, his audacity amazed her. Moonlight shadowed his handsome face; still her eyes searched his for a reason for his preposterous claim that he could teach her to dance.

"Why are you doing this?" She struggled to free herself again. "Let go of me. You're being cruel for no reason. You know I can't dance."

"I don't know that, and if you haven't tried, neither do you. You have a choice to make, Miss Wright. You can either give me the cane or I'm going to kiss you."

Katherine stopped struggling and stared at him in disbelief. Her senses whirled at the very idea of a kiss from the man. "We are practically strangers."

"You don't seem like a stranger to me." He looked down at his hand on her arm. "You don't feel unfamiliar beneath my grasp."

She wasn't sure what he was doing to her, but she agreed. He didn't appear a stranger to her either. "You wouldn't kiss me."

Lord Greyhawke leaned his face close to hers. "Of course I would. I've been wanting to kiss you all night."

He really wanted to kiss her?

Katherine's hand tightened on the handle of the cane. Her breath seemed to collect and pool in her throat.

A knowing smile lifted one corner of his mouth. "You'd rather I kiss you than give up your walking stick?"

Would she? Tension like she'd never experienced swirled and sparked between them.

Silently she digested what he said as a tingling awareness gripped her. She hoped the turmoil she was feeling inside didn't show in her eyes or on her face. From the moment she looked up and saw him standing in front of her, there had been an inexplicable, unrelenting attraction between them.

Finally, she drew in a long uneven breath and said, "I'm not afraid of a kiss, my lord."

Continuing to watch her carefully, he said, "So you've been kissed before?"

Her chin lifted defiantly. "No, but the thought of it doesn't trouble me. I've always expected to be kissed one day." But she had never expected to dance.

"Afraid to dance but not frightened to be kissed by

the man they call 'the beast'? That makes you very intriguing, Miss Wright."

He moved his face so close to hers Katherine thought for sure he was going to kiss her. Shivers of dread and anticipation coursed through her and mingled together so rapidly that she didn't know which emotion would be the victor.

Instead of placing his lips on hers, he hesitated and said, "How can I refuse such a tempting invitation?"

Tightness bound her chest. For a fleeting second she felt close to swooning for the first time in her life. Her knees were quivering but not from the cold or from standing for so long. Was he or wasn't he going to kiss her?

And did she want him to or didn't she? All she really knew was that she'd never met a gentleman who stirred her senses the way Lord Greyhawke had.

She took in a shaky breath and managed to say, "That wasn't an invitation."

His lips hovered so close to hers it was if she could already feel them. Anticipation had won.

"It was. You are seducing me and I accept that. What I haven't decided is whether or not you know you're doing it."

Lord Greyhawke threw his hat toward the front gate and with one fluid motion circled her waist with his hands, lifted her off the ground, and trapped her against his chest as his lips came down on hers with firm, mounting pressure that startled her at first. It was a powerful sensation. Katherine swallowed a small shivery gasp and closed her eyes.

His lips molded impatiently, eagerly, to hers. It was as if he were starving and only the taste of her lips would satisfy him. Caught up in the shelter of his embrace, she felt safer and more whole than she'd ever felt in her life. The warmth of his body and the strength in his arms seemed to sink into her soul and nourish her. Spirals of wonderful sensations curled tightly in her abdomen and then seemed to shoot through her body as she surrendered to the first stirrings of passion that had awakened within her.

Time seemed to be suspended. Katherine relaxed and concentrated on the pleasure soaring within her.

The thrills that swept through her were shattering all she had ever imagined a kiss would be. Thoughts, dreams, and wishes were no comparison to a real kiss delivered passionately by a real man. Their kiss gathered intensity once again. Katherine felt as if she had been waiting for this experience all her life. She welcomed it with open arms and open mind to explore it all.

His lips left hers and he kissed her cheek, under her eye, and down to the corner of her mouth before returning and melting his lips to the contours of hers once more. As they kissed, the movement of his lips upon hers became more languorous and less frantic. It was as if he treasured what he was doing and how he was feeling.

Lord Greyhawke lifted his head a little and looked down into her eyes. "What do you think of your first kiss?"

She moistened her lips and inhaled a deep shaky breath. "That I expected it to be softer and shorter. Much like when Papa used to kiss my forehead or my cheek."

He chuckled and then in a reassuring tone said, "Miss Wright, a gentleman's kiss to a lady is not supposed to be chaste like a father's buss to his daughter."

"I think I understand that now, and I'm wondering why I've never allowed any of the gentlemen who've wanted to kiss me to do so. Surely I've been missing many opportunities to experience these wonderful feelings it causes deep inside me."

He gave her a rueful grin. "That's not the answer I expected from you, but do not think that every man will produce the same response in you that my kiss did."

She eyed him curiously and watched shadows of moonlight play across his handsome features. "Why not?" she asked.

"I'll just say that every man kisses differently."

"How do you know this?"

His lips twitched with a little humor and so did hers. Katherine could tell he was considering how to answer her question so she playfully goaded him by adding, "Have you kissed many men?"

The earl laughed. It was an easy, natural sound that was pleasing to her ears.

"I have never kissed a man. Since no two ladies kiss alike, I will assume it's safe to think no two men do either."

"And have you kissed many ladies?"

His gaze feathered down her face and back up to her eyes. She could tell he appreciated her curiosity.

"Enough," he answered.

Katherine stared into his golden brown eyes and said, "I like the way you kiss."

"I'm glad to hear that, Miss Wright. I liked your kisses, too. Immensely. Perhaps we should do it again."

"That would be lovely, but dangerous. We are standing out in the open on my front lawn."

"It won't be the first time I've done something dangerous. And for reasons I don't begin to understand and have no desire to contemplate, I am of a mind to tempt fate one more time tonight and kiss you again."

His words tempted her and eased her fears. "I think I would like that, too, my lord."

The earl bent his head to hers and sought her mouth once again. Katherine knew what to expect and began to kiss him back. She dropped her cane and wound both her arms around his neck, pulling him closer, urging him to kiss her harder. And he did. She skimmed her hands along the width of his shoulders and down the breadth of his back.

He trembled beneath her searching hands. His arms tightened around her possessively, pressing her breasts against the firmness of his powerful chest as if he were trying to bind her to him.

"Open your mouth," he whispered against her lips. "Let me inside to taste you."

She followed his instructions without hesitation and his tongue flicked across the inner surface of her lips and around the corners of her mouth, surprising her. Shivers of exquisite pleasure soared through her. She had never experienced anything as wonderful as being held tightly in Lord Greyhawke's arms and kissing him.

She wanted to taste him, too, so she eased her tongue forward, slowly at first, until she heard him moan softly. That spurred her to respond to his kisses with the same aggressive eagerness he exhibited and their tongues teased and played

Katherine knew she was the one being seduced, but she didn't care. She was enjoying every moment of it. She answered every gasp, every moan, and every breath that fell from his lips as they kissed long, deep, and savoring. He slanted his lips over hers again and again. She welcomed the feel of him, the smell and taste of him to all her senses.

"Am I doing it right?" she questioned breathlessly.

"Perfect," he answered, kissing his way down her chin to her neck and around behind her ear.

Her breath trembled in her throat, but she managed to whisper, "Are—are you feeling the same unexplainable things I am feeling?"

"Oh, yes," he murmured in a shaky gasp. "And probably many more than you are enjoying right now."

An unexplained wanting grew low in her abdomen. She had no idea that two people could create such long, delicious, and wondrous feelings of delight by their lips and bodies touching and coming together so intimately. Now she knew the meaning of all the love poems she'd ever read. What she was experiencing with Lord Greyhawke was the reason they had all been written.

Katherine felt as if she could go on kissing him forever until suddenly the front door opened. She felt the muscles in the earl's arms jerk and flex with tension. She twisted around and saw the duke, Uncle Willard, and three other gentlemen standing in the doorway, gawking at her and the earl.